BITROUX

First published in 2025 by Digital Jazz Communications

ISBN: 978-1-7637202-2-0
Fiction - science fiction, speculative fiction, metaphysical fiction.

Also by Jordan Harcourt-Hughes

Bitroux: The Metalsmith

For all the Star Seeds

CHARACTERS

The Metalsmith and his close circle

Merouac: Head of the East-West Line Subcamp (Bitroux)

Evra: Merouac's niece

Malaena: Merouac's twin sister and Evra's mother

Heyla: Ayuherica market trader

Hieime: gemologist and gem trader

Salvette: Evra's father

The Transcontinental Railroad Project

Seb: 2IC, Bitroux workshops

Harlin: Seb's wife

Tielder: Supervisor, Metalworks

Sanat Leron: Architect of the Transcontinental Railroad Project and
Governor in Waiting, Suron

Tor Anale: Head of Logistics, Transcontinental Railroad Project

Suron City

Gartounne Leron: Governor of Suron, father of Heyla and Sanat Leron

Delsaine Leron: wife of Sanat Leron

Ophrin Leron: son of Agrippa and Sanat

The Faurin of the Remneur Ranges

Afourla: Head of the Faurin Royal Family

Asta: mother of Kii and Kultan

Kii and Kultan: twin brothers, grandsons of Afourla

1.
Shaft 4, Wangresse Mines, North-West Ingrue.

Timar was dusty and hungry as he wiggled along the width of the mine shaft, suspended in his harness, disregarding the plummeting drop below him. He wiped the surface layer of the rock and brushed away the silt and the soil, which crumbled quickly under the light pressure and fell away. He was looking for glimmers in the rock; green or pale pink, sometimes the thinnest of lines, which might indicate that somewhere deeper there was a vein of precious stone worth cutting in for.

He was not, in any way, expecting to find a deep white vein of stone, right there at surface level in front of his very eyes.

He looked around quickly, an instinctive reflex despite the fact it was only him and Rala harnessed and suspended in the shaft. With a thundering heart he leaned in and looked closer, bringing his eyes almost right to the stone.

'Rala,' he called out softly. 'Get yourself down here.'

Rala looked down in annoyance. 'Amoura, if I rope it down I just gotta rope it back up and that's hard labour I'd rather avoid. Whaddya want?'

'You gotta see this,' Timar whispered.

'Later, man. I got enough to look at right in front of me.'

'Rala. Now.'

Rala cursed, but began levering himself down and pulled himself alongside Timar with a grunt. He followed Timar's gaze.

There was silence.

'Damn! That can't be what I think it is.'

Timar traced the layer of white rock amid the dark sediment around it. It looked as if it were positively glowing. 'We gotta get it out of here before they see it. You and me.'

'How the hell are we gonna cut it out, stupid, without the bosses noticing?' Rala retorted. He, too, leaned in to touch the stone, wiping the last remnants of dust away so they could both see the marbled white and silver streaks in the rock more clearly.

'We're gonna cut it out now. Then we're gonna tuck it in close. Then we're gonna sneak ourselves outta here any which way we can,' Timar decided.

Rala swallowed but was unable to take either his hand or his gaze away from the rare stone. 'We'll end up in the clink for sure. It's too dangerous.'

'Man, do you know what this is? It's *white pala*. On Maarte's own broad and tall shoulders, I swear it is. Rala, listen. This'll make us. We're looking at the rarest gem rock on the continent. Maybe the whole planet of Ahm itself. We'll never have to work another day in our lives again.'

Timar and Rala fumbled in their attempts to affix small lights either side of the rock where the stone was positioned. A rivulet of water trickled down the stone in front of them, making the edge of the shaft slippery and dangerous.

Rala blinked as Timar ground the cutter around the edges of the white pala. Dust rose as the whirring sound filled the shaft. It was an unwelcome noise that rattled them both.

Finally, Timar had cut in deep enough to dislodge a hand-sized square of the stone and reached into his overalls, placing it between his belly and the belt of his trousers. 'Alright. Let's get ourselves out of here. We can't go up from this shaft, of course. They'll be expecting us in an hour. We gotta go out another way. Now.'

The two men pulleyed themselves down quickly from their perch. On the floor of the shaft, they pushed their gear against a dark corner and turned to quietly make their way through the base tunnels towards the old test shaft.

'This is it just up ahead,' Timar whispered. The test shaft had been closed since the mine officially opened.

'It's not safe,' Rala said, looking up, pulling on the ropes unhappily. Sunlight was only faintly visible at the very top of the shaft.

'It's the only way,' Timar said flatly. 'Buckle up. I'll go first, you follow.' With that, Timar locked his harness into the rope lever and then flicked it over to Rala so he could strap himself in next. They began to pulley the carriage box up towards the light.

'This rope's probably rotten,' Rala complained as they jerked and bounced upwards, only to lose momentum, dropping and swaying precariously as the shaft lever whined and creaked with the weight after so many months of being unused.

'Shhh,' Timar said vaguely to the lever.

'What's it gonna do?' Rala said with a nervous titter.

They were half way up when another rope began to creak and moan. Rala blinked. A cool shiver ran down his back.

Seconds later, a rope snapped.

Both men yelped as they dropped height with a jarring motion. They hung in the air for a moment collecting their wits. Then, with a fierce crack, the last rope snapped.

The men, pulley and carriage box dropped into the darkness.

2.

Merouac and Evra recover

Merouac was running. He tried to wake, but couldn't.

He was back in the the Remneur Ranges, the home of the Faurin monks. He was running at pace up the side of a mountain, with a dozen others. His breath was heavy, his chest heaving.

Far below was the temple compound. Merouac knew he was on Tenogru, the most northerly of the four mountains.

He had been there recently, and so knew the mountain for what it was, but knew also that there was a difference. The temple seemed smaller. The mountain landscape was denser, more like jungle. The climate felt different, hotter.

He realised that in the dream, he was not himself. He was not Merouac, Head Metalsmith, formerly responsible for the Marville Line, now relegated to the interior of the continent to prepare for the East-West line. He was one of the Faurin monks, and he was in training with an elite group of similar monks.

He was running with a group of them, but no one he recognised. Those in front of him and behind continued to run, the light fading around them. They ran on through the undergrowth, in the dark, as if time meant nothing at all. He could feel his body fading, as if it was turning from something physical into something like a vapour, something airy and without weight.

He wondered where he was, why he was running, what they were training for – as it was obvious they were training for something. The steadiness of the footfalls in front and behind him, the breathing that was only slightly quicker than normal, the focus, the power and sustained energy they all had.

This was the purpose of the run, he realised. To take them beyond normal senses. Beyond rational response. Into something else. He realised his entire body was beginning to feel different. It in fact felt like it wasn't there at all.

Another shout.

The monks ran on, and soon the undergrowth began to clear. Deep in the trance state they had sunk into during the long trek, the monks worked and fought in an alternative state of awareness. They heard no sound through their eardrums. Instead they were listening to molecules of energy particles. They were fighting their opponents based on reading the intelligence of sub-sound. They were the Intangien, the monks who could hear the sounds beyond silence. And, one by one, they began disappearing from the training field into thin air.

At some point the running ceased. He, and the monks around him, stood still, listening deeply.

As he dreamed on, he realised something else – Malaena was once again present. She was somewhere close, connected to what he was seeing. But it was still unclear – what exactly was he seeing?

'Look to the visitors,' Malaena said.

He looked north of the fields where a cluster of Faurin stood. They were facing three figures who had appeared. The visitors were different. Merouac strained in the dream to try and identify who they might be. But their visage shimmered and shifted, as if they were not quite there.

They've crossed over with a frequency bridge, he realised. *They've crossed from another dimension.*

'Who are they?' he murmured. 'Where have they crossed over from?'

There was no response. The dream faded.

The next day, Merouac woke late. He found himself lying and simply staring at the ceiling.

Things were changing. Had changed. Like a rising tide; there was just more and more to comprehend. Things he previously didn't see, understand or care to think about.

For instance, this sense that Malaena, his twin sister, was with him. Not always. But on occasion, she'd drop in. Be right there. And he could feel her presence across the dimensions.

He stared up at the ceiling of their shack. His bed was little more than a camp bed, low to the floor, nothing more than thick canvas stretched across metal frames. They had made camp more than six months earlier, but it was a sub-camp, and so the huts were temporary accommodations; nothing more than frames with wooden walls boarded together. They were watertight, and they kept out the weather, but that was largely it.

Merouac's sleeping arrangements were similarly functional. Evra was still asleep in the other small room next to his; really, it had been one room, but he had added a partition.

His niece had also started out with a camp bed, but Harlin had protested and said the girl needed a real bed, even if Merouac didn't.

So she slept better than most others working on the railroad. He was glad to have Seb and Harlin around; they loved to spoil the child and sometimes knew what to do more than he, the eternal bachelor, ever did.

In any event, he and Seb must have done something right – the five shacks they had built on the hill above the East-West workshops had stood firm in the dust storms and no repairs had been required. The workers' camp would be another matter, of course.

Sitting up, he was aware of just how much his body was still hurting. He allowed the dizziness to clear and placed his feet on the floor. As he rose, he took a moment to examine the black and blue bruising that stretched all the way down from his left hip to his knee, angry and dark. He winced as he tried to put weight on the leg.

Sore and aching, he hobbled over to the stove and turned on the hahma current to make tea. Evra, also sleepy, heard him and sat on her own bed, in the other small room that opened out into their makeshift kitchen.

Teas made for them both – Evra's made with half cold water, Merouac put his boots on and stepped slowly down the porch steps and around to the front of the hut, which provided a view down the hill to the workshops and to the vast open landscape beyond.

He sat on one of the boxes on the porch with effort, and lit a cigarillo to smoke with his tea.

Evra followed him. As always, she seemed relaxed and happy. He wasn't sure why or how this was, given the ordeal they had just been through – and the fact that by all accounts her mother was gone for good.

But, a voice said. *She knows.*

He reflected on that idea. The idea that a child of only five shades could still be connected to her mother across the dimensions. He had been feeling it, so why would it be surprising that Evra would, too?

Merouac wondered if having that ongoing connection was why she had never seemed to fret, even when she had first come to live with him. She was a child still assured by a strong parental bond with her mother, even though Malaena was gone, living now in some other dimension he was yet to understand.

Merouac motioned for Evra to come and stand in front of him and hold out her arms. He checked them again for breaks, bruising. Nothing. He made her turn around. He probed her small back, prodding here and there to test if there was any pain. 'It doesn't hurt?'

His niece shook her head. She'd submitted to many such gentle examinations from him over the past few days.

ooo

Merouac walked slowly around the cabin, following the path through the small cluster of other shacks around their own, to look down the hill towards the railroad sub-camp he had been placed in charge of.

He surveyed the sky and smelled the air. The sky was pale and almost clear again; the thick cloud that had blanketed the atmosphere had now mostly dissipated, with only wisps and threads of charcoal smog still visible.

Merouac looked beyond the sub-camp sprawling out below. Rolling out for miles and miles, vast open plains, empty other than long dusty grasses, shrubs and rocky outcrops and small clusters of rolling hills. Clusters of grassy plains painted the land a light shade of green, but otherwise it was tawny blond dirt and unoccupied stretches of land.

The continent itself was large enough that there were many vast spaces like this, especially across the middle belt where the East-West line was marked out to run along.

For a while longer, the land would stretch, bare and absent of intent, for as far as the eye could see. But only for a while. Even though it was hot, dry and largely barren right now, they knew from the Great Northern, the first line of the Transcontinental Railroad to open, that the railroad changed everything. Once the East-West line threaded its way through this middle tract of the continent, it would attract business at each intersection and at every point where a station was planned.

Merouac traced the ground with his foot. He felt too stiff and sore to bend down and pick up the strange dust but it was the same silt that covered everything in the wake of the dust storms. The morning was cool, but wouldn't stay that way for long. The Summerial Start, the stretch of days that saw the beginning of the hot seasons ahead, had arrived. The sun would start to set later, and from early evening, they'd at least start to see the stunning pink-purple skies and purple hazy sunsets this part of the continent was renowned for.

It was time to get moving, he thought. He and Evra had had a few days to rest and recover. He wasn't quite ready to get back to work, but at least he could start inspecting the workers camp after the dust storms.

Dressed, he left Evra in Harlin's attentive care, one shack over, and went to see Pearl, hobbling at a snail's pace. He had his crutches with him but he could be damned if he could figure out how to use them going downhill. He was more likely to topple right over, he thought, doing that.

Pearl was a hardy woman of fifty shades or so. She had worked for him for a while now, as caretaker of the East-West workers' camp. The role was not a small one. As well as looking after the camp, she oversaw the kitchen and communal eating areas, where, outside of the workshops and the camp, families and working men could eat. She also managed the supplies stores for those who cooked within the camp itself, with her team on standby to receive deliveries from supply trucks weekly and then daily when the camp grew larger.

Merouac walked past the stores and the open areas where sheets of wood had been set up on thick tree trunks and stumps for men to sit on while they had their cups of tea and smoke breaks. The camp had about a hundred families currently. It was relatively small for a railroad workers' camp – the ones for the Great Northern had around a thousand families; the big camps were more like small townships. Often it would take hours to walk from one end of a camp to the other.

Here was much smaller. But Pearl did a good job and made sure everyone did the right thing and kept things clean. There were latrines and public areas and wash stations all around, which she and her team took care of; communal areas and the living, breathing camp itself that was never dull or quiet. She had six women who worked for her, often the wives of metalsmiths working with Merouac or the workers who came into the camp.

It was mid-morning, so just women around and young children. Seeing all the kids around in the camp reminded him that it wasn't just Evra who needed a school.

He found Pearl at the inner camp kitchen.

Pearl stopped her work to greet him. 'Well, look who it is. Good to see you upright, boss.' The woman was short, with large, intelligent brown eyes and fuzzy hair that constantly required pushing away from her face. She did that now, brushing the side of her head with one hand and blowing upwards to displace the ringlets that had fallen over her eyes.

'Pearl, how many kids of school age do you think are in the camp?'

'At least twenty, I should say. Mebbe more. I'm not counting the babies of course but lots that'll be jumping out of their mama's arms soon enough. You looking to set something up?'

'I'm thinking about it. But first things first, we've got to get things sorted here. Much damage from the storms?'

'We got a bit, nothing that can't be fixed though. How are you, more to the point?' Pearl, without shame, had walked right up to him, bent down and placed a hand on his leg, testing it with a gentle prod.

Merouac winced.

'Heard you've been holed up in your shack for a few days, recovering. How did it happen?'

'Long story,' Merouac said. 'I'll be back on the job tomorrow.'

'How's the kid?' Pearl stood up again and placed her hands on her hips, her gaze still unrelenting.

'Evra's alright. She's pretty resilient. Doesn't seem to get bothered by much.'

'I heard her Daddy's turned up, eh? Salvette. He's settled into the camp these last few weeks.'

'How did you hear that?'

'I got ears. Anyhow, you able to take care of her okay, with that limp?'

'It's not the limp that's the problem. It's just taking care of a kid in general. That's why I need a school.'

'Harlin's looking out for her, eh, in the meantime? But make sense to get us a school.'

'That's the next fight I'll be fighting. Tielder thinks it's not needed because we're just a temporary camp.'

'Temporary don't mean a short while though, does it? Anyways, school aside, you know what you need, Merouac? You need to get yourself a woman. How long you been a bachelor, anyhow?'

Meruac felt himself colouring slightly. 'Always.'

Pearl nodded. She turned away and began rummaging through the kitchen's collections of pots and pans, inspecting them for grit and grime.

'Well, it's time to change your ways. You're a grown man. Why you want to be a bachelor for anyway? Where's the fun in that?'

'I don't have time to think about anything else but the railroad,'

Merouac retorted.

'Well, you need to make time. You need a woman to take care of you and you need a woman to take care of Evra.'

Merouac exhaled. 'Thanks, Pearl, I'll keep that in mind. Meanwhile, tell me what needs to get fixed.'

'I'll take you around. We'll look at the awnings first. There's a few tears in them. Harlin should be able to get through it in a day or two. Other than that, it's just a good old mess, really. I've got the girls on clean-up duty. The dust is nearly sorted.'

Merouac nodded. 'That's good.'

'What was that storm, Merouac, you think?' She led Merouac out of the kitchen and to the seating areas, which were covered with rough tarp awnings. He saw immediately where they had loosened and ripped. He helped Pearl lever them down and untie them from their rope holdings. They folded the tarps. 'I mean, we've never had anything like it, what with the sky and the dust. And there's rumours swirling left, right and centre, I have to tell you, amoura.'

Amoura was the Tustennuit word for friend, but Merouac found the tone most people used it with irksome, as though it predicted a lecture of sorts, which is what he felt coming from Pearl.

'I suppose you're going to tell me about this talk.'

'Well, I hear you and Evra were off down in the grid, Merouac. That's the rumours. During the storms, you were away down in a place no one should be, and with a child, and with half your workshop crew joining you for some emergency. Is that how you got the limp? Did that have something to do with everything going on?'

'Slow down. What do you mean, everything?'

'You know what I'm talking about. That big damn planet that just appeared, out of nowhere, in our very own night sky. It appeared, it got bigger and closer and then we guess it imploded, which is what caused all the dust storms and what not. Were you involved in that somehow, Merouac?'

'Well, there's an argument it wasn't even a planet,' Merouac said, trying to evade the conversation.

He didn't want to talk about it with Pearl and yet, at the same time, felt distinctly uncomfortable about lying. He'd never had much occasion to lie before, and it didn't sit well with him.

It surprised him, in fact. When he was doing his job, things were all very clear, very practical, very hands on. He was good at what he did and, generally, when people respected what you did, they followed instructions and listened to you and that was that. Then, just as he was planning to make his escape from her endless questions and commentary, she stopped him.

'Now, Merouac, why don't you sit yourself down for just a moment. Rest your leg and let me give that hair of yours a clipping. You gotta stay decent to command all those men, don't you? You're looking a real sight with those long locks.'

Before he knew it, she'd sat him down, found a sheet to cover his shoulders and had gone to her supplies locker in the back of the kitchens to find herself some clippers.

He decided to succumb. He was tired. It wasn't worth fighting. And besides, on this point, she may be right. He couldn't remember the last time he'd even thought about cutting his hair. As he sat there, Pearl returned and he let her chatter flow over and around him. He closed his eyes. Pearl had moved onto another topic now, which was the imminent influx of men into the workers' camp and how many more women she was going to need to keep the camp up to scratch. It wasn't urgent chatter and he had heard it all before, so he let himself tune her out momentarily.

After only a moment he felt something shift. It was his sister. Malaena, once again, was making her presence felt. Not in a dream, this time. Pearl was still talking endlessly. She didn't notice a thing. He opened his eyes. Nothing new to see.

And yet, he felt her. They were, after all, twins. They had once been close all the time, day and night. So the feeling of her presence was something he knew well. And this wasn't the first time she had made contact in daylight hours. There had been a handful of moments in recent days, when he and Evra had been recovering. She had used these moments of contact to confirm things, new information he had been guessing and wondering about.

She had confirmed that when the shield was active, it blocked signalling pathways. Which was why even if a person could tune metal to other-world frequencies, it wouldn't have any effect – the shield would block the signals. If the shield was working at full strength, then no contact with outside worlds, realms and dimensions would have been possible.

But, with the shield now thinning, everything was different. Things were changing, and changing fast. *Think of it like an ocean,* she had told him, in this strange way they had started communicating, a telepathy across the dimensions of sorts. *That's how you'll be able to navigate the universe. Just look for the energy currents.*

He closed his eyes again. There was stillness; the colour blue came into his mind, and then, there it was. More information arising in his waking state.

Malaena was telling him that their planet, the planet of Ahm, wasn't alone in the universe anymore. The shield would continue to fade until it simply wasn't there at all anymore. Then, Ahm would have become a mature planet and part of the Broadsphere, the galaxy that was home to many different ecosystems that contained conscious life. Some of these ecosystems incorporated physical planets, some didn't.

'Ouch!' Merouac said, startled.

'Sorry boss,' said Pearl, tussling his hair and brushing over a section of skin she had accidentally grazed with the sharp end of her clippers.

Merouac grumbled but let her continue. It hadn't really hurt, he supposed.

He turned inwards again, to the new bloom of knowing that was emerging.

Malaena was still present, still sharing information. *The Broadsphere is a bandwidth of frequencies. Every ecosystem has a unique frequency signature and exists on a different level of the Broadsphere. Frequencies may observe, depending on their levels of awareness, other ecosystems of life on other frequencies. But to actually communicate requires a frequency bridge. Both frequencies must be willing to contribute to the frequency bridge from their own end.*

That was it, it seemed. The sense of his twin sister faded. Of course, it was becoming clear they were not separated from the rest of the universe by their protective shield any longer. It was also becoming clearer they had not been alone on their own planet either, possibly for some time, as long as the shield had been thinning. And hadn't he, himself, been the architect of an event so grand he could barely remind himself of it? Wasn't there a race of creatures, from beyond the shield, recovering in the caves below the grid because he had created a frequency bridge that allowed them to take shelter there?

Afterwards, with his freshly clipped and shortened hair, he limped back up to the cabin.

He realised Pearl, with all her ideas about what the planet was or could have been, wouldn't be the only one coming up with theories. But despite the enormity of the idea that other worlds could be in contact with them, that other life forces could be coming and going from their own planet with the shield down, his main focus was still to take care of the small child who had come into his life. The child Malaena had left behind in her journey beyond the shield, to wherever she was now.

3.
Hieime intercepts the white pala

Long after Ahm's sun star had faded and the two moons had inverted, Hieime tossed, sweated, turned and then suddenly awakened. It took him a few moments to get his bearings. The room was unfamiliar. The fanciest hotel in the town, he recalled after a moment, because he'd had a good day and it had seemed fitting.

He looked across the empty bed, felt a moment of regret it was so empty, and remembered it had been his own foolish decision to leave Delsaine to her marriage, at least for the time being.

Parched, he rose reluctantly and crossed over to the ante room that contained the toilet, a lavish bathing chamber and a petite sink. He turned on the tap, leaned over and splashed his face with water.

He made his way out of his hotel room, down the stairwell and out onto the front verandah, which was dusty but silent. He walked out onto the road that stretched out to the wide open spaces of the west Ingrue. He fumbled in his pocket for a box of cigarettes and pulled one out and placed it between his lips, searching his shirt pocket for matches. As he prepared to light his cigarette he looked up at the night sky.

It had started to clear now; the dust from the storms had for days lain not just on the ground, but seemingly in the night sky as well. Hieime wondered if there had been any movement down in the caves below the grid. He shook his head and turned back towards the hotel, returning to his bed where he lay staring, his eyes wide open, until finally, he fell back to sleep.

The next morning, Hieime woke, disorientated and groggy, to the sound of a fist banging on his hotel door.

'Go away,' he shouted.

The knocking became a more insistent banging. Hieime swore.

'Alright. I'm coming.'

A short time later, with a pounding behind his eyes that was not made any softer by the bright refractions of the rising sun star, he was seated on the verandah outside his hotel room, his gem grading table and instruments set up and laid out in front of him. The man who had woken him now sat opposite him, his shoulders hunched anxiously. He was a sight. His face was streaked with sweat and dirt. He looked like he'd been on the run for days.

The man looked back anxiously at the road and then back to Hieime again.

Hieime shook his head and sighed. The gem was probably stolen. But Hieime was known as a man who wouldn't ask too many questions about a gem's origins, and as a result half of his work came from black market gems.

The man looked at him oddly, frowning. He drew a kerchief out of his pocket and wiped his forehead. 'Will you look at the gem now?'

Hieime nodded and held out his hands for the man to pass over the stone, which he'd wrapped in paper.

He unwrapped the stone and looked at it. And it was then that the clamour began. Whispers, all around him, radiating out from the white stone. Beads of sweat broke out on his neck. The stone was, in some strange way, talking to him.

He looked back at the man, who was flushing red and shaking. He returned his attention back to the stone, and examined it for a long period of time. When he was done, he looked up from his table and stared out at the gritty desert landscape for moment, his heart hammering. He looked back at the stone. It couldn't be the white pala – the rarest stone on the continent. Most never laid eyes on it in their lifetime. And yet he knew that it was. The purity was incomparable.

He cleared his throat and sat back. 'It's catalyn catalyte. Congratulations. A nice stone.'

The man blanched and went pale. 'You're fucking with me.'

'No. It's found mostly in the Remneur ranges, but but it has been found in most other states across the continent.'

'It's not white pala?'

'No. It's similar in colour, but no. It's definitely catalyte.'

The man swore again, and stood up and paced back and forth across the dusty ground in front of Hieime and his grading table. He rubbed his face with his palm.

'I'm sorry it's not the gem you thought it was. But it's not a bad stone,' Hieime said carefully.

The man heaved a big sigh and blew into his handkerchief and patted the kerchief over his face.

'Look, why don't I buy it off you? Then you won't have come all this way for no reason.'

The man looked at Hieime and then blew his nose loudly. 'How much?'

Hieime named a generous price.

'You sure it ain't pala? I got a feeling it was as soon as I saw it.'

'Well, yes. I'm sure, that is.' A bead of sweat trickled down Hieime's back. He stood up and went into the hotel room behind them to retrieve his wallet. His hands were shaking. He returned and placed a thick wad of notes on the table. 'Here. It's a good sale. And you never know. Maybe you'll come across white pala next time.'

The man, still red cheeked and puffy faced, nodded. With thick sausage-like fingers, he reached out and took the notes slowly, folded them and put them in the breast pocket of his shirt. He got up, nodded to Hieime and turned to leave.

Then he stopped and turned back around. 'Maybe I should get a second opinion,' he said slowly.

Hieime shrugged.

The man nodded to himself and took a step back towards Hieime, his gaze suddenly suspicious. 'I'll do that. I will. Could be pala and me just giving it away for a catalyte.'

Hieime swore under his breath. 'You could do. But here, let me show you.' He leaned over and picked out his mallet from his tool box, stood over the stone, which was still sitting where the man had left it in exchange for the money, and brought it down hard on the stone. The resounding crack as the stone broke in two made the man jump.

'If it was pala, I wouldn't have been able to break it,' Hieime explained.

The man's shoulders slumped as he stared at the stone. With a final sigh, he nodded and turned back around to the road. He gave Hieime another nod and and began his slow walk back to the road.

He stopped once, then again, seeming to want to turn back, but stopping, collecting himself, and walking on.

When the man had disappeared completely from sight, Hieime allowed his knees to buckle under him and he sat down heavily in his chair.

He looked at the white pala in front of him. He retrieved a soft cloth from his toolbox and gently wrapped the pieces of stone in it.

Breaking the stone in pieces had not diminished its power. The murmuring had quietened down, and yet the stone still pulled and tugged at him. He took the wrapped stone inside, found another cloth and wrapped it in a second layer and put it on the dresser while he packed and donned travelling clothes.

It was a two-day trip to Suron.

That night, he stayed at a hotel on the west Ingruan border. Sleepless once again, he left his room to gaze up at the glittering night sky. The two moons crossed and inverted overhead.

Close to dawn, as the moons were setting, he returned to his room. The gemologist and rock trader took the pala stone out of its wrapping and simply stared at it for a long time.

4.

Merouac and Evra visit the workshops

'Hey, boss. You're up and about, then,' Seb, his second in command, called out.

Merouac had decided that after three days recovering, it was time he and Evra stretch their legs. They walked, or hobbled in Merouac's case, down to the workshops, which comprised two long metalsmithing and fabrication workshops, courtesy of the Transcontinental Railroad Project, and a series of cabins and storage sheds behind the workshops. The workers' camp was a few hundred yards away, completing the triangular arrangement of managers' huts on the hill, workshops below and workers' camp adjacent.

While Seb and Merouac had been in charge of making their own huts, the workshops had been custom built and fitted out by the railroad proper. That, at least, had soothed some of the bite. Merouac still seethed at the fact that he'd been let go as Head Metalsmith at Endren, only to come out here to the middle of nowhere to oversee tearing up old lines before the new East-West line could be built. But at least the workshops were decent.

About a hundred men had been clearing old tracks and preparing for the coming months when the new track would be laid.

'Morning, Seb.' Merouac winced.

'Alright? Eh, I like your haircut,' Seb said with a knowing grin. 'Pearl got you, did she?'

Merouac nodded, rubbing a hand over his shortened hair. 'She did, yes.'

'Alright, Ev?' Seb asked. Evra nodded vigorously.

Merouac's second in command was a short and stout fellow with thick, silvery-grey hair. Despite his workman's physique, he had a gentle face and a ruddy complexion. Blue eyes, a moustache, and always with one pencil behind his ear and three or four poking out of the breast pocket of his overalls.

Seb had one uniform and that was overalls and that was that. Most days, they were the same bright blue, industrial issue, buttoned up all the way. When they had visitors to the workshops, official railroad men and what not, he'd move into his pair of black overalls. That was Seb's version of formal wear.

'On the mend, then? Looks like you've got a way to go, yet,' said Seb, nodding to the crutches Merouac was leaning on in a somewhat awkward fashion.

'Still a bit to go.'

'I take it the Doc came, sorted you out as much as he could?'

'Yes. He thought Evra looked fine; told me to stay off the leg if I could. I said I'd give it a few more days.' Merouac nodded towards the workshops. 'How're things here? Are you right to keep on for a few more days while we rest up a bit more?'

'All under control. We've started on the clean-up. Dust

everywhere, of course: the workshops, the huts, storage supplies. It'll take a few days yet. Oh, and another thing. All the good scrap'll be coming in from the old tracks. I s'pposed you'd want a new pile, so I've got it started just yonder behind the wood sheds.'

Merouac paused. He hadn't even thought about the scrap being pulled up from the old lines. Much of it was worthless, but there would be a certain amount of metal fixtures and components that could be repurposed.

There was another underlying suggestion there, of course, which was that Merouac may like to use them for his sculptures. His *tuned metal sculptures,* as it were.

Merouac felt a surge of affection for his second in command. Seb didn't really get it, this idea that his boss's sculptures seemed to be able to do something arcane, something only ever heard of in myths and legend. But Seb knew enough to want to make things work for Merouac, and if Merouac needed a supply of good-quality metal for his sculptures, then it was Seb's job to source the supply and make it just so.

Seb led them over to take a look at the growing pile of scrap metal.

'Look here, Ev,' said Seb, bending down to crouch beside Evra, who was doing a close-up inspection. 'You see what we have here?' He pulled a number of the small pieces of scrap off the pile and turned them over in his hand. He traced the various imprints and insignias on each. 'You got some real good bits here. These are the marks of the best metalsmithing houses on the continent.'

Evra bent closer to have a look, picking the pieces up in her hands and drawing them close to her face for inspection.

'Look. This one's the mark of Shelton House. From the Northern Ingrue. This one's Gould, from the South. You see, they're like stamps, or signatures. They tell you the metal's real good quality.'

'Good enough for sculptures?'

'Well, sure! Here's the mark of Manne House and Arvenne, the other Southern metal houses. And then the last one is Sereville, which is in the North. Well, imagine that. You've got the full set, Ev.'

Evra beamed. She looked expectantly at her uncle.

Merouac nodded with resignation. 'Take your pick, then. I'll have a look at them soon.'

As Evra started a new, small pile of special pieces for his sculptures, Merouac noticed his niece had taken her long-sleeved top, another gift from Harlin, and tried to push the sleeves back up to her shoulders.

She had arrived in the winter, when they were at Endren. But with Summerial in its gradual ascent, and the warmer weather already upon them, he'd have to sort out some new clothes for her. And bigger – she had grown since she arrived.

He'd ask Harlin what she could come up with. These were the kind of everyday things Merouac was still navigating, still working out as they came up. His parenting skills, his experience, was so limited he didn't even know how much he didn't know. The kid was still here though – just – and he was grateful.

'Alright, Seb. I guess we'll head back up the hill, now. Can you bring me up a few things from my office when you have a minute?'

'Aye. The maps, perhaps?'

Another timely suggestion that Merouac appreciated. The final map would mark out the exact route for the line and was required before they could start laying down the new track. The last Merouac had heard was that Sham Leoch was still giving his final advice about what bridges needed to be factored in. There wouldn't be many; the East-West largely cut across the flat, dry and dusty middle of the continent, so it was relatively easy terrain for a railroad, without any large bodies of water to cross.

While they waited for its arrival, Merouac could spend some time reviewing the latest drafts to see if there were any sections that required special thought or planning.

'Yes. And anything else that's coming in from Endren. I'll be back in the workshops in a few days. We can have our first briefing then.'

'Aye, sounds good.'

'Also, Seb, there are a few tarps that need fixing from the camp. Can I get Pearl to run them up to Harlin? A few repairs for her, after the storms.' Seb's wife, Harlin, was a seamstress whose skills had come in handy more times than Merouac could count when it came to repairs around the camp.

'She'll be happy to do it, no doubt about that,' Seb replied with a quick nod. 'And Harlin's real happy to take care of Evra when you come back to work.'

'I appreciate it, Seb.'

'No trouble, boss. No trouble at all.'

5.

Merouac returns to work

Merouac and Evra had a routine in the morning of gruel with sweet molasses and tea. They sat at the table in their cabin kitchen.

'We did a good job with the scrap heap, didn't we Uncle Mer?'

Merouac nodded, observing that Evra's cheeks were rosy and that his niece had already had a go at putting her hair into her usual pigtails with some ribbon Harlin had given her. Her small hands grasped the molasses as she held it over her plate, trickling it slowly and with determined focus.

Her pinafore looked somewhat grubby, and shorter than before. He'd had no idea how fast children grew. He still had only minimal ideas about children generally, he reflected.

He thought of the day a few months earlier when his boss, Tielder, had gotten wind of Evra.

Tielder had given Merouac an odd look. 'She's really your kid now?'

'She's my niece, T. Her mother's gone and she's not coming back. So yeah, I guess that makes Evra my kid.'

Now he looked at the bare-boned shack they were living in and wondered if he shouldn't be doing better. Their living abode was as basic as it came. It had a kitchen, with a stove and a table. Two small rooms with beds for them to sleep in. It didn't seem enough, somehow. He had a kid now, who needed a decent place to live, something that felt like home.

A thought emerged somewhere inside and told him that Evra didn't care. *He* was home to her now, and as long as he was around, she'd be happy. But still. There was a lot to this situation of being guardian of a young child.

They had been down to the workshops again the day prior, as Evra had wanted to see how the pile was coming along. As soon as Evra had laid eyes on the new arrivals of discarded railroad metal, she'd let go of Merouac's hand to run over to start inspecting all the pieces of track, bent rail, spikes and endless ties and nails.

'Evra, be careful.' Merouac had shouted louder than he had planned to and had felt his face flush as some of his men popped their heads out of the workshops to see what their boss was yelling about.

'That metal's likely to have sharp edges,' he had explained more quietly, limping over to the scrap pile, which was taller than him at full height. He still felt unable to bend over and stood watching as Evra, with more dexterity than he would have thought for a child of five shades, extracted one piece after the other from the wedge and tumble of the junk pile.

'Look, here's a good bit,' she told him, holding up a tie plate. He had nodded vaguely. Taking care of a child was hard. They just did things. They didn't stop to ask permission, they didn't think about whether things were safe or not and if it was right to be touching them. The whole scrap heap was something most children would be cautioned to stay well away from, he thought to himself. He really needed to get better at this thing, he thought to himself, once again. It was a thought never far from his mind at the moment.

Now, at the table, Evra was already talking about returning to her piles. 'I'm collecting bits from the pile for you to use. In your sculptures. I'm keeping them aside especially.'

'I can see we've got quite the collection out on the porch.'

'Yes. And my favourites are now on the shelf.' Evra pointed to the meagre shelf he had affixed to the shack wall as a place to keep his notebooks. In them were sketches or ideas, both about his sculptures and his work for the railroad. He took them back and forth with him each day to the workshops.

Now, he saw that his notebooks had gone from being loosely piled up to neatly stacked in a vertical, orderly fashion, making room for some of the small sculptures he'd made the shade before last.

'Harlin helped you with that, I suppose.'

'Yes. I told her what to do.'

There were a few quiet moments as they ate.

Merouac pondered the question for a moment before asking, but decided there could be no real harm to it.

'Ev, did your mother ever tell you the story of Maarte?'

'Yup.'

'What did she tell you?'

'She was taller than anyone who ever lived. And she just walked around and around. Like Heyla does.'

'Well, I guess Maarte and Heyla are a little bit alike. They're both tall and they both walk a lot!'

'Maarte was taller. She could touch the sky.'

'That's true. What else?'

'Maarte created the shield.'

The shield, of course, was the term used for the seventh layer of hahma current that encased the hahmasea – the layers of Ahm's atmosphere. There were seven layers of atmosphere that sat, one on top of the other, between the ground and the furthermost limit of sky.

Each layer had a different structure and differing levels of current. The hahmasea's lower four levels had the strongest charge, gradually ascending to reach the strongest charge at the fourth level, at around a mile above sea level. The next three levels were weaker in hahma current, but worked to exert pressure downwards towards the core of the planet, serving to hold the lower levels in place.

The seventh and outermost layer exerted the strongest pressure, and was for that reason known as the shield, a protective layer that both locked the atmosphere in place and protected the atmosphere from outside energy.

'Why did she create the shield?'

'To keep everyone safe.'

'Uh-huh.'

'But we don't need it anymore. It's going away,' his niece explained in a decidedly manner-of-fact way.

It differed across the continent but the origin story of the shield was always based on the story of Maarte. The story of Maarte was strongest and most frequently told in Tustennuit, the lawless country that still drew mystics and Maarte scholars who wanted to return to the source of divinity. Maarte, a young child who grew into the tallest person ever to have walked the planet, realised Ahm was precious, sacred, and needed to be kept safe from any other inhabitants of the wider universe who might seek, at one point in time or other, to occupy or take over the planet.

Maarte spent her lifetime thinking on the problem and, in the hours before she died, drew into life a shield that encompassed the whole of the planet, an invisible, protective barrier that would forever keep the planet safe and keep all other life out. The actions so exhausted her that she expired immediately after, but promised to exist in the aether, continually guarding and protecting the planet.

Merouac reflected on what Malaena had told him; that she had prayed to Maarte, the creator of the shield, the protector of the planet, as a child on the cliff, waiting to be rescued.

Maarte hadn't answered. And that's when Malaena knew. Maarte wasn't there anymore. Maarte was gone and so was the shield.

After they had finished their gruel and washed up, they sat on the porch step. Merouac massaged his thigh, which was still sore and stiff. The bruising was still a purplish-black, but the pain had at least lessened to a gentler throb.

He winced as he leaned over to lace up his boots. He drilled his niece. 'Okay, Ev. I'm back in the workshop from today. You'll need to be good for Harlin, you hear?'

'Yup.'

'What are you going to do if you want to see me today?'

'I have to ask Harlin.'

'And what if Harlin says no?'

'Then I can't see you. I have to wait till you come home.'

'When will I be home?'

'For dinner.'

'That's right. So I'll most likely see you at dinner.'

Evra nodded. 'Yup.'

He sat on the small porch of the hut and laced his heavy boots. Evra leaned against him, humming under her breath. She wrapped her arms around his arm, cheek placed against his shoulder.

Merouac nudged her. 'Here comes Harlin. Hand me those crutches. And be good today.'

'Morning, boss,' Seb greeted him outside the workshop, eying first Merouac and then his crutches and then the necessary path he would have to take to get to his office. Seb went to work immediately, moving obstacles out of the way.

In the workshop, Merouac's men greeted him warmly. It was the habit to shout out to greet the boss and so shouts rose up from each section of the shop in the usual way and he replied with a grin and a wave. He made his way through the general work spaces to his office, at the rear of the second workshop, closest to the stores and incoming arrivals of goods and materials.

'Here you go,' said Seb, as they made their way into the small rectangular office. Seb pulled Merouac's chair out from under the desk and directed Merouac to sit.

'You don't need to do that, Seb,' Merouac said, somewhat embarrassed.

'Just for the first few days, boss, while you're getting settled. It's no bother.'

Merouac sat. It was somewhat comforting to be back in a world he knew and was, well, far more normal than the world he had started stepping in and out of these last weeks and months.

His large tools – the saws and the mallets and the hammers hung on the wall near the bench, all marked out, each with a specific place where only that one particular thing could be hung.

Still strewn across the bench, from when he had last been in here more than ten days ago, now were sections of round bar, goggles, gloves, abrasive blocks, a pile of rags and next to those another pile of polishing cloths, all radiating the aroma of farlen oil. Hammers, pliers, spanners and clamps covered the surface of the bench, under which were plans, railroad maps, hand drawn sketches and piles of paper work orders, now marked and grimy. Open jars of various sized screws and rivets sat here and there, some holding down the sketches so as not to allow them to float off the desk onto the even dirtier workshop floor.

'All under control? Paperwork, I suppose. What do I need to look at?'

'I've got tea on the burner.' Merouac's second in command returned with the papers from the last few days on his desk, along with two mugs of steaming marla tea.

'We're due for a near final update on the tearing up of some of the old lines, so I'll see to that and come and let you know what's what after. Here are the latest supply sheets; that lot's come in today, this lot tomorrow. And these order forms need your signature. Also, more men are coming off the Marville line; should be here in three or four days. We'll need to let Pearl know.'

Merouac took the papers and the tea and sat them at the desk in front of him. 'Thanks, Seb.'

'No bother at all, boss,' Seb replied. 'I'll just be next door should you need me.'

Merouac took a sip of his tea and leaned back. It was a comforting to hear the shouts of his men across the workshops and the eternal clatter, ringing and banging of hammers over the hot forges. So too, the smell, of smoldering hot metal and smoke and the grit of it all; you never left the workshop without a layer of grime and soot covering your skin, no matter how light the layer might be. Merouac hadn't worked on the tools so much these last few shades, and even he left at the end of each day with the same layer of black grit glistening and mingling with sweat.

The men were busy with the production and ordering of the track components; nails, fasteners and so on, making sure their supplies were ready as soon as they were able to start laying down the track for the first five stages of the line, which would be any day now. Even though many of their supplies were delivered ready to use, it was their job to ensure the railroad tracks fitted and adjusted to the terrain. Some additional customisation was required for different sections where tracks merged, crossed other tracks or passed over water on bridges.

The hahmatricians were in another section of the workshop, ensuring the L4 hahma current would be connected all along the track route, ready to turn on and activate the railroad's power supply, at least what was not supplied by steam itself. Then there were the general carpenters who had arrived in order to start building all the maintenance sheds that would dot the line on every mile of its route, to ensure signals were kept working, the tracks were clear and the stations themselves were kept in good order.

After a time signing off on paperwork and settling back into the sounds and smells of the workshop, Merouac looked across his desk and saw the pile of newspapers mounting up. He pulled over the pile of broadsheets and started flipping through them.

The sub-camp's newspapers came with the overnight mail from Endren and arrived with any number of other papers or instructions for Merouac. The papers usually got disseminated among the men, purely because Merouac rarely read them. Most days, by the time Merouac got around to reading them, their thin pages were well-worn and covered with fingerprints, with large sections of copy illegible as a result of the ink getting smudged by his men's thick fingers.

There were three different newspapers that were delivered: a union paper, which came once a week, a high society daily paper and the trade paper, the one Merouac mostly looked at.

He didn't think he'd ever read the high society paper in his life, but now he picked up one of the latest editions and opened it. *The Mantle,* it was called. At least the paper was weightier, and cleaner, too. This one didn't get read as often by the men and so wasn't in such a bad state. The first page he opened up had a story on the railroad. That surprised him. He looked more closely, squinting his eyes and bringing the paper closer to his face to see the details.

'Alright there, boss?' Seb had reappeared at the door.

'Did you see the story on the railroads in here?'

'Nope, not yet, at least.'

It was a story about the Marville line, the second line of the railroad and the one that had been causing Merouac a whole lot of grief, and was yet to be fully opened. The feature image on the left-hand side of the spread was a face he recognised.

'Delsaine Marville, daughter of the well-known Marville family, and wife of the Governor-in-Waiting of Suron,' Merouac read aloud.

'She's the lass who paid for the line, didn't she?'

'Hmm? Oh, right. Yes, apparently. Family money equates to naming rights, I guess, hence the Marville Line being named after her. You remember, she was out here not long ago.'

Seb nodded slowly, pulling up a chair and sipping his own tea. 'She came here to find that other fellow, didn't she? The one you brought back down from Banne to help with … with …'

'Well, naming rights or not, this story isn't as much about her as it is about us, Seb.' Merouac's frown deepened the longer he kept reading.

The story in the paper covered the connections to Delsaine and her own family line, but then quickly proceeded to cover the fact that work on the line had been held up while they addressed unnamed issues.

Merouc swore as he looked at the photos on the next page; one of him, Sham Leoch and a few others, taken from a distance, but at the site of one of the derailments. Merouac didn't remember a photographer being close by.

There was no caption, no mention of who it was in the frame. But it pointed to the railroad men being clearly perturbed about the situation.

'Since when does *The Mantle* cover the state of the railroad?'

'Since it's got a pretty well-placed high society lass involved, pr'aps,' Seb mused.

'Well, we look pretty damned guilty in this shot. They're essentially pointing the finger at us for something they know nothing about. They should stick to taking photographs of social events.'

Merouac felt aggrieved by the commentary on the delays, the issues and the insinuations that the track errors were the result of the workshops not doing their work. It wasn't anything he hadn't heard before but it continued to be a sore spot for him.

He kept reading. There was another story, about the possible appearance of an odd planet in the sky, seen by thousands of people across the continent, and which may have caused the recent dust storms.

Merouac sat back. 'Seb, I haven't seen much of this kind of coverage in the other papers. Has the society rag been writing this kind of stuff for long?'

'I ain't sure, to be right honest about it, Mer. I read them less than you do.'

'Can you get me some back-copies, from the last annalshade or so? Give us more of an idea of what they've been covering?'

'Back issues, you mean? Well I can't see why not. I'll go look into it now.' Seb got up and took himself off to his own, smaller office next to Merouac's.

Later that morning, a stack of older editions of the broadsheets had arrived, and Seb piled bundle after bundle against the wall in Merouac's office. 'Should keep you busy for a few days then, boss,' he remarked, somewhat proud of his efforts in delivering on Merouac's request.

'Hand me some of the oldest ones, will you?'

The pages of the older editions were more fragile and a faded yellow, but still legible.

Merouac read stories of the Great Northern, the first line of the Transcontinental Railroad being launched to great fanfare. Quotes from society folk declaring it a great success, this ability to travel from north to south without having to change trains even once.

There were photos of the new carriages, of the new stations, of travellers themselves looking out the large windows and waving to the photographers.

It was a Suroni publication, and focused on matters relevant to the country itself. So amid stories of the railroad there were stories of about architecture, new buildings in development, the sale of estates, the state of the sandstone quarries and about development, and much coverage of cultural and social events.

There was coverage of the Governor of Suron, Gartounne Leron, and the fact of his seventieth birthday, which had come and gone with less celebration than would have been usual for a Governor due to the fact that he had been bedridden for some years now and was rarely seen out.

There was also commentary about the fact that the Governor Leron had not, as was the tradition, passed on the governorship at the age of 70, to his first-born son. In this instance Gartounne only had one son, and that was Sanat Leron. Merouac noted that no mention was made of the other sibling, the daughter. He was beginning to understand why Heyla had fought against her upbringing and left Sanat Leron to deal with their father himself. He was a miserable piece of work.

Merouac sat brooding throughout the morning, nursing his leg and drinking mug after mug of marla tea. His attention was only partly on the job, as he got through the stack of paperwork and supply requests that had started to pile up. The other part of his brain was working through the injustices of being blamed for train derailments when there was no clear evidence at all that the metalwork was to blame.

Late morning, and with Merouac already feeling a sense of exhaustion despite not yet having moved from his desk, another face popped its head around the doorway of his office.

'T,' Merouac said in surprise. 'What are you doing here?' His boss, Tielder, was sturdy, hairy and had a thick bushy beard he'd been proudly growing for as long as Merouac had known him.

'I came to see how you're doing after all the storms, for a start. Would have come sooner, but the silt made a good old mess up north. I've been up helping them clear the lines so the Great Northern can get back on track. Then I heard you were laid up good. What happened?'

'Bruised thigh,' Merouac replied.

'Is that so? How'd that happen?' Tielder said lightly, inviting himself in to Merouac's office and pulling up a chair.

'Want some tea?' Merouac asked, trying to buy himself some time.

'I do. Good idea,' Tielder said, getting up and shouting out for someone to bring him a cup.

Merouac considered how much Tielder really needed to know about the situation. A little, because he was his boss, and a good one at that. Tielder had, after all, made him Head Metalsmith only a year after he'd arrived at the Endren workshops. Merouac decided to focus on the thing that he himself wanted cleared up.

'Evra and I went out for a walk near the Jacks the other day. I went too far up; and I fell.'

'Well, she shouldn't be going with you on jaunts like that, Merouac.'

'You're right, T. The kid needs to be in school. I want a school built here so she's got somewhere to be. You've got one at Endren for the families. It's time we built one here.'

'A school? How long are you planning on staying here, Mer? This is a sub-camp. It's not permanent. You won't likely be here for that long, and neither will your workers. It's not worth taking the time to set it up. You'll be coming back to Endren soon enough, and Evra can go back to school there. I don't get it, Merouac,' Tielder said, exasperated. 'There must be ten families here who can take care of Ev. Why does it need to be a school?'

'Because it does. It's what her mother would expect. She's a quick kid, T, and she doesn't deserve to get less just because she's with me. I want her schooled.'

'Look. I'll tell you what. You get these first five sections of the East-West lines delivered on time, I personally guarantee you your school.'

Merouac looked suspiciously at Tielder. 'How are you going to do that?'

'I'll figure out something. But when the time is right, Merouac. And it'll be better coming from me. Not you.'

ooo

Merouac was starting to feel like he might have done his dash for his first day back, when Fernell appeared.

'Hey, boss. Good to see you back. Meanwhile, we've got issues with some of the deliveries. They tried to make delivery to the East-West sub-camp and were told this camp was now called, what was it, here … Bitroux. And so they took their deliveries back and now we don't have the supplies we need.'

'Yes, that's the right name for the camp, now.'

'Bitroux? Since when? And what does it even mean? And who decided on the re-naming?'

'I did.'

'Why?'

'Because I told my niece she could name the camp, and that's what she came up with. So that's what it is.'

'Well, that's real nice, boss, but now our orders are now heading back to Banne.'

Merouac swore. More delays were the last thing they needed. 'Well, call them and tell them to turn around and bring them back. And, just to be clear, that's the name. Manage instructions for all deliveries and ensure the rest of Stores know about it.'

Fernell sighed and shifted from one foot to the other. 'Might not have been the wisest thing, Merouac. We need to go through official channels for that kind of thing. We can't just go around changing the name of the railroad sites.'

'I'll send word,' Merouac replied. He felt exhausted already, and he'd only been back on the job for moments.

Fernell looked unhappy about it, but nodded and retreated.

Merouac was about to collect his gear and head out when Mingus and Jan appeared. Merouac sighed, sat down, and waved the two men in.

6.
Mingus and Jan query Merouac

'Got a few moments, boss?' Mingus asked, tapping gently on the wall next to the door to Merouac's office.

Mingus was a man on Merouac's crew who Merouac had long appreciated. The man, not much older than he, was thoughtful and often held his tongue where others would jump in wanting to be heard first. He had dark hair often tied back in a knot near the nape of his neck and wore a kerchief around his neck. He was reed thin, and moved with an ease that was almost elegant.

Unlike most of the men on the railroad who were hailed from the Ingrue and Banne Country, Mingus was from Tustennuit, the wildest, most lawless and secretive country on the whole continent. And yet he was remarkably intelligent and civilised. He listened with patience and mulled on things for a long time, and then spoke slowly and quietly. He was known to offer thoughts or remarks days after a conversation had taken place, and most others had moved their attention on to other things.

Merouac didn't know much of his background other than the fact that he'd had a unique sort of apprenticeship up at the Banne Port workshops. He had stayed there for his whole apprenticeship and worked with visiting metalsmiths specialising in one technique or another rather than travelling round a larger selection of workshops across the continent as Merouac had done. Still, it seemed to have served him well and he'd earned Merouac's respect and trust early on, when they were working together on the first railroad to be laid as part of the Transcontinental Railroad project; the Great Northern.

He, his wife and four children had been based at Endren, and he had moved directly onto the Marville line as part of Merouac's crew. Then, after Merouac was sent out to the middle of the continent to start preparations for the East-West line, Mingus had duly followed, just as soon as Merouac was permitted to start pulling men in. Mingus's wife Aya and the boys were now based in the worker's camp.

Jan was another of Merouac's crew who had been with him since the beginning. More practical and emphatic perhaps than Mingus, Jan spoke with his hands and liked to draw things out to get ideas and plans straight in his head. He'd often drawn Merouac into rapid-fire question and answer sessions about what was required for railroad production specs. Jan would collect Merouac and bring him over to a table where a bunch of the men had already convened. Jan would indicate with a quick flick of his hand where the group was up to in the process of thinking or planning things out, and then rattle of a bunch of questions for Merouac to answer.

'What's up?' Merouac asked lightly, while at the same time sensing that the two of them waiting till the end of the day to catch him meant something could well be up.

'Well, for a start, we just wanted to see how you and Evra are doing,' said Mingus. He and Jan stepped into the office and closed the door behind them.

'Getting there, thanks.'

'That was some fall, Merouac,' said Jan. 'We've been talking it over, the two of us, and we still can't figure it out. How that kid of yours is still with us. Thank Maarte she is, of course, but you know what we mean.'

'I do,' said Merouac. 'And I'm grateful for your help.' Both Mingus and Jan had been part of the rescue party, deep in the bowels of the caves, to get Evra back.

Mingus waved the thanks away. 'Aye. Of course. But, still.' Mingus offered one of his long, pregnant silences and Jan also let it hang in the air. It seemed both Merouac and Jan knew Mingus well enough to understand how much was being said in that silence.

Merouac sighed. 'Pull up a chair, both of you. Everyone gone for the day?'

They nodded.

Jan coughed. 'So, boss, as we said. We got to talking, and the more we talked, just Mingus and I, mind you, the more confused we got. So we thought you could help us better understand what exactly is going on.'

'I can try,' Merouac said.

'Well, to begin with, boss, what took you down there in the first place? How was it that you and Evra were down in those caves? And to take the question one step further, why was the kid down there with you? Not that we want to get personal, boss, but with all the other questions we got, those seem like the most sensible ones to start with.'

Merouac wished he could start collecting shekels for every time he found himself in the position of having to decide just how much to confide in the people around him, and what the right level of information was to provide. But these were the best and most trustworthy of his men. In addition, Merouac was starting to feel like it might be good to have a few people in his confidence.

He looked from Mingus to Jan and back again. He took a breath. And then reached into his pocket and pulled out the map of the caves he'd been carrying around with him, and placed it on the table. Both men leaned over with interest to take a look.

'Alright. First things first. This is just between us and goes no further for the moment, do you hear?'

Both men nodded.

'Just before the dust storms, I was given this map of the caves. There's quite a deep and complex network of them under the grid below Suron. A few of us have been down there exploring, because, as you say, no one ever really knew about them. Then, I got word that there was a generator down there, generating L7 current.'

'L7, are you sure?' Mingus asked.

'Yes, it was L7. The generator was also found directly below the Marville line, where the derailments had been happening. I wanted to see if there could be a connection between the hahma current and the derailments.'

'An L7 current would definitely muck around with the railroad,' Mingus said slowly.

'That's right. But, hold onto your hats, there's more to say.'

Both men nodded expectantly.

Merouac paused, and took a beat before he spoke again. 'Let me start this by asking you both - are you ready for an esoteric, *planetary* conversation?'

Mingus and Jan looked at each other and shrugged.

'Half the continent is claiming to have seen a new planet appear in the night sky, only to have it disappear days later', Mingus remarked, seemingly unvexed by the direction his boss was heading in.

Jan nodded his agreement. 'If there was any time to be having a planetary conversation, as you call it, boss, now would seem to be the time.'

'Alright then, he we go' said Merouac. 'It's quite likely that the shield is down. It seems it's been thinning for quite some time and, if that's the case, then we, as in the planet of Ahm, aren't really alone any more. The working theory has always been that if the shield fades, we'll become part of the wider universe and other beings, races, energies and frequencies will be able to make contact. And, essentially, they have.'

Merouac paused. Silence. Both men waited for him to continue, seemingly eager to hear more and without the judgment Merouac had been dreading.

He continued. 'There's been a particular kind of being that's been making its presence known to both me and Evra. I've called them the Top Hats. I've been seeing them for some time and I think they're connected to the railroad somehow. Anyway, they made an appearance down in the caves. Evra followed one of them. That's how she fell.'

Mingus and Jan were quiet, brooding. Mingus fished a box of cigarillos out of his hip pocket and offered them around. All three took one and they sat in silence for a few moments.

'She fell, but she still survived, Merouac,' Mingus said.'Almost without a scratch. It seems you're worse off than her, and only because you wouldn't wait till we found more rope.' It was true. Merouac had jumped the last thirty feet because they hadn't found the rope needed to lower him any further.

'I know. She tells me the Top Hats caught her, saved her in fact.'

More silence.

'There have been rumours about the shield fading for a while, now,' Mingus said, leaning over and opening the door to Merouac's office so the air could circulate. 'Those Top Hats, boss. Friendly, then, if you said they've been appearing and talking in some way to both you and Evra? Why did they let her fall, then?'

It was at this point that Merouac realised he'd reached his limit, at least for the time being. He'd tell them more, but explaining his theory of the Top Hats leading him to the place where the Helara could journey to, to escape their imploding planet, was a big leap. He'd wait.

'I don't know. But I do think they were trying to show us more of the caves. In fact, I'm thinking about going back down there.'

'You really want to try that, boss?' Jan said doubtfully. 'The grid's got a pretty close eye on it at the moment. I don't like your chance of getting past the Ingruan watch dogs.'

The underground hahma grid stretched right across the continent. The grid itself was managed by the Ingrue, the only country these days to produce hahma current, sell it and disperse it across the grid. Many of the Ingruan men moved constantly through the grid, employed to tinker, test, fix and clean to keep the flow of hahma current steady. Merouac imagined there might be more of them around now than before, with so many people having taken refuge down there in the storms. The Ingruan men were no doubt in the process of clearing out all the folk who had thought they might take shelter down there for good.

'Well, that's true about the grid. But the caves aren't owned or managed by the Ingrue. They're in Suron, and it seems as though nobody really knows much about them. How deep they go. How far they stretch. If it's just in that one site, or if they stretch further below ground into other countries. I'm thinking it just requires a dip into the grid to find the passage to the caves, and then the map should point the way to get back down to where we were. I wouldn't mind a few extras if you men were keen to join me?'

ooo

They were going underground. They had waited another two days before setting out, allowing Merouac's leg some more time to come good.

Merouac, Jan and Mingus set out for Suron Junction before dawn, while the two moons were still large. The junction would be busy as soon as the sun rose. A key intersection for trade deliveries crossing the country and transiting over to other lines, many people also changed here to make their way into the capital of Suron, to spend a day in the gardens or on the promenades – a particularly popular pastime especially in the warmer seasons.

'Merouac,' Jan had said with a warning voice, the morning they set out. 'This isn't about us proving anything, remember? It's just about getting a better understanding of things.'

'What if they're one and the same?' Merouac had retorted. He knew his men were concerned; they had repeatedly told him to stop worrying about the issues with the Marville line.

'I want to see this generator again for myself,' Jan had continued. 'But let's take it one step at a time, eh, boss?'

Most entrances into the power grid were not marked by anything on the ground other than a small post with a numbered code and a heavy lid covering a man-hole that was latched and locked, and would potentially have to be jacked open, unless a worker had been careless enough to leave it open, or crafty, or generous enough, Merouac thought, thinking of all of those who had descended into the grid to find shelter during the dust storms, and those who had then found their way even further underground, into the caves below the grid in Suron.

Only the Ingruan power crews had business being in the grid, maintaining and fixing power connections underside in the famously complex and never-ending tunnels of the grid.

They had timed their journey for when a shift change would be occurring in the grid. Like the shifts at Endren, the grid shifts went around the clock. Jan had done some reconnaissance at one of the bars out near the Junction the previous night, talking to some of the workers to try and see if he could hone in on the exact time of the pre-dawn shift change.

It seemed Jan's intel was correct; with no one else in sight, the men easily jacked the man-hole and stepped down the short ladder into the grid. The air was warm and dry. The passageway was lit by the small bulbs of hahmalight positioned at regular intervals along the walls of the tunnel.

Merouac had a flash of the first time he had descended into the grid; some weeks ago, when the pale pink imposter of a planet had loomed softly in the night sky and hordes of people had likewise flooded the grid, looking for shelter.

Evra had been on his shoulders and she had reached up and brushed her small hands against the pipes above them, asking why some were warm and others not.

He had explained that only a fraction of the grid was in use any more. Most of the pipes were cold and many rusting from not being used anymore, not because hahma power wasn't in high demand, but because they had streamlined the gridline to focus on key veins of current threading across the continent.

Of course, it was just another reminder to him that children's hands and fingers went everywhere, touching things they had no idea could harm them. The pipes were not hot enough to burn Evra's fingers, but they could have been. It was one more reason he wanted to get a school for the child, so she could be safely under the care of someone who knew more about what children were likely to do, and know in advance not to let them.

The three men, assembled at the foot of the ladder, took stock. It was quiet.

Having grown up in the Ingrue, Merouac knew what to look for;

you could tell an Ingruan by their thick, red, often curly hair. He and Malaena had been a strange anomaly in their youth; the only children of the camp they had grown up in to have jet-black hair. All the other kids' hair had ranged from a soft goldish-blonde to a shrieking carrot orange. The union workers also wore the Metal union insignia on the left-hand side of their tawny-coloured shirts and overalls.

The way appeared to be clear, at least for the moment.

'Let's get moving,' said Merouac, quietly.

Mingus nodded, as did Jan. 'Keep your back against the walls, and then retreat into the offshoot tunnels if we hear anything,' added Jan, reminding the other two. This was the main thing that was going to help them steer clear of trouble. Even though the main tunnels were well lit, there were so many offshoots leading into other parts of the grid that they would easily be able to melt back into darker corridors if any of the Ingruans passed.

It was certainly a lot quieter than the night he had been here with Evra, Merouac thought to himself. Either the crowds had all returned to the surface and started getting on with their lives, or they were even deeper down, in the complex and previously unknown cave system below.

They examined the coding on the map Epoque had crafted for moving through the tunnels of the power grid to find the access point to the caves. Most of them had a vague sense of knowing where they were. Mingus, Jan and several others from Merouac's workshop crews had all travelled this route again the night following the one when Merouac had first descended. That was the night they had been working against the clock to find and retrieve Evra from the very deep cavern she had fallen into.

They walked at pace, moving closer towards the centre of Suron proper, towards the only access point to the cave system anyone seemed to know about. They turned left, and then right, sinking back into the shadows whenever they heard distant voices. But thankfully, none came close. They continued.

Twice, they paused and revisited the map. Then, finally, they reached the drop down.

The man-hole leading down into the tunnels was discreet, to say the least. It was hidden away in an obsolete, unused and unlit tunnel of the grid, almost as if it had been put there purposely to only be found by those who had made it in the first place.

The three men jumped down; there was no ladder this time, simply a short jump into the first tunnel of the caves.

Merouac felt assaulted by conflicting sensations as they jumped down.

First of all, the caves, eight layers of interconnected tunnels going deeper into the belly of the planet, should have been a place of extreme discomfort for Merouac. He hated being underground at the best of times. It was one of the reasons he'd known to stay away from a career in the mines.

But the caves were different; the rough-hewn tunnels were warm, the air clean and fresh and not musty and damp as would be expected. They felt safe and warm and so his body went through an automatic response of being uncomfortable, shortly followed by a sense of all-pervading wellness. It was strange.

Despite the positive sense of energy in the caves, which he had remembered from last time, it was still the place where he had reached breaking point, where he had been scared for the life of his niece and had very nearly lost her for good. And so the terror and the desperation flooded through him momentarily also. The fact that her fall had not been fatal was part of the big mystery he was now embroiled in, and part of the reason he had wanted to return here, to see that drop again and know for sure it was deeper than she could have survived alone.

He remembered the exact moment Evra had seen Tunga, the

name she had given to one of the Top Hats, the pale floating blue creatures they had both started to see in the late, dark hours. The difference between Merouac and his young niece was that where Merouac felt cautious and unsure, Evra was confident and had wasted no time befriending the creatures.

'Tunga!' Evra had cried out, recognising her friend. Evra had started moving at pace towards the tunnel on the other side of the cave.

'Evra, come back here,' Merouac had called out, stepping towards her, blinking at the same time.

Epoque, their young guide, had been behind him, and had also cried out as she had seen Evra run off. 'We haven't mapped that tunnel,' Epoque had gasped, the fear in her eyes ramping up his own terror more than a notch.

He recalled the sense of paralysed terror that had flooded his body, freezing him, and how slow he felt himself moving as he ran after her.

It was the last they had seen of the young child until Merouac had heard her voice as he was being lowered down into the chasm she had fallen into.

He'd never been so relieved to hear a voice in all his life. After a long night of trial-and-error recovery efforts, and despite his rough landing at the base of the chasm, he had taken the child into his arms and hugged her harder than he ever remembered hugging anyone.

'Which way?' Mingus asked.

'Back to where we were,' Merouac replied.

'Where Ev fell?' Jan probed, a look of concern shadowing his face. 'Are you sure you want to go back there, boss? Might be easier just to go straight to find that generator, eh?'

'Aye,' said Mingus. 'I agree. Better to avoid that place, Mer. It'll only be upsetting, wouldn't it?'

Merouac gritted his teeth. At some point in the next few moments he was going to have to front up and tell them the next part of the story, the story of what had happened after they had rescued Evra.

'Let's go. I'll explain as we move,' Merouac said.

The Helara, the very fact of them, was something that had been keeping Merouac awake at night. He was dubious about telling his men about what the full situation was, but it was important for at least a few of them to understand that the generator they were down here to inspect was a bigger part of the story than they yet knew.

The tunnels of the cave were round and looked hand-hewn, the floors soft and sandy. The rock walls were covered in a chalky surface, small sediments that came off with a brush of the hand.

'Does anyone know who even owns these caves?' Mingus said quietly.

Jan shrugged. 'Suron, I assume. It's not part of the grid, so the Ingrue wouldn't have any jurisdiction down here. But I'm guessing they'll be all over it if they think people are coming through the grid to get down here.'

They made their way through uneven passages that narrowed, became wider and then narrowed again After a time, the passages became wider and started to lead off into their own labyrinth of tunnels, and it was then that they started to see that in fact there was still a substantial number of people around.

Some of the passages led to chambers and caves which whole families seem to have moved into. Some tunnels led to deep recesses that smelled of food and cooking and yet the tunnels were not smoky; ventilation must have been thought out at some point to make the caves actually livable, Merouac thought to himself.

Jan moved off momentarily to speak to a small family group, crouching in front of them as he asked questions and nodded his understanding. 'Their guess is that there are around 150 families, groups and individuals set up down here, in various nooks and crannies. Apparently, most of them haven't gone down too far. They're mostly up here on the first level; some have gone down to the next level but not many.'

Continuing, they passed through a large, open cave Merouac remembered. Its domed ceiling and echoing acoustics seemed impossible, but Jan pointed out as they moved through the space that they had possibly been travelling downwards as they went, and so the height may not be so surprising after all.

Merouac remembered when Evra's own father, Salvette, had made the connection between the generator and the railroad. And so, as they got closer to the place where the massive generator sat, Merouac stopped his men and started to explain the extended theory about tuning metal, creating frequency bridges and all that had happened to lead them here, to the generator.

ooo

'So Merouac, what you're saying is that the generator's been doing double duty, of sorts,' Jan said, as the three men stood over the crevasse where only darkness lay. They had reached the point of the recovery efforts, the generator looming behind them and an odd assortment of ropes strewn across the floor. Both confirmed to the men that they had reached the site Merouac intended; the place where Evra had fallen.

Merouac nodded.

'And following that, you came back here, after Evra was reclaimed, and you brought her here again.'

Merouac detected a note of frustration in Jan's voice but he nodded. 'Aye.'

'And you moved this big beast of a machine here, from where Salvette originally found it, to power up this thing that you're calling a frequency tuning, to create a bridge of sorts, is that right?

Alongside a dozen Faurin monks, you charged up the generator to full L7 current and created some kind of frequency bridge that allowed the Helara, an alien life species, or foreign energies of some kind, to escape their imploding planet, into the caves, down there into the abyss, and even further down into some kind of vast empty chamber, where they are now, resting and recovering?'

'That's one way to sum it up,' Merouac agreed.

He thought back to that experience, among the strangest, most surreal and yet most moving of all the unique experiences he had been part of since the conversation about the shield being down had started.

He remembered the deep chants of the Intangien echoing through the caves, pummelling at the edge of Ahm's frequency range.

He remembered striding over to the generator, switching the levers to full, feeling the shift in static charge. 'It's starting,' he had shouted.

The contact had faltered and then broken before reasserting itself and opening a space across the realms. The pressure in the air kept rising as the chants of the Intangien rose and fell.

A rumble sounded in the distance, a rolling seismic wave that travelled closer and closer until eventually it surrounded them. It was followed by another and another. Frequencies collided, whitewash and foam. There was a deafening roar of static, a sense of confusion and displacement that peaked and dropped as the resonance match took hold.

Across the realms, across the tides and the frequencies beyond the shield, they locked their grip. They had felt it with a sharp, halting sense that had a physical effect. A judder, like a ship crashing into a mooring. The frequencies of the two realms merged, sharing a single vibration.

A murmuring, carried on the air, came and went. The Helara had begun to appear. At first one, and then two and then groups of three, and then there were more than could be counted. The cavern became immersed in a field of orange light. A strange song insinuated itself through the tuned air. There were so many of the strange other-world creatures arriving that they became a white blur.

They had watched, awed, at the silent, urgent journey taking place in front of them. Merouac had not thought there would be so many of them, not realised they would come so thick and so fast. But of course it made sense. An entire realm, a whole planet of sentient energy.

The mist had thickened; there was a final rush and then everything went quiet. The chasm below faded into darkness. The Helara had migrated. They were safe. The transfer had worked.

Even though they had been deep underground at the time, Merouac had had the sense that, above them, high in the sky, the Helara's former home had held its last breath as long as it could. It breathed out, releasing its entire particle structure with a magnificent, resounding crack that finally splintered inwards into a million fractures, splitting apart all layers, all parts of its structure and disassembled into itself.

And now, back here at the scene, Merouac felt sure that what he thought had happened, had in fact really happened. His memory was true.

Below them, further below than even where Evra had fallen, were the final known depths, where the Helara now slept, an alien race who at some point in time would surface, be recalibrated to the dimension they had migrated to and ready to live again.

Mingus had been sitting, crouched on his knees in deep thought as Merouac had told them the story of his ability to tune metal, the confirmation from the monks of the Remneur Ranges that frequency tunings could be the thing required. And the fact that after having rescued Evra, there had been a second, much larger and stranger, rescue mission. A rescue mission to save an unknown race of creatures from a dying planet.

'Merouac,' Mingus now said slowly. 'You said the generator was already down here. And it was already tuned to L7 current. If more people are aware the shield is fading, then is it possible someone else had already been down here, trying to do the same thing? And if so, who?'

7.

Tor gets word of the generator and the white pala

'Good to see the weather starting to settle down, wouldn't you say, Sir?' Tor Anale's driver had to shout over the rumbling of the car motor. You would never know it by looking at Tor's expressionless face, but the head of Suron's military and railroad logistics did in fact enjoy being chauffeured in his new, very modern, automobile.

They were nearing the Transcontinental Railroad's Central Supplies Depot, a massive, temporary camp north of Suron city that functioned as the logistics base for the Transcontinental Railroad. Hundreds of supply stores had been erected to manage the centralised distribution of steel, timber and other supply goods to where they were most needed in the production schedules of each new line.

The depot was where Tor could be found most days. It was where his role had been based since the start of the railroad project, and he liked it because it provided both purpose and camouflage.

The depot was managed by over two hundred of Tor's military enrolments, and at least a quarter of those had been hand-picked by Tor himself. The selection was informed by a list of critical skills and sensibilities such as the ability to follow orders without question, some disregard for government oversight of military logistics, strong connections to black market networks and the ability to carry out tasks that overlapped with Tor's outside activities without batting an eyelid. Tor looked for both men and women who had the same desire he did to engage in profitable side-ventures with the requisite amount of secrecy and unflappability.

The roads were dirt and the vehicle bumped and jolted. The black exteriors of one of the first A-Class hahma-powered cars to be sold in Suron would be covered in fine orange dust by the time they arrived, but Tor's driver knew better than to open the door for his boss without having wiped the vehicle down first. Tor would only step in, or out, of a spotless vehicle.

Tor Anale waited quietly as his driver parked and cleaned the car. As he sat, he processed the news that had been delivered to him that morning. It was not good news. In fact, it was alarming and the more he thought about it, the more riled up he knew he was likely to get.

His generator had gone missing. His L7 hahma-powered generator, specifically procured, engineered and set up to support his experiments in frequency tunings, had vanished into thin air.

He would attend to it that afternoon, he decided. He would depart early from the depot under the guise of official business in Suron, and make his way down into the grid. But first, the work of the railroad needed his attention.

When the door was finally opened for him, he stepped out and down. A slight breeze ruffled his hair, and he patted it unhappily into place. The previous week, Tor's military whites had turned orange within minutes of being outside. Perhaps he had been optimistic in thinking there would be no wind at all today.

Tor Anale strode towards the guarded open flap of the map tent; he had it guarded because he could, and it cemented the impression that it was the most important place in the depot. He ignored the nearby workers who were subtly shaking their heads at the lunacy of anyone wearing whites in a place like this, especially after the weather that had ripped across the continent recently. Most of them adopted far more sensible attire: hardy canvas pants and shirts, some with scarves over their heads or, at the very least, tied around their necks, to be used to wipe the dust clean when required.

The fact that Tor's team had been recruited for a diverse range of activities didn't change the fact that the business of logistical management for the railroad still had to be done, and done well. In fact, the official work was indeed part of the camouflage – the 'nothing to see here' screen that had worked so well for Tor, for all the years he had been working in Suron, after leaving the Faurin ranges at the age of seventeen.

He arrived at the depot daily at midday and manned the map tent until late afternoon. He reviewed plans, gave orders, approved cost sheets and ensured the supplies kept moving and arrived where they needed to be, for each line to meet its completion dates.

His people knew well enough to stick to their official roles at the depot, with no mention of any other activities underway unless they were directly asked for an update from Tor, in the privacy of the map tent. And, in addition to attending to the roles given to them, the expectation was that they would be good at them, discharge every duty without complaint and be quick about it. Some were better than others, of course.

Today, seven men were standing to attention at their respective tables, ready to show him charts, maps, surveys, tally reports and plans.

As Tor had expected, most looked more worried than usual. The mess the dust storms had created had been nothing short of a complete disaster, and had everyone across the continent scurrying and screaming for answers. And of course supply deliveries were off schedule, and men, who had been in short supply for as long as he could remember, due to the vast scale of the project, were now in even shorter supply as gangs were dispatched to the Great Northern line to clean up the debris from the storms. With an inward sigh that was imperceptible to anyone else, he began at the first table. 'Tell me', he said.

Early that afternoon, there was a second flurry of activity and movement across the camp, similar to the one that had rippled through the camp when Tor Anale arrived. This time it was the Governor-in-Waiting, unannounced.

The arrival displeased Tor Anale. He didn't like spontaneity. And Sanat Leron required careful management at the best of times.

Sanat Leron was a natural statesman. He had the ability to actually do things that people cared about. When Sanat had proposed that the seven countries of San Aurelle start collaborating again as they had when the continent had been federated, people had taken notice. When he had proposed his idea for the Transcontinental Railroad, a united network that would work better for everyone, people had listened and supported him. It was exactly the reason Tor took care. The less Sanat knew, the better.

One of his men stood apologetically in front of him, having delivered the news that Sanat had arrived and had requested to see him.

'Take him to ten-two.' The smallest of five reception tents was used mostly as a cloak room for visiting officials. But better to meet in a small space with little luxury than to take Sanat to the tent that actually served as a tea-room and have him stay longer than was absolutely necessary.

'Sanat.' Tor greeted the Governor-in-Waiting in a noncommittal but polite manner.

'Ah. Tor. Good afternoon.' The two men greeted each other with a handshake.

'Well, Tor, this is a very small space to meet in, isn't it?'

Tor looked around them and shrugged. 'It's perfectly acceptable to me. Nothing like what you're used to, but it serves us well enough.' Tor's expressionless face gave no indication of the delight he took at seeing Sanat stooping, to avoid his tall frame coming into contact with crates and boxes on one side and the canvas ceiling above.

Sanat slapped him on the shoulder. 'Come on. Let's take a walk. I feel like a bit of air and, anyway, I'd like to see the camp. I don't get out here often enough.'

Without asking for Tor's approval of the idea, Sanat strode back out through the tent entrance.

Tor Anale would have argued but as it was he was already talking to thin air.

Like the workers, Sanat was dressed in hardy travelling gear: thick corduroy slacks, linen shirt and a scarf around his neck. With his height, his blond hair and congenial nature, Sanat charmed wherever he went. Already, he'd made his way over to a group of workers, asking questions about what they were working on. They all loved to talk with him. They'd be here till the moons crossed if he didn't intervene.

'Sanat,' he called out sharply. 'This way.'

Sanat excused himself from the group that had quickly gathered around him and caught up to Tor, who had begun walking in the opposite direction, towards the depots, which he had decided were the safest things to show Sanat if he was in the need to be inquisitive.

Besides, it was a stretch away from the rest of the tents, and away from as many eyes as possible.

'What is it that you want, Sanat?' Tor said as they walked.

'I'm chasing that report from the shield survey team that I asked for. There's an enormous amount of discussion going on across the continent. Lots of rumours about the reason for the severity of the dust storms. I asked for a full report and all I've had are a few messages from your men saying everything is fine and there's nothing to worry about.'

'There isn't anything else to tell you, Sanat. The shield is stable. The dust storms were unfortunate, but the shield and the weather aren't connected. I do understand the concern about the impact on railroad logistics. I can show you the new schedules we're working on at the depots.'

Sanat had slowed to a halt, so Tor attempted to cover his annoyance and also stopped, simply pointing at the section of the camp he was taking them to. 'This way.'

But Sanat didn't budge. 'I don't need to know about the logistics, Tor,' he said, crossing his arms and standing firmly, taking a moment and turning to survey the camp at large. His visual survey seemed to only take a minute, and then his attention was steadfastly returned to Tor.

'Ah. So there is no need to show you the depots. Well, we can turn back around.'

'The report, Tor.' Sanat's voice had become a little firmer. 'What's happened to the survey team? Surely they can provide a status update on the shield, and why we've been having all this strange weather. That's their only job, isn't it?'

Tor was silent.

Suron's Governor-in-Waiting paused. His perceptive grey eyes scanned Tor's and he paused for a moment, reflective. 'Tor,' Sanat offered, 'Why don't you just give me a real assessment of the situation, right now? Do you really believe there's nothing going on with the shield? You've got your ear to the ground, and you've been overseeing the shield survey team for some time now. If the report isn't ready yet, why don't you simply tell me what you think, and then we can continue that discussion with the team after they've presented their report.'

Tor remained stubbornly silent.

Sanat's expression set. 'Alright. By tomorrow, then, please,' said Sanat. 'A full report. Leave the logistics for a day and get me this. Please.'

OOO

Already irked by the news of his generator disappearing, and then by the appearance and demands of Sanat Leron, Tor Anale left the map tent early and made his way down into the hahma grid. His experiments with frequency crossings had started three shades prior, and to keep his operations quiet and secure, he had closed off a section of the power grid underneath Suron.

It was completely out of his purview to do so, of course. But oddly enough, he'd gotten away with it. A few discreet signs indicating that maintenance was underway had done wonders to keep things low-key.

It was an art to navigate travel in the grid without drawing attention to himself, but Tor had a well-worn route he utilised to make his way towards the area of the grid directly under Suron city. It was the benefit of the grid being old; many of the tunnels were unused and therefore unmanned.

His Green team, code for the underground operations focusing on the frequency tunings, had been told to be ready for him, and ready they were, assembled and trying, each of them, to avoid his direct gaze.

'It was here, in an enclosed part of the grid that I'm paying you to patrol. How the damn did you not see it go missing?' he asked the group of twelve.

'Well, we didn't see it actively getting taken, that's true,' Henk agreed. 'Apologies.'

Of all his secret projects, this was the most important. Which was not to say it had been the most successful. Far from it. But he couldn't stand the idea of his pet project taking a further step backwards.

Tor gave Henk a look. There was something in the man's tone that gave him pause. A distinct lack of respect, and apparently no fear of the consequences. This was a little new and different for Henk. He'd consider that.

'In any event, boss, it was in a section of the enclosure we only monitored occasionally, due to the fact that it was enclosed,' added Sybil. 'There are signs everywhere not to enter.'

Tor scowled. The fact that someone had breached the perimeter was an insult; the fact that they had stolen something from him he cared about was downright diabolical.

'Of course,' Sybil continued. 'It could have been one of the Ingruan teams. They could have found it, confiscated it, and we'll never hear about it or see it ever again.'

'That's exactly the point,' Tor howled. His voice echoed down the corridor and they all turned, listening to the echo as if it were an embodied person of its own. 'That's why you were guarding it.'

It was true that only Ingruans were allowed to be down in the grid, but, by Tor's own reckoning, they didn't need to be anywhere the hahma current didn't run through.

The last round of frequency tunings had, in fact, been a complete failure. And so the generator had been relegated to the back burner until Tor came up with a new plan. But how would any kind of new plan help if the generator had now gone missing? He would be back to square one, and he was running out of time, especially with Sanat on his case about the shield survey team.

'Why am I paying you all to patrol and monitor the area, if a generator can just go wandering off, all of its own accord?'

Silence from the group.

'Find it,' Tor snapped. They were still in a research phase. There were still adjustments to experiment with. They would figure out the art and science of frequency tuning if it killed him.

'Er … Sir …' Tor turned to the voice coming from behind him. 'What?'

Felarne, one of the other guards on Tor's payroll was approaching from the western perimeter.

'We might have a more immediate problem.' Felarne took off his cap and wiped the sweat from his cheeks. 'I've got an Inspector from Power wanting to access the enclosure. Told him to mind his business, but he's demanding to be allowed through. Says it's illegal for any part of the grid to be closed off like it is. Says there have been reports from different teams recently of this area being inaccessible for works, so he's come down to sort it out.'

The Ingruans' purview was limited to trafficking hahma. Everything else fell into a kind of no man's land, as far as Tor was concerned. And if it hadn't been for all the extra activity in the grid with people trying to shelter from the dust storms, the Ingruans wouldn't have noticed and no one would be any the wiser.

'Well, what do you usually tell them when they ask that? Surely this isn't the first time in three shades that they've come demanding access.'

'True. But in the past, I've told them it's been signed off by the Governor of Suron; special duties. That's worked every time without fail.'

'And this time?'

'It seems they checked.'

'They checked with who?'

'With the Governor. And then the Governor-in-Waiting. They were told they didn't have any concerns down here, and to go ahead and investigate.'

Tor swore. 'Go back and tell them they didn't check with the right people, and to go back and check with the Head of Military.'

'Isn't that you, sir?'

'You know it is, you dimwit.'

'And you don't want to go and talk to them yourself?'

'No, I do not.'

'And you don't want me to bring them through to you here?'

Felarne clocked the deepening scowl on his boss's face, patted his face once more with his handkerchief and nodded, turning and walking briskly in the way he had come.

Later that night Tor Anale left the logistics camp and directed his chauffeur to take him to the Marline Club at Ryelle Market. The precinct was on the Suron City's outer circuit, and home to suppliers of industrial fabrics and fibres, as well as also being the location of quiet meeting places behind nondescript bars that allowed him to conduct much of his off-book business meetings and negotiations.

Attending the Market for meetings after-hours was something he did more often than not, and it was the part of his day he most looked forward to. His pet projects often came to life here, in the shady alleys, secret rooms and quiet corners of an unremarkable part of town.

The Marline Club, however, was not a place Tor Anale frequented often, despite so often being in this precinct, largely because it was a place he knew his logistics teams drank at. It simply would not do for the Head of the Military to be seen drinking with his direct reports, who all collected here, nursing their agras and moaning about the tedium of their duties. Tor agreed with them about the railroad logistics work being unfathomably uninteresting. But it would have been unprofitable to share that with his men. Being eternally unreadable was the seat of his power.

Tonight's meeting, though, had not been organised to further any project he currently had on the go; rather, it had been arranged by the man who ran his off-fleet booking arrangements for him. Dorren was rough, but sharp – at least most of the time. He was a red-head from the Ingrue, one of the rare men from that part of the world who didn't spend their days in the power grid. He'd been Tor's man for the last five shades and had done a decent job of quietly finding trading groups around the continent who wanted to use the excess from the Suroni military vehicle fleet – for a price, of course. The main requirement of any such role of course was that he could keep his mouth shut and ensured others did the same.

Dorren was there to direct him to the private room where three nervous and red-faced men were standing, their hats in their hands.

They were from the mines; that much could be seen from their clothes, which all bore dark stains.

The three men stood awkwardly until Tor motioned for them to sit down.

'Well, we'll be quick,' the taller of the men said. 'Don't want to waste your time.'

Tor Anale gave a brief nod.

'We three here are all partners in the Quaillan mines in the West Ingrue. A few miners got loose with cuttings of gem stones. Smuggled them out, so to speak.'

'Unfortunate,' Tor said.

They nodded. 'We want them back.'

Tor Anale shrugged vaguely. 'Yes, I suppose you would.'

'Well, we heard you might be able to help us out.'

Tor Anale narrowed his eyes.

The man continued, unnerved but stubborn. 'We heard you could access resources. Or, perhaps, put the word out to the market.

That kind of thing.'

'Which market would you be referring to?' Tor Anale asked dangerously.

'Ah … the black market … or so we heard.'

Tor Anale stared at the men. 'Suron does not put its resources to helping out private industry in the Ingrue.'

'It's a white pala stone, Sir,' one of the others continued weakly. 'We could pay a handsome reward.'

Tor Anale shook his head in amazement. 'I will pretend not to have heard that.'

Tor proceeded to explain that the men had heard incorrectly, and that no help could be provided. All the while, his mind was racing, thinking about the fact that what they had just told him was barely believable.

There were three different types of pala – green, the gentlest of them all but easy to find in the Faurin mountains. Black pala, stronger but rare. And then white pala, the most powerful of all and rarest of all the three pala stones.

He'd been using green pala for his tunings to date – which should have worked, and yet nothing had been happening. His one attempt at negotiating for black pala with a trader from across the ocean had fallen through. White pala could solve all his problems in making a frequency tuning actually come to life.

If there was any chance at a shot at grabbing the white pala while it was in circulation, he needed to try. He'd have to make his move soon, but with absolute discretion.

On his way out, Tor Anale cuffed Dorren across the back of his head. 'How dare you,' he snapped.

8.

Salvette comes to dinner and Merouac heads out to the Rolling Jacks

Merouac was deep into the maps of the area around the Rolling Jacks, even though the final version still hadn't arrived. The one detail which had appeared in the most recent version showed that there was a complexity in the route he hadn't anticipated; they were being asked to tunnel through a substantial bulk of mountain. It wasn't going to be easy and it wasn't going to be fast. He'd have to get his demolition crew lined up and ready to move as a priority.

Seb appeared at Merouac's door. 'Ready?'

Merouac nodded and indicated for Seb to take his usual seat, so they could start their morning meeting.

'We've got to start the decamp soon. We'll need to create four sub-camps and then allocate men to each one.'

'Aye.' Seb nodded, writing down a few notes with his pencil and paper.

'We'll need Central Logistics on board to help set up the new camps. We'll also need to get them to send the track materials to each of the minor camps, rather than here directly. They'll need exact lists of what we require for each section.'

'Aye.'

'And we need to hurry Endren along with the final map of the route. We're out of time, especially since they've moved up the schedules. We need to know where the stations are going to be. If they want the first four sections laid quick smart, then that's five stations to be marked out and built.'

'I'll chase them today. I can get on over there if need be.'

'The hahma crew will need to get out there as soon as the map's in. They'll need to start working on the signalling and power connections. And then we're going to have to sort out our labour problem. We've got men coming, but when? I haven't heard anything more from Tielder, so chase him and find out dates. They need to be here within the week. And then they need to get their assignments pretty quick after that. Tell them not to set up camp here because they'll be moving out to their assigned minor camp within the day.'

Seb nodded. 'Got it. I'll need a few men with me for all of this.'

Merouac nodded. 'Take five men, whoever you think is the best fit, and get them onto it.'

'Also,' said Merouac, through somewhat gritted teeth. 'Check in with Stores. They need to be across what's going on and work with us to manage deliveries, both to here and to the minor camps. They were grizzling about the name change here; make sure everyone's clear on it and, if we need to, I can send word to Tielder today. I don't need any more complaints about supplies being further delayed because of me, in addition to the issues we've got with hard wood.'

'Uh, Salvette, hello there,' Merouac heard Seb say.

He looked up to see Salvette standing awkwardly at the entrance to Merouac's office. He had a light sweat on his brow, and he shuffled from one foot to the other.

'Mornin'. I came to have a word with you, Merouac. I weren't sure if you were up and about yet, with the leg and all.'

Merouac sat back. 'No, I'm not quite up and about yet, Salvette,' he said slowly, trying to think a few steps ahead. 'I suppose you're wondering about Evra.'

Salvette nodded. 'I wanted to check in. Perhaps see if I could visit and say hello, if she's on the mend, a'course.'

'Well, she's fine actually, Salvette.' Merouac scratched his cheek. He wasn't particularly happy to have seen Evra's long-disappeared father surface again, and not overjoyed that he was now employed by the railroad. But, at the end of the day, he was family. Evra deserved to have as much family around her as possible. And Salvette had proven his worth during the dust storms, in more ways than one.

'But look, it isn't a great time this morning,' Merouac continued. 'Seb and I have got a lot of things to get working on. Why don't you come on up to the shack later this afternoon? Stop by and see Evra then.'

Salvette nodded eagerly. 'Right. Thanks. I'll do that. Thank you.' And with that, he raised an arm in farewell and stepped back towards the workshop floor, making his way out quickly into the daylight.

'I'll leave you to it, boss,' Seb said.

Merouac nodded but had drifted into deep thought. Despite his seemingly slow wit, more than likely brought about by years of drinking, Salvette could put a thing or two together. It had been Salvette who had first come across the generator down in the grid, set to generate L7 hahma current. It had been Salvette who had made the connection between that generator and the location directly above where the derailments on the Marville line had been occurring. And he'd had the sense to bring that information to Merouac, explain his thinking and help Merouac see the connection as well.

As well as that, Salvette had at one time been married to his twin sister. Malaena had seen something in Salvette. Possibly that early flair was long gone. But people deserved a second chance. And he knew Salvette was aware of Malaena's mercurial nature. He understood she had been doing something rare and arcane, had been long journeying into her own mystery. And that mystery had to do with the crossing back and forth between worlds. Salvette had told Merouac that Malaena had been doing that as long as he'd known her. That she had the gift, but chose not to speak of it. And he'd chosen never to ask, after seeing her disappear into thin air more than once.

Merouac decided he would work with Salvette to find out the best way forward, for Evra, and possibly for himself, as well.

By the time Merouac finished up in the workshop and walked slowly back up to the shack, Salvette had already arrived.

'I hope it's alright,' said Harlin somewhat fretfully. 'He said you'd told him to come on up.'

'It's alright,' Merouac assured her. 'Thanks for looking after her again today.'

Merouac patted Evra on the head as passed her. She was sitting with Salvette at the table at the back of the shack, looking at his scars.

'Look, Merouac. Sal's got marks on his arms.'

'So he does. Hello, Salvette. I'll just get tea on – will you stay for something to eat?'

Salvette nodded. 'Thanks.'

'We'll come back over soon,' Harlin said. 'As soon as Seb's washed up. I'll bring some pudding.'

'Thanks, Harlin.'

Merouac watched from the kitchen as his niece played with

Salvette. Early on, she'd decided to call him Sal, and it suited him, he thought.

Evra had now launched into a game of tag, leaping off the outside bench where they often ate their supper, tapping Salvette and running away, calling out for him to chase her. Salvette was up on his feet and trying to play the game as best as he could, but he couldn't beat a nimble girl of five shades threading and weaving around him.

Again, Evra was showing her remarkable aptitude for being comfortable with things as they were, without any need to know more than what she was presented with. In the same way she had quickly adjusted to her mother's absence, she had adjusted to living with Merouac. From the first day, she had reached for his hand when they were walking, like it was the most natural thing in the world. Now, her father had reappeared in her life and she was as relaxed with him as she was with anyone else. She seemed to harbour no grudge for the fact he'd been largely absent up until now.

The chasing game over and Salvette slightly the worse for wear, Merouac indicated that all three of them should sit. Merouac passed an ale over to Salvette and opened one for himself. Evra sipped from the mug of cold tea he put in front of her.

Evra had returned her interest to the marks and scars on Salvette's hands and forearms. 'What are all these scratches?'

'Those won't last. Just a bit of thistle from all the clearing work.'

Merouac glanced at Salvette's hands, blanched and looked again. The brittle tangles of mirrahedge had wreaked havoc on them. It grew wild, tough and gnarly along many of the wide-open belts of the continent's interior. Salvette was downplaying a thick web of scratches all over his hands, wrists and lower arms. 'All that's from clearing? Why didn't you ask for some gloves?'

Salvette flushed red. 'I didn't even think to ask, truth be told. Thought it just went with the territory.'

'But didn't you see that the other men were protecting themselves from exactly this? The bushes and scrub in these parts are tough. Lots of thorns and things that will tear at your skin.'

'Well, I don't know. It doesn't hurt too much. Next time I'll know to ask.'

Merouac wasn't impressed, but didn't pursue it because Salvette was looking somewhat embarrassed. And he was a railroad rookie, and so it made sense he hadn't thought to ask. He also wondered if Salvette had been given the worst sections of track to clear. The lowest of the low always got the worst jobs.

'Well, we appreciate your work, Salvette. All that clearing means the new track's ready to start laying down. So you and your gang have done well.'

Salvette still looked a little flustered. 'Uh, Merouac, you got anything else I could sip on? I'm off the drink. Drying out, as it were.'

Merouac swore quietly to himself. Of course, he should have asked before he assumed anything. 'Sure. Tea?'

'Like mine?' Evra asked holding up her mug.

'Kind of. Salvette's is going to be hot though, because that's how we drink it. You're the only one around here likes to drink their tea cold and a day old.'

Salvette turned to Evra. 'Is that right?'

Evra nodded solemnly.

'Just like your mama, then.'

Evra grinned and nodded. 'Yup.'

Merouac, who had gotten up to get Salvette a tea, stopped and turned back to Salvette. It was true. Malaena had always liked to let her tea cool before she drank it. He couldn't believe he hadn't made the connection before. 'Huh,' he said.

Evra returned to her activity. 'What's this, then?' she asked, tapping her small finger on Salvette's shoulder, the site of a large blue tattoo. Merouac had noted it previously; it was a large V, surrounded by scrolls and tiny orange macra flowers.

'Well, I used to play the games. I was good once, you know. I travelled all over.'

'What are the games?'

'Card games,' Merouac answered without thinking.

Salvette nodded. 'Card games. I used to play in the rallies. Go up against opponents. Go into the big games with ten or more players.'

'Where did you do that?'

'All over. Pubs and taverns in the Ingrue, to start with. That's where I met your mama. She saw me play once. I used to be real quick. One time, I won a whole season of games. Every place I went to, I won. And so I got this tattoo to remember it.'

'When will it come off?'

'They don't come off, Ev,' Merouac said as he returned to the table with a steaming mug for Salvette. He waved at Seb and Harlin, who were making their way over to share the evening meal with them.

Salvette got up to shake their hands as Merouac introduced everyone.

Salvette was a little rough around the edges, but he was obviously trying. He stood up, forever awkward, it would seem, to shake Merouac's neighbours' hands. His blond hair needed a cut but he looked to have at least tried to brush it. His face had had a shave and a wash, and his blue eyes were clear, a testament to not drinking, Merouac presumed.

'Sal, your pants are falling down,' Evra said loudly.

Salvette looked sheepish. Merouac and the others laughed gently.

'All the work on the railroad's probably getting you into good shape,' Harlin said warmly. 'I can bring your trousers in, if you like.'

'That'd be good, thanks. Might be I need to get a new pair, as well.'

Salvette was still thick around the waist, but it was clear to see that he had in fact lost weight. Merouac scanned him to see if there were any other marks that Evra had inherited. It was mainly the sandy hair, really. Merouac and Malaena had both been born with jet-black hair, which had lightened as they grew up to a dark brown, but Evra was fair like her Dad.

Merouac stepped back from the conversation as Seb and Harlin settled in. Truth be told, he was still sitting on the fence about Salvette. He wanted to do the right thing, but he also still had a reasonable level of resentment towards the man who'd walked out on his sister. It was a slippery, mottled feeling that was hard to define. Even harder was the knowledge that he himself hadn't behaved much better. Last time they'd spoken of such matters, Salvette had pointed out Merouac's own absence for long periods of Malaena's life. And he'd been right, too. They were both culpable.

After dinner, when Seb and Harlin had retired to their own cabin and Evra had gone to bed, he sat outside with Salvette and broached the topic as frankly as he felt he could.

'Salvette, look, I want to trust that Evra having you in her life is a good thing.'

Salvette nodded.

'Tell me again when it all started. With Malaena, I mean.'

Salvette took a breath. 'I don't know. It was always there. I reckon it really started when she was younger. She spoke to me about it one time, when we first met. I was just playin' along 'cause she was such a catch. I was a bit drunk, at least enough to be in a bit of a lull. She was talking about the time she fell. Being on a cliff face for a while.

'That's when it happened, she told me. She didn't just stay there on the edge of the cliff. She stepped right over. Maybe the reason you didn't find her the first two days, Merouac, is 'cause she weren't there. She were elsewhere then, and she's oft been elsewhere since. She comes and goes, and she's good enough at it that no one really notices all that much.

'I didn't ask her again. But I saw strange things that I didn't really know how to explain. She didn't offer to talk about it again, either, after that first time. It were like now she'd told me, she didn't have to mention it again. She just went about her business.'

'Do you think she told Evra?' Merouac asked, even though he knew, deep down, Evra was cognisant of everything that was happening, and possibly understood even more that he did.

Salvette looked pained. 'I don't know. I weren't there for any of that.'

'Why did you walk away, anyway?'

There was a long pause. 'I just couldn't do it,' Salvette said.

Merouac let the words hang there. Only a few words, yet intermingled was a definitive sense of shame and perhaps some sadness as well.

'What about now?'

Salvette lifted his head, a new kind of hope written on his face. 'Well, it's different now. I'm off the drink. I haven't had a pint for a good few moon-crosses, now. Sometimes it's hard. Maybe it's always going to be hard.'

'I can't be the one to keep you on the straight and narrow, Salvette. I haven't got time.'

'No. No, of course not.'

'But if you think now it's different, I think it's different, too. So how about we just take it at that?'

Salvette nodded and stood up quickly. 'That'd be grand,' he said quietly, and offered his hand for Merouac to shake.

Merouac shook the man's hand and watched as Salvette made his way down the hill towards the workers' camp.

Perhaps there was something that could be done to get Salvette into one of the other crews. The man's hands were a disaster. There might be some better work for him, and it might help relationships to give him a hand up in the world. There was only so long a man could stand being the lowest of the low in the rankings of men on the railroad.

Merouac's left hand touched his thigh. Now all he had to do was to get his own body back in working order, he thought. The clock was ticking. He had a railroad to build.

ooo

It was time to get back on the job proper. Merouac's leg still ached but they could take the jeep out to the Rolling Jacks and get the trickiest part of the sections sorted and underway. He would take Evra out with him, he decided. It would be a nice change for her, from being with Harlin every day, although Harlin adored the girl. And it would give him some time to talk with her, before the schedules really started heating up.

Cirrel Mendaron would be his man to lead the demolition team, and he made plans for Cirrel to travel down from the north and meet them at the Jacks.

Harlin had helped Evra wrap a scarf around her head earlier that morning. Now, Merouac packed her up into the old buggy they used when travelling around the railroad sites. It was open, no doors, and dusty.

'Keep that scarf on, and mind you stay in your seat. Don't take the belt off, or you could fly out, you hear?' he instructed his niece.

Evra nodded obediently, a look of anticipation on her face. It was the first time she'd been allowed in the vehicle.

'You can get the extra bits of the scarf and put it over your mouth when it starts to get really dusty, okay?'

As Merouac sat himself down in the driver's seat and checked his niece over one more time, he realised her hair was growing. Harlin had made her a new dress, but it wasn't particularly practical. Perhaps he could ask her to make Evra some pants. Possibly get some new shoes as well; the ones she was wearing were scuffed and dirty.

'Good day for it anyway,' he said to no one in particular, looking out at the blue sky and crystal clear morning as he gunned the rackety motor and signalled to Seb, who waved from the front of the workshop.

Evra chortled with glee as the buggy rumbled and chortled across the grounds around the workshop and turned out onto the open road.

The road leading to the Rolling Jacks was narrow and straight, requiring Merouac and Evra to pass right through the Tellehara Valley, which wasn't in any way a valley – only another sparse desert scape – until the Jacks came into sight before them, rising in height and power in a manner that cut the landscape dramatically.

The crags and the sloping surfaces of the Rolling Jacks could be treacherous at heights. Some men had, in the past, been mad enough to scale them. It wasn't unheard of for there to be the occasional death reported in the papers, of men falling from the Jacks from some crazy height. Merouac couldn't grasp what they had been thinking.

The Jacks would certainly protest invasion into their hard core and it was exactly the reason Merouac was furious the proposed line had them tunnelling through rather than going around them. The rock formations were stunning in their own right, part of the dramatic landscape of the open plains; why not leave them alone? The explosives that were going to be required to put a tunnel through their core would be phenomenal, more than they had ever used before.

If they had to go through, rather than around, Cirrel and his explosives team would need to get to work quick-smart. This was the element of the East-West line that that had the most unknowns.

They still had to get a better understanding of the hardness and depth of rock, before they could even estimate how long it would take to tunnel through, let alone build the railway line through the completed tunnel.

Merouac glanced at his niece. 'Ev, I know life's a bit funny at the moment. If we'd stayed at Endren, you'd be at school now. They have a small school with about twenty kids. You'd get to learn interesting things and be around kids your own age. You'd like that, wouldn't you?'

Evra nodded.

'I'm trying to get a school set up at Bitroux, but it might take a while. In the meantime, you're stuck with me, Harlin and Seb.'

'And Heyla?'

'Well, yes, Heyla as well, although she's a gypsy at heart. But she's very fond of you, Ev, and will be wandering back our way soon.'

Evra turned her head to watch the scenery go past.

'What about the ... Hel ...'

'The Helara. That's good you were able to remember their name.' Evra was referring to the energies slumbering deep down under the catacombs beneath the power grid.

'What about them? When will we see them again?'

'We won't see them for a long time, Evra. They had a big journey to make and they will be very tired. Imagine if our planet disintegrated and we had to find another place to live. It must have been very stressful for them, and we really only understood what they were asking for at the final hour.'

'Ophrin helped us, didn't he?'

'He did. And they're safe now. But they need time to adjust to our frequency, as well. The air we breathe, the energy here on our planet, it's all different. So I suspect they'll acclimatise while they sleep.'

'What does that mean?'

'Acclimatise? It just means to get used to things.'

'Do you think they have enough room down there, where they are?'

'I hadn't thought much about it,' Merouac said.

'What if they are all squashed together and can't stretch out? And how many legs do you think they have? Was it three?'

'I really hope that they're not all squashed, Ev. I don't think they are, because I don't think they have quite the same kind of bodies as we do. Do you remember when we created the frequency bridge, and they all came past?'

'Whoosh!' exclaimed Evra with gusto, demonstrating with her arms the fast and furious movement of the Helara during the event, at least as much as her belt would let her.

'Yes, exactly. I think they probably have bodies that are less substantial than ours. As in, they may be more air-like.'

Evra, as ever, seemed unperturbed by the tangent their conversation had taken. They were essentially talking about an alien race that he, Merouac, had allowed to find safe passage and safe harbour in the interior of their own planet. There was no way to really tell if it had been the right thing to do, or if it would lead to outcomes not worth thinking about. The young girl showed no surprise or no fear at such a thing being possible. There was only curiosity at who they were, and how they were doing, and what their bodies were really made up of.

'Like a breeze?'

'Yes, kind of. Not so heavy as you and me. So they may not need as much space as we would.'

'Maybe that's how they can fly,' Evra reasoned.

'That's a probability,' Merouac agreed.

'When will we see Ophrin again?'

'I'm not sure, Ev.'

'How many do you think there were? I think lots.'

'How many Helara? That's a really good question, Ev. It all happened so quickly. And of course they may have different kinds of bodies to us. All we really saw was a big rush of energies pass us by. It could have been hundreds, or it could have been thousands. Anyway, it was a lot.'

'What if they grow and it gets tight down there?'

'I think if anything happens and they need our help, we'll know.'

'How?'

Merouac shrugged his head. It was another good question. He didn't know how he would know anything at this stage. And yet he felt confident the Helara would know to make contact, in the same way Malaena was making contact with them: through thoughts, impressions, feelings and things simply popping into his head. Of course, with her it was different; they were twins and they had always been able to communicate telepathically.

'Ev, you know how we stay in touch with your mama? How we feel her and sense her?'

'Yup.'

'Well, it's like that, I think.'

Evra seemed satisfied with that answer. Then, 'What about Kultan?'

'What about Kultan?'

'When will we see him again?'

'He's gone back to the mountains. He lives up on Tenogru, remember, in the Remneur Ranges?'

'Will we go there again?'

'I'm sure we will. I'm not sure when, but yes. We'll see him again. Remember, even though he's still young, he's going to be the head of all the Faurin when he's older. He's in training for that now. So he has lots to do where he is. And we've got a railroad to build.'

'Are we nearly there?'

'No. But look over there. What can you see?' Merouac pointed to the eastern horizon, where the shimmering peaks of the Rolling Jacks could be seen.

Evra had time to investigate the rock formations and collect a few specimens, as Seb has told her she might like to do, while Merouac met with Cirrel.

The arcane formula of blowing up a mountain was not one known by many. But Merouac knew Cirrel's history well: as a boy he had apprenticed with many mining groups who wanted to go deep into this mountain or that to mine rock and gemstones. There was far more to be found deeply embedded in the hard core of mountains than anywhere near the surface, and so ways and means had been engineered to get there. That being said, blowing up the interior of a mountain to allow passage, while retaining a stable environment around it, was a far more delicate matter and an art form that Cirrel had been in apprenticeship to perfect for five shades before he had been brought in to assist with the Great Northern railroad. On that first railroad he had demonstrated remarkable skill and understanding of what was required, despite still being only twenty-odd shades old. Which now meant he was a rare specimen indeed.

Cirrel's experience working with engineers to figure out the structural requirements of tunnelling safely through the side of a mountain meant there were few other people Merouac would have called upon to navigate the work required out at the Rolling Jacks.

'This is going to be tight, understand? It's not like the Great Northern where we had a whole shade for the explosions required for the line. We got a hundred days total for four sections of the East-West, so we've got to hustle.

'You'll need to start within the week. You can set up your own camp out here, or else settle down at the minor camp closest, which we're striking up soon.'

Merouac diligently went through the protocols with Cirrel, who was under instruction to, in turn, brief his own crew of four.

'You'll need to submit your explosives plan to Seb in ten days,' Merouac said. 'Any idea roughly how long it's going to take?'

'I reckon eighty days at least to tunnel through all three mountains,' said Cirrel.

'It can't take that long.'

Cirrel thought about it. 'Well, I had thought to do about twenty small explosions to get us through. But we could do ten bigger ones, instead. That'll make us go faster. But we'll need more men and more explosives. I reckon that granite means a hundred kegs of Gee Vee a day.'

'Is it safe?'

'It'll be fine.' Cirrel chewed on a piece of grass. He always looked dirty, Merouac thought, largely because he was prone to wiping his face while he still had black powder on his hands.

'I'll get you a crew.'

'I'll need forty.'

'I'll get you at least twenty, maybe ten more.'

'That should do it.'

'The explosives plan needs to come in for sign-off, and then I'll get the Gee Vee ordered and sent out here for you to get underway. Each day there are explosions scheduled, you need to send a runner to me to confirm it's happening on schedule and then that they've been completed.'

On the way back from the Jacks, Merouac broached the topic of Salvette with Evra.

'Ev, you happy to have Sal around?'

'U-huh,' Evra mumbled, sleepy now after their day out in the sun.

'He wasn't there before, but he wants to be in your life now.'

'Yup.'

'I think we should give him a go. But I want some time to see that he's really ready, okay?'

'Huh?'

'I mean we'll just take small steps, alright? To see if Salvette can be good and safe and reliable and if he's careful and if he's really on the straight and narrow. Sound good?'

'Yup.'

And then Evra was asleep.

The trip home was quiet and the sun was golden as it set.

It had been a decent day, all told.

9.

Salvette out at the Rolling Jacks

Salvette didn't know anything about blowing up mountains. But he was damned happy to be off the clearing work. Maarte knew he never needed to see that prickly, stubborn and hard-to-wrangle mirrahedge ever again.

Being on the rubble clearing team was a good change, he mused, but at the end of the day, it was still hot and dusty work. And it was fair to say that being around Gee Vee was something else entirely. The Rolling Jacks were sharp. They were imposing. They were big. He dreaded to think about what might happen if the explosives weren't set off right.

Salvette had found the meeting with Merouac to be fair and reasonable, and he was appreciative of being assigned to a new crew. And he was awake and sober, which was good. The difficult thing about sobriety was the thinking. The inability to avoid the thoughts that surfaced. His mind worked slower than some, no doubt a result of so many years on the drink. But now he had a clear head, he was being troubled by the things he could no longer drink away.

In the past, whenever thoughts of Malaena had surfaced, he could push them away with a drink or two. Now they had nowhere to go and so he'd been remembering her more and more of late.

He thought back to when they'd first started courting. She would come and watch him when he played a game. There had been a particular drink she liked. A gin of some sort. She'd sit on one drink all night, and flash her big, happy smile his way, egging him onto victory. She told him she loved the energy, the cheering that went on in the middle of a game when the stakes were high. That was back when he was still okay, before he'd really started to lose control of things. But even then, there was a restlessness about her. A need to be going here, going there. Moving about. He had just thought she'd been a fidget.

But then there had been the reality of it that had become clearer over time. She was here, and then not. She was absent, before returning. It wasn't just a sense, it happened before his own eyes. Often, in the blink of an eye. Where she had been only a moment earlier, there was now absence. A vacant space that was empty and then filled again. It confused him, but he didn't question it. He kept the knowledge to himself because, at the end of the day, what was there to do or say about it?

And then she'd told him she was pregnant. He was at his worst, then. The drinking had set in and the gambling had taken a turn for the worse and he hadn't been winning any games at all. In fact, his fortunes had completely turned around and he owed far more money than he was able to make.

In any event, the explosives schedule was now well underway. Salvette was getting used to the work, getting used to his crew, but he was watching the head of the explosives crew with a sense of wary unease.

Now he stood in the dry, early morning air alongside his crew, stiff after a night trying to get comfortable on the hard ground where the crew had made a temporary camp, rather than having to go back and forth from the sub-camp each day. It was crude and basic. Food supplies were being brought out to them but they were in essence sleeping under the stars without cover.

Black-handed Cirrel was in good form that day. He'd earned his nickname because his hands were, in fact, quite literally black, stained for all time with Genus powder, or Genus Vitricide more formally, or Gee Vee for short. Gee Vee was the black powder lodged into the rock and set alight as part of the explosives. Cirrel had been working with the stuff for so long it had soaked good and well into his skin, never to wash out, all the way up his forearms. When it was dark, they disappeared. It was an odd sight to come across him at night, with seemingly no hands to speak of.

The first morning Salvette had joined the newly formed rubble-clearing team, one of the crew had pointed out Cirrel to him. Moments later, the man had passed Salvette close by and he had smelled a stench so strong and so sour that he had flinched.

The smell of having peed your pants and not washed them. That smell was overlaid with the smell of tobacco, which was perhaps a blessing. Then, layered over that, the smell of liquor. Even in the early hours of the morning, those layers of stench were present. It was the smell that told Salvette something was up.

Salvette recognised a man going off the rails in Cirrel. He knew, early on in his own journey, that there was a time when you could still act capable, when people didn't yet know it was all coming apart. That's the way it was with Cirrel. Sometimes he looked very capable and others he looked like he was just barely holding on. On a good day, Cirrel's eyes were clear and cloudless as the summerial skies. But

Salvette had seen the other days when there had been dark circles and the thickness of mind that came after a night heavy on the drink.

He'd been there. Many times. You could get away with a bit of drinking in the morning on the railroads. You could get away with a beer for breakfast, if you had any handy. But to smell of it, that never went down well. You were most likely to be laid off for the day to sober up and then you lost a day's wages and went hungry. It had never really been worth it, although admittedly that hadn't actually stopped him most times.

Cirrel was still young. He was probably still able to take a certain amount of booze without slowing down. There was a quickness about him that made sense for someone who worked with explosives. But there was also something reckless about Cirrel that made Salvette very, very nervous. He'd never worked anywhere near explosives before. The rumbling sounds of the detonations made him feel unsettled and anxious. Often, the reverberations just made it all feel too close for comfort.

Cirrel was squinting in concentration as he moved back and forth in front of the mouth of the mountain as the hole got deeper and darker before them with each explosion. Hands on hips, frown in place and cigarillo hanging loosely from his lips. He was inspecting his supplies and making various calculations, muttering to himself as he extended leads and affixed them to his instruments.

Black-handed Cirrel was pedantic when he was in good form. His need for detail and accuracy was intense; he was trying to instil the same focus into his recruits, but Salvette wasn't convinced it had transferred yet. They seemed to respect their boss and would follow his meticulous instructions, but it was he alone who could execute a carefully laid out explosion. They were still lackeys.

Now he stood back and looked at the mountain, sizing it up.

Often, Salvette felt Cirrel was literally pitting himself and his black powder against the hulk of the mountain, made solid over hundreds, possibly thousands of shades. A competition of might, perhaps. Would Cirrel be able to make the rock budge? He always seemed certain he'd win, one way or the other.

Cirrel made a motion with his hand, and a shout followed at the mouth of the mountain: 'Fire in the hole!'

There was a rumble around them, as the Gee Vee made impact with the solid interior of the mountain. The ground shook and the mouth filled with white, dusty, crumbling rock. Salvette's crew waited as the ground continued to shake. After the noise and movement abated, they brought up their scarves to cover their mouths. The dust was slowly settling and they could now move in to start clearing the rubble.

The need to have more than one Cirrel had already been identified, though. As it was, he'd been instructed to build a team around himself in order to start training others in the same skills. But recruiting potential talent and training young men was a different kettle of fish than natural aptitude being applied. Cirrel was an average trainer of young talent and still quite taken with his own rareness – it was possible he hadn't invested as much energy into training his apprentices as would have been preferred.

'Ain't we going to go in faster, Cirrel?' one of the clearing crew called out.

'What's that?' Cirrel spun around with an annoyed look on his young face.

'Nothing. Well, damn it. Shouldn't we be deeper in by now?'

'Hey. It ain't a fast process. What, you want the entire mountain to come down? We go in, we blow a bit up, we clear it, we secure it, and then we go in again.'

One of Cirrel's crew called over. 'Cirrel, it's a decent point. We just used a half keg of powder and barely scraped another yard in.'

'Well, could be the rock's harder than I supposed. Get more powder ordered up. Today.'

'Yes, boss.' Cirrel's crew were taking notes and nodding their heads.

The following day, the crew stood waiting for instructions that didn't come. Cirrel was having an off day, it seemed.

Salvette wondered if Cirrel was in debt and chasing money. That wouldn't be surprising. With all the games going on at night across the different railroad section camps, all the boozing and betting and gambling and so on, half the men working on the railroad were chasing one debt or another. Otherwise they were hiding from those doing the chasing. He'd been on both sides of that particular coin.

He himself was trying to stay well clear of that kind of life now. He was determined not to lift a finger to express interest in being part of any kind of game, despite his technique and skills earned from long years at the table. He needed to stay sober, and to keep his money in his own pockets. To make his way for good out of the land of easy bad habits. They were hard to break, that was for sure. Every day was tough. Every time he went to bed sober was a small victory, even if no one else appreciated it.

But it was easier now Evra was in his life. His own daughter knew him, called him Sal. She'd hugged him, not just once but a few times, now. Did she know he'd left them, her and her mother, those five shades earlier?

'It ain't the gambling,' one of the men said to Salvette as they stood under the hot sun watching Cirrel, who was sitting, looking at the mountain, despairingly. He seemed to be in a world of his own, muttering quietly under his breath and smoking one cigarillo after the other.

'Cirrel's got himself some trouble with the ladies.'

Salvette had observed Cirrel's lean build and bright blue eyes. The blue eyes were common in the people of Augrelle, although many worked the land and were of a more solid build. This young man was sharp as a wit and burdened with good looks. Salvette imagined he might have an easy way with women.

'Turns out he's got three women on three different farms across Augrelle who are convinced he's going to marry them. He finished up on the Great Northern, then returned home to the horror that he's been found out. He's been drowning his sorrows ever since.'

'That's not good,' Salvette remarked.

'No, I'll say it ain't.'

The next morning was another where explosives had been scheduled, but none happened. Black-handed Cirrel was gone. The team were told to stand down while a crew was dispatched to find him and bring him back.

One of his working crew, a man by thee name of Alb, slapped Salvette on the back and continued his feed of Cirrel-related information from the day prior. 'Our friend's gone on a bender, by the looks of it. We've got ourselves a day off, good and fair. Join us for a drink?'

'No … thanks. Where has he gone?'

'We reckon he's gone running back to Augrelle to assuage his lady friends. Better he goes and sorts it all out, I reckon. He's no good to us in his current state.'

'What about our schedule?'

'I don't care about that today, but Lenny's getting fidgety, that's for sure. He'll be wanting a crack of it himself if his boss doesn't show up by end of the day,' reckoned Alb.

Salvette looked dubiously over at Lenny, Cirrel's new second in command. He looked very young, scarcely fourteen shades, perhaps.

'He ain't got the skills, of course,' Alb said.

Sure enough, that afternoon Lenny had called a meeting of all the crews that were standing around waiting for the explosions to start back up again.

'We're going to get moving,' Lenny announced. 'I've learned all that Cirrel does. We'll start at noon.'

ooo

Cirrel had still not returned the following day. Salvette felt conflicted, but it was a new feeling and he was struggling to make head or tail of it. He went for a walk and sat himself down in the shade offered by one of the towering Jacks.

A lot of trust was being placed in Cirrel, he thought slowly. He'd done all the explosives on the first line of the railroad. Merouac wouldn't have chosen him if he had any doubts about his ability. But on the other hand, Merouac wasn't here every day, and Merouac didn't seem to know that anything was up with Cirrel. Salvette thought perhaps he needed to give Merouac a tip that something was afoot.

Feeling such a sense of duty did not sit comfortably with Salvette. It was the penance he felt he was paying for being sober, it seemed. He had a reason for being sober, of course. And that reason was a small child who wasn't more than five shades old and yet seemed to know and regard him with affection. And there was a chance he could maybe turn things around and become some kind of a father and make up for the lost time since he'd walked away from his duties as a parent.

But building up trust with his daughter also meant building up trust with Merouac. He felt sure no one had sent word about the Cirrel situation to Bitroux. And he wondered if someone should. The more he thought about it, he realised that no one would. Union men covered for each other, and every man on the team would pull together to ensure the Cirrel situation was managed without Management Intervention. And now, they had the young spark Lenny looking to make decisions he wasn't experienced enough to make. Maarte help them.

Salvette didn't sleep well that night, but it didn't matter much. He was up before dawn. The two moons still making their late-hour journey to opposite horizons, he began his uneasy journey towards Bitroux. The walk would take most of the day, and he'd rather get as much of it out of the way before the heat arrived as he could. He didn't want to give himself time to change his mind. Merouac needed to know about the situation at the Rolling Jacks. And Salvette was going to be the one to tell him, even if he had no idea how one did such a thing. He'd figure that out later. For now, he focused on putting one foot in front of the other.

10.
Salvette plays the game

The man standing in front of him looked vaguely familiar. A shock of orange hair. Tall. What curls he had. Like the ringlets of a small child. He only thought that because a ringlet had broken loose. The rest were pulled back in a band at the nape of his neck.

He wore spectacles. There were pockmarks on his face and he had a few days' worth of stubble, as though he'd been on the road himself for a few days.

How did he know this man?

'From the games, a good ten shades ago,' the man said. That's what you were wondering, ain't it? How we know each other?'

'Well, I guess it was,' said Salvette slowly, not sure he had gotten that far in his own mind, but nevertheless.

'You know me because we played across from each other, a dozen or so times, I figure, when we were both younger and faster. Well, I was young and fast, I reckon you were already on your way to being old and foolish. Dorren's my name.'

'Dorren, eh? Well, I'll ignore that stab momentarily, as that name might well ring a bell. My memory ain't that good anymore, but I reckon something's stirring.' Salvette thought some more. 'You might have beat me one time, and one time only, I'd say. Selegree Creek, weren't it?' Dorren was starting to look more and more like someone he could have spent time with in the past. 'Green kroanite on the table. I could have done with the poulas from that one, but you pulled a fast one on me. I was sorry to see it disappear into your dirty old pocket, that's for sure.'

'I reckon you're right about that' agreed Dorren. 'I whipped that kroa right out from under you, didn't I? I recall it was quite satisfying. Surprised you remember it, though.'

'So am I, as a matter of fact. In any event, what are you doing standing here in front of me now? Come to give me half your gold for old time's sake?'

'Hardly. Seems like we could have some business together though, if you're up for it.'

'Not likely. I ain't on the circuit anymore, as you'd well know. I got kicked off shades ago. And, in addition, I've come good. I cleaned up, since I got a kid of my own to think about.'

'You got a kid?'

'Aye. Cared for by her uncle, but I got some involvement now, so I gotta be up to the task, don't I.' It was a statement, not a question, Salvette realised. The certainty of it felt good.

'Huh,' said Dorren. 'Well, no matter, I can get you back in the door. There's a game coming up. My boss told me to find someone good, and I thought to come looking for you. Word about the place told me to head this way, to the railroad camp. You got work here?'

'Aye. And that means I can't go running off to play a game. What's on the table, though, out of interest?'

Dorren grinned. 'Well, you'd never guess it, but a white pala's surfaced. It's gonna be a big game. And there's good money on the table for you, Salvette. Said you got a kid now? Well, think about it like an investment. Boy or girl?'

'Girl.'

'Well, ain't she lucky then, to have a daddy that's gonna earn some big cash and put it aside for her. Kids take money, you know. You got much put away?'

No,' Salvette said slowly, pondering. 'White pala, you say?'

'That's what I said. How about it? We play in two nights' time. I take you with me, get you set up and have you back on the third day, with your pockets loaded. Of course, you gotta win. That goes without saying. I ain't got nought to give you if you don't win. But I believe in you, Salvette.'

'Why don't you play for it yourself?' Salvette asked.

'Conflict of interest. I'm supposed to be winning it for my boss. I put my hands on that white pala? I'd never be able to hand it over, I reckon.'

'Can I think about it?' The idea of being able to buy nice things for Evra was tempting. Salvette had never even thought about that before. He'd barely had the chance to think about it now, but the idea was growing on him by the second. What he wouldn't give to see Evra in new things he'd bought her. See the respect in Merouac's eyes, the acknowledgement that he might have Something to Offer.

'What do you say, old friend?'

'Well, as I just reminded you, I got thrown off the circuit,' Salvette said.

'Nothing a few poulas won't take care of. I'm all over it.'

'Well …'

'Alright, I'm gonna count to ten. That's how much longer you've got to think about it.'

'I'll do it,' said Salvette almost instantly, without even realising the words had left his mouth. 'Only, I've got to take care of something. I need to get a message back to the sub-camp. It's important.'

'Alright, I have wheels just down the road. I'll zip you up to the camp – you can drop your note off and we're on our way.'

Salvette frowned. 'No drinking, you hear? I ain't touching a drop and you can't make me.'

'Salvette, as long as you win this game, you can drink your mother's milk and I won't bat an eyelid. Not a one.'

'There's no need to be coarse,' Salvette muttered, trotting after Dorren as he whipped around and started pacing down the track, a man on a mission if there ever was one.

Word of the new game spread quickly.

A lean, thin faced man in a small pub deep in the West Ingrue was one of the first to hear of the steal. 'I'm in!' he cried.

Another in Tustennuit leaped up when he heard the news. 'I'm in!' he shouted.

And so it went all around the mining bars, the news that the biggest game of all time was in play. The entry fee was the biggest anyone had ever heard – outrageous, many claimed. But it was, after all, the white pala stone.

OOO

The game was played in the dark of night in an empty store house deep in the west country of the Ingrue. The play table was brightly lit by overhanging lights temporarily installed that hung suspended from the rafters.

The circle around them was dense, heads bobbing to see the faces of the final round players, who had made it through the hundreds of early participants and several minor rounds the night before.

The hands of all players were clear to those around but guards were watching to see no one whispered a single word to alert players to their competitor's hand.

Salvette, seated at the table, looked out in the crowd to find Dorren. Dorren was there, not too far away, and saw Salvette look his way. Dorren ignored him. Salvette looked past Dorren at the handful of shady personalities that sat beside him. They all wore dark glasses and some kind of hat, making it impossible to see who they might be. One man was particularly small; even when seated he had the height of a child. That made Salvette think. Who did he know who was that small, who Dorren might be working for? And if Dorren was in his employ, would the man paying Salvette's fee even need to make an appearance?

In any event, Salvette knew there would be little to say about anything, since the game was about to start. His throat felt parched, and he swallowed, patting his head. He felt nervous and the crowd, larger than he'd ever seen at a game in his life, wasn't making it any easier.

The vestor shouted out to get the crowd in order. Once the noise had quietened down, he held up his hand to show the crowd to listen. 'Alright, you lot. Listen up. These are the rules, for anyone who is unclear. The game plays out in one night.'

Tor Anale. The name popped into Salvette's head unexpectedly. Distracted, he tried to push it away, but he lingered and his gaze returned to Dorren and the small man sitting near him.

It couldn't be, he objected to himself. The head of the Suron military, funding a player to win a white pala, and showing up at what was essentially a black market event? Then, he thought, with a heavy feeling, that's exactly who it was.

Talk about high stakes. He'd been around long enough, both on the black market circuit, the games circuit, and every dark and shady bar and pub from the Ingrue to Tustennuit and in between. He'd heard the rumours, several times over, about the way Tor Anale went about his business. Fingers in every pie, so to speak. He played a calculated and complex game in the shadows, and trading the gem markets would fall right into that space.

A tense, brittle silence filled the air. The vestor continued. 'There are no breaks. No rests. You walk away from the table, you're out. Once the play has begun, it does not stop until there is a winner. Anyone who falls asleep or passes out at the table is out of the game. Likewise, cheaters, card hufflers, sign language users and deck swappers.'

Why would he be here? Salvette thought, as he clocked every other player around him, many he knew from times of old. Why risk it? He had already commissioned Dorren to find a player, Salvette was here as that player, the game was starting, so why the damn had Tor Anale decided to come along, however discreetly?

He had no more time to think about it. The game was on. The dealer, positioned at the top of the table, dealt the deck. Twelve cards each hand. Five suites. Twenty-six different combinations to make, all varying in value. The player with the highest point score led and got to choose the next round's suite. If a player dropped a hundred points below the winner, he was out. The player was announced the winner when he was the last man standing.

Two hours in, ten players had dropped out, six were left. As the game went on, Salvette did one of the things he was expert at: keeping an eye on his competition and adjusting his play accordingly. Fermhell was looking exhausted but Salvette knew he'd play through, and so a long-flare strategy was required. Hanven had been looking entirely distracted from the get-go; it was likely he was too unnerved by the rock they were playing for. He'd be out soon enough, and in fact he was already swaying on his seat. Likely he only had moments left in him, but his eyes were still open, and so he couldn't be removed while that was still the case. But soon after, despite all his best intentions, he slid off his stool, slipping to the ground. 'Leave me be,' Salvette heard the man mumble as he was dragged clear of the table.

The room smelled of stale sweat and the booze that had sloshed from people's drinks onto the floor. Salvette turned his attention to Sareg, who was holding his cards tight, flipping over one after the other, singing quietly to himself as the game sped up with fewer players. The vestor shouted out a command, placed a card on the table and then brought it up for the crowd and all others to see. In response, all the players still in the game threw down an additional card, face up for all to see.

'Oh man,' said Valen, on Salvette's left, as he laid down his card. 'I'm out.'

'Ha!' shouted Raleine triumphantly on Salvette's right. 'So you should be. I'm still standing.'

'You got a flat deck, man,' said Felra, seated on the opposite side of the table, as he spat out a piece of gristle and slid his finger over his teeth, needling the last bits of the sandwich he'd been passed by one of his support cronies and sucking the places between his teeth where bits were still lodged.

The dealer shook his head. 'The deck is fine.'

'Cheat!' someone screamed across the room at the man tapping his chin with his finger and looking at Tonare, next to Valen, who was about to lay down his card. On the sound of the word the man lowered his hand with automatic reflex, and that combined with the fright in his eyes seemed to provide clear permission for the room to jump on him, which they did.

After the fight had been picked apart, and Tonare officially removed from the game, play resumed.

Three more hours of play, and without Salvette really knowing how, he was one of four players still left in the game. Another hour and there were two. And then, sometime later, and quite suddenly, it seemed to him, there was cheering and din and movement and men slapping him on the back and the dealer nodding at him in approval. A blur around him, Salvette sat unmoving as the noise grew louder, more men came up behind him and he saw the dealer take the cards and begin packing them away, all of it happening in slow motion and all of it seeming to happen to someone other than him.

Salvette's eyelids were half shut. 'Are we done?' he murmured.

The vestor arrived at his side and raised his arm. 'This is the winner,' he shouted.

He felt a distant, and faint, surge of pleasure.

The vestor shouted in his ear. 'Sir, I believe the pala stone is now yours.'

Salvette dropped his head on the table. 'Thank Maarte,' he said.

'Give it over.'

ooo

Outside the store house, hours later, Salvette met Dorren and handed over the prize stone. He did it reluctantly, knowing its value and also having felt a strong sense of wellbeing having it tucked in his pocket. The stone was a creamy white with small slivers of sparking silver shimmering across its surface. It wasn't large – he could close his fist around it, but it felt supremely solid, powerful – mighty, even.

Dorren in return held out a bundle of notes, the promised payment for the white pala.

'I think you should make yourself scarce,' Dorren said quietly. 'You don't want folk chasing you down for the stone, and I don't want anyone knowing you sold it to me. You understand?'

'I got it, I got it,' Salvette said, feeling drunk with delight at the thick wad of cash weighing down his hands. 'And by the way…' Salvette was about to ask if it was Tor Anale he'd seen in the crowd, when the small man appeared behind Dorren, calling him away. Well there it was, Salvette thought to himself. He'd just won the Suron Head of Military a white pala stone.

Dorren turned to follow Tor Anale, giving Salvette a quick nod, and a wave indicating his should scram, pronto. With that, the two men went their separate ways into the quiet night and Salvette walked quickly away from the noise of the bar nearby, ensuring he wouldn't give in to any silly ideas about a drink to celebrate his win. In fact, as the thought occurred to him that it would be so easy, he picked up his pace and walked faster and faster away, in the direction of Bitroux and his daughter.

11.

Tor meets with Gartounne

Tor Anale took a deep breath as he walked briskly along the corridor of the Leron Estate, towards the large wing that housed the ailing governor, Gartounne Leron. The man who had been his sponsor this past ten shades, a man who was holding on to power by the skin of his teeth, even as his mind and body wasted away.

He hadn't slept. If the past week hadn't been bad enough, the day prior had certainly taken the cake. He'd walked right into a trap he should probably have seen coming.

He'd been tricked. And tricked by two women, imposing on his turf and territory in a way they had no right to. He'd done his duty. Responded to a meeting called by Sanat Leron – or so he thought. He'd turned up at the estate, only to find that Sanat was nowhere to be found.

Instead, he found Sanat's sister, the woman who'd snubbed her nose at Suroni life and left to walk the roads with the gypsies, or so he'd heard. Heyla. And, with her, Lavilla Whelme, the Governor of the Ingrue. It was a distasteful mix to see the two of them together. As he had entered the room, he'd seem glimmers of something in their eyes. Curiosity. Power. Danger.

This was the trap. They told him that since Gartounne had repeatedly refused to meet with them, they'd called for Tor, the head of military and the next best thing. They had questions; could he sit with them a while and help them get clarity on matters?

He had turned and walked out of the room. If Gartounne had refused to meet with them, he certainly wouldn't. But the fact that they were so close meant that Gartounne getting wind of the situation was imminent. A change of tactics was required.

Close to dawn that morning, he realised that things had shifted in such an extraordinary way that he was going to have to confess to a number of activities. It was a bitter taste in his mouth indeed.

As he came closer to the Governor's personal rooms, Tor noted the usual queues of administrators lining up to meet with the old man. He had been carrying out his governing duties from his bed for almost as long as Tor had known him. Tor moved past the queues and stepped into the dark bedroom, where the same stale, sickly smell hung as ever.

Gartounne's nursing staff acknowledged him as he stepped into the old man's chambers. He wrinkled his nose.

'Can't you do something about that smell, or at least cover it up?' he asked the head nurse.

'You know he won't let us open any windows, Sir. A bit of a breeze would sweep things clean, but he won't allow it. And if he finds out we've opened them when he's asleep, he'll get into a fit and you know that's not healthy for him either. Best to not antagonise him, we've decided.'

The old man was propped up on the bed, numerous cushions

behind his back. He observed Tor with a narrow, sunken expression, his grey eyes watery and bloodshot.

Tor's usual approach was to simply come and sit with the man, who was more often than not dozing. He occasionally woke to bark out an order, only to sink back into his cushions with a hacking cough that seemed to go on interminably. Despite his agenda, he did the same thing today, giving the man a courteous nod and moving to sit by his side. He distracted himself by offering Gartounne a drink of water. The old man waved it away.

The thing Tor had seen, as a Faurin cadet serving in the Suron army and seconded for special duties with the Governor, was that Gartounne hated both his children. Heyla had already left Suron, but he had heard enough to know she had thrown it all away – her entire family name, her inheritance, everything – and walked clear of the city, rarely to return.

Gartounne truly disliked women – Tor had observed that enough to know it to be true. But with Sanat it was different. It was jealousy. Gartounne resented his son and his achievements, and it was Tor who benefitted from it. Gartounne punished Sanat by favouring Tor, and over time Tor came to be the other son, the one who received favour simply because he was not a threat.

'What have you got say for yourself today, my boy?' Gartounne rasped with a gravelly voice. 'All under control? That damned Ristelle is chasing the numbers for the fleet, by the way. He'll be coming your way soon enough.'

Tor was quiet. He watched as the nurses closed the door behind him, and took a moment to take in the quiet of the room.

'Gartounne, did you know Lavilla Whelme is here at the Estate?'

'I'm not talking to that woman.'

Tor decided to take it slow. 'Why? I'm sure that as Governors, many of you have information and knowledge that help each other.

Isn't that so?'

Gartounne sniffed, then wheezed, then coughed. Tor stood up and found napkins on the bench. He moved over to the bed and patted down the old man's face. It was damp and cold. Tor would have recoiled if he hadn't trained himself over the years not to.

'She's come to speak to me about some rubbish. Sounds like a blatant lie. She's convinced there's some circus of activity going on in the grid. I know nothing about it.' fumed Gartounne.

Tor returned to his chair and sat down.

'Sir, she's here for a reason. And it's true. There is activity going on in the grid that you don't know about, but only because I haven't told you. She came here to ask you why you were allowing the Suroni military to section off an area of the grid, right here in Suron. I wanted to let you know that it's me. I've had activities underway down in the grid.'

Gartounne gave Tor an annoyed look. 'The grid's out of our jurisdiction. Whatever you've got going on down there, shut it down. Or deal with Lavilla yourself.'

Tor swallowed. 'Ah, yes, quite right I guess, Sir. However, there's more to tell you.' Tor felt his heart begin to pound. He wasn't going to enjoy this. Then, out of the corner of his eye, he noticed that the medicine cabinet against the far wall was open a fraction. The nurses must have forgotten to close and lock it.

'Ah … but first, have you had your medicine yet? Your cough sounds like it needs some soothing.' Tor jumped out of his seat and went to the cabinet. The vials and bottles were all neatly arranged in front of him. 'How about I give you your afternoon treatments?'

Gartounne still looked irritated but shrugged. Tor prepared the syrups and, returning to the bed, spooned them one by one into the old man's mouth.

Placing the empty vials and spoon on the bedside table, Tor sat back down next to the old man's bed and watched his eyes begin to close.

'It's probably time to tell you I've been undertaking some experiments you're likely to disapprove of quite strongly, Sir.'

The old man sighed and nodded, emitting a low grunt. He looked at Tor with the distinctive glaze of a medicinally induced fog.

'You probably don't know, but ten shades ago, when Afourla came to talk to you about the shield disintegrating, I heard the conversation. I heard him tell you that things were changing. And that there had been visitors. Visitors who appeared in the mountains and returned on two further occasions to share knowledge with the Faurin about what lay beyond the shield.'

Gartounne snorted. 'That damned Afourla didn't know what he was saying. It was all lies.'

'I don't agree,' said Tor quietly. 'And so I did my own investigations. I found out everything I could, and for the past three shades I've been experimenting with frequency tunings down in the grid.'

'You're as much of an idiot as he is then,' Gartounne said slowly, his words slurred.

'Of course, in order to manage my own experiments, I disbanded the Shield Survey team. The shield being down means my experiments have a good chance of success. But I want to do it my way, and I want to be the one in control. I told the team they were not required any longer. They have all been moved to other units now.'

'Hmmph,' said Gartounne.

'Just in case Sanat asks,' Tor said. 'With all the storms recently there have been questions about the stability of the shield. Of course, if the shield is dissipating, then the storms probably have everything to do with it. But we don't need the whole continent causing a stir, do we? I thought you'd agree with that.'

Suddenly, Gartounne sucked in a deep gasp of hair. He let out a deep hacking rattle that was loud enough to bring two nurses running back in. They moved directly to the bed to attend to the Governor, whose eyes were now streaming with water as he fought for air. His face was turning a deep purple. The nurses worked quickly to sit him up, thumping his back to get the air moving again.

'Get out,' Gartounne shouted at them once the worst of the fit was over.

Tor stood by, nodding to the nurses as they acquiesced and made their way back out of the room, but not before each one had cast their eyes over the vials and spoon on the bedside table and given him a dark look.

Gartounne fixed his grey eyes on Tor, far more sentient and aware than he was comfortable with.

'You fool,' he said. 'The shield can't fade. That's not how it works.'

Tor was trying to recover the situation. On one hand, he truly wished Gartounne had fallen asleep. On the other, maybe it was better that the truth was out there, and his boss had actually clocked what Tor was saying.

'I don't agree with you, Gartounne. I'm sorry.' Even saying those words, Tor felt himself to be outside of his body. Never, in his entire career, had he been so outright as to disagree with Gartounne in such a way.

'Get out,' Gartounne ordered.

Tor turned on his heels and walked out of the room, somewhat glad to have been dismissed.

12.

Seb and Merouac head out to Meurre Fells

Harlin placed her hands on Evra's shoulders. 'All set? Said your goodbyes?'

Evra spun around and darted back to Merouac. He knelt and gave her a hug. 'What are you going to do, today Ev?'

'Stay with Harlin.'

'That's right. And what about tonight?'

'Still with Harlin. We're cooking together and then I'm sleeping over.'

'Exactly. When will I see you again?'

'Tomorrow afternoon.'

'That's it.' He held her at arm's length and gave her a grin. 'No trouble, you hear? Be good.'

Evra nodded vigorously and shook clear of his embrace, taking Harlin by the hand. The woman hugged her close and gave Merouac a reassuring smile. 'We'll be fine,' she said.

Mingus and Jan emerged from the workshop. They had agreed to hold fort while Seb and Merouac went north to sign off on the shipment of wood that was coming to the Bitroux camp, given the laying of the new tracks was imminent.

'Here's the paperwork,' Jan said to Merouac after a quick nod and smile towards Harlin and Evra. The papers were affixed to a clip board, duplicates for their record of the papers they needed to sign off on later that day.

'Harlin, how are you going with the tarps?' Merouac thought to ask. 'Mingus here could organise to have them picked up if they're all stitched up and ready to go.'

'Aye, they're ready,' Harlin confirmed. 'You can send up Evra's new sculpture collection and bring down the tarps while you're at it.'

Mingus nodded. 'Right you are,' he said.

Mingus turned to Merouac. 'Truck's ready for you. Shame to lose it from the tracks for two days, but it'll help in the end, I suppose.'

Sham had sent a call asking for the sub-camp to sign off on the latest wood shipment directly, so it could be delivered straight there rather than going through the central supply depot. It worked in their favour, other than the short-term production delay. But it meant a trip north to Meurre Fells in a vehicle that could go the distance, and their line truck was the best choice.

'All set then, Seb?'

Seb gave Harlin a peck on the check and waved to Evra. 'See you both tomorrow, then.'

Merouac and Seb jumped into the truck, waved as they rolled out of the sub-camp, and made the first turn north, on their way to the woodland state of Meurre Fells.

The truck rumbled out. Merouac had taken the wheel to give Seb some time out. It took a while to adjust to the truck, which handled heavily and was far more unwieldy than the small jeep he got around the tracks on most of the time.

They watched the wide-open spaces roll past, climbing north for a good while and then arcing north west, towards Meurre Fells.

Meurre Fells had long stretches of woodlands and forests and was a key source for the railroads and most other industrial projects that required hardwoods. The other thing it had was space, and it used a certain amount of that space to house prisons.

It was the only country to keep prisons generally, but also the only one to maintain an asylum, aptly named Ruptor Delle.

Prisons were a mainstay of Meurre Fells' commercial enterprises. The people of Meurre Fells had at least proven themselves to be good wardens, good at keeping people guarded and locked up and under control. The last time he had checked, the country ran eight large prisons. They ran their prisons so well it had become the machine that kept their country in business. Where other countries across San Aurelle sent their molta to the Ingrue to be refined into hahma power, they sent their criminals to Meurre Fells for punishment, imprisonment and safeguarding.

The country had thereby grown into its capabilities as chief warden, not just as warden of prisoners who had committed crimes and done foul deeds, but those who fell outside the cracks – the strange and delirious, the ones who could not be helped.

Meurre Fells was small by the standards of the continent, and land-locked. It abutted Banne Country to the north, overseer of most of the continent's large commercial port trading. To the east, the rural heartlands of Augrelle Country, and to the west, the power and metal titan, the Ingrue. To the south, the more civilised and cultured Suron.

As well as being the smallest country, it also had the smallest population and, along with it, a palpable sense of scarcity, which had hung in the air whenever Merouac had spent time there.

The folk of Meurre Fells weren't wealthy, there was nothing underground to mine and in fact they were thinning their supply of natural above-ground resources every annalshade that went by, which is why some of the wood for the railroads had started to be sourced from elsewhere.

Too many times in recent production pipeline schedules, the country had failed to turn up the goods. Merouac wondered why their governor wasn't doing more to manage their woodlands to keep business moving.

'Did you bring the papers?' Merouac asked Seb.

'Didn't I just see Mingus hand you the clipboard before we left?'

'No, the other papers. The broadsheets.'

'Oh, aye. I brought a few.' Seb leaned down to a pile of papers at his feet and lifted them onto his lap.

They looked to only be a small selection of the pile they had recently accumulated in the workshop.

'Seb, I hate to say it, but I'm starting to think telling Tielder about the generator down in the grid might not be our best move.'

'Eh? That's a surprise to hear you say that. Especially after all the stories in the papers you've been reading out to me these past few weeks.'

Merouac grinned at Seb's quiet jab. He had suspected his second in command had been getting somewhat weary of his continuous updates on the backlog of railroad commentary.

'Well, I do care about my reputation being restored. All of ours, who were working on the Marville line before we got shipped out here. And that generator fits the bill in terms of what was destabilising the network hahma currents. But there's two reasons for keeping quiet. The first is that we want to give our new friends the chance to acclimatise.'

'The Helara,' Seb said slowly.

'Yes.' Merouac felt he needed to tread carefully here, in order to not make Seb feel too uncomfortable. Seb had a vague understanding of what Merouac told him had taken place with the frequency bridge, but no more. 'And there's also the fact that the generator was down there in the first place. Mingus and Jan got me thinking about who else might be trying to do what we've been doing here, with the frequency tunings. You know, the experiments behind the shacks, with Helya and Hieime.'

Seb nodded slowly. It was another area of activity he was on the periphery of, but he had known right from the start it had been important to Merouac. From the beginning, Seb had been part of his quest to discover what had happened to Malaena. He'd even built Merouac a small workshop where he could work on his metal sculptures whenever he could find the time away from the workshops.

'In any event, since we moved the generator further away from the surface, the derailments have stopped. And I can go and reclaim my reputation a bit later.'

'Makes sense, I guess,' Seb agreed.

They watched the small townships come and go as they drove through the Meurre Fells countryside. Signs for one of the large prisons began to appear, and they passed the road leading off to it without seeing a single vehicle. It was uncannily quiet.

They passed farms and smallholdings and eventually found their way to the timber depot, where their cargo was awaiting quality inspection and review. Once Merouac had signed off, the wood would be sent straight to Bitroux. They had a quick lunch from the supplies Harlin had loaded them up with before they left, and spent the rest of the afternoon going through the inspection process, which proved to be more thorough and time consuming than either of them had anticipated.

By late afternoon, they were ready to call it a day. They got directions to the nearest inn, where they would stay the night before making one additional trip for some workshop supplies in a township on the border of the Ingrue, before returning to the sub-camp.

After throwing their gear in their respective rooms, they made their way to the inn's public rooms for a drink.

The public room was quiet; it was late enough that Merouac and Seb felt deserving of a beer, but early enough that many were still working.

'Might not be as early start and finish here, without the mines and the factories,' Seb suggested as they found their way to a booth near a window.

The bar looked and smelled like any other bar Merouac knew, perhaps even a little cleaner; as Seb had noted, the work that went on here wasn't as dirty as other parts of the country.

'I suppose we might see a few from the forestries soon enough though,' Merouac said. 'Assuming they work an early start and finish like other power and metal.'

'Aye, true,' Seb agreed.

Merouac went to the counter, where an old woman was serving the only other customer in the room. Merouac nodded to both the man and the bar woman and stood waiting his turn to be served, in no hurry and in fact quite enjoying the chance to stand at the bar and enjoy the different scenery.

'What can I get you?' the woman asked soon after, wiping down the bar in front of him as she went. She had short blonde hair and deeply wrinkled skin; Merouac thought she could be sixty-five shades or older.

She went about the business of pouring the two beers he'd ordered and placed the wet, dripping glasses in front of him. She looked up, just about to say something, and then seemed to freeze.

What was she doing, he wondered.

She seemed flustered. She was looking at his neck. Then, she looked at his face, then back at his neck.

'Everything alright?' he asked, looking around to check if

anything was happening behind him. But no, it was all quiet.

'Well, I … it's just that I know you. I know that scar.'

Merouac felt his hand go instinctively to his neck. 'You do?' he said, puzzled. He felt sure he'd never seen the woman before.

The woman looked flustered, and wiped her hands on her apron. 'That birth mark. Your hair. I do, I know you. And I know the others just like you. I just haven't seen any of you, well…'

Merouac shook his head. 'I'm sorry, I don't understand. You know me, from my scar?' Merouac looked over at Seb, who seemed unworried and was turning the pages of what looked to be another broadsheet.

The woman looked puzzled herself. 'Forgive me.' She took a breath. 'It was just such a curious time. It's been so many shades since I even thought about it. Must have been what, forty shades ago. Is that how old you are?'

He felt his heart lurch in a way that was quite uncomfortable. 'Yes, that's about right,' Merouac said slowly. 'But what do you mean, all of us?'

'Well, you were just babies, of course. But you all had the same scar. And yet only two of you had the jet-black hair, another thing that was strange. Of the whole one hundred of you, only two with black hair. You have a twin sister, don't you? That was the other one. Yes, I remember.'

Merouac noticed three, then four men walk into the bar, tall and dark like many of the Meurre Fells folk, and not too clean, either. He wondered if they'd come off a shift at one of the mills; more would follow, if that was the case.

Two of the men came up to the bar and the woman gave them brief nod, but kept her attention on Merouac, a strange look still.

'Where is it that you're talking about?' Merouac asked.

'Well, you were all in my care, dear. At the orphanage.'

'An orphanage? No, you must be remembering someone else. I'm not an orphan.'

'Well of course you were. You all were. A hundred of you, all newborns, brought to us, and other orphanages, to find homes for.' The woman was persistent, and now frowning. Almost on autopilot, she drew another set of beers for the newcomers and landed them on the bar; they nodded and took their drinks away. Presumably they had a tab, Merouac found himself thinking.

'That's where I worked. That's how I know you. Or *knew* you, I guess. Not that we really knew you, and then you two were gone so suddenly …'

'Er … I'm going to take my friend his drink, alright?'

The woman seemed to come out of her reverie and saw Merouac had visibly paled. 'Oh,' she faltered. 'You were never told, were you?'

'Everything alright?' Seb asked as Merouac placed the drinks down on the table.

'Well no, in fact everything isn't alright,' Merouac said, sitting down. 'That woman at the bar just told me she knows me from my scar and my hair colour. She thinks she knew me when I was in her care at an orphanage.'

'That's odd. Must have you confused with someone else, I suppose.'

'She knew I had a twin sister.'

Seb looked over at the woman, who was staring at them intently. On catching their gaze, she looked away. Then, seeming to act on impulse, she came over.

'Look, I'm sorry to startle you,' she said to Merouac. 'Can I sit down? This place will fill up momentarily, and I don't want to leave you looking like you do right now, like you've had a good shock. Can I sit down?'

Merouac and Seb exchanged looks. Merouac nodded. 'Alright. Take a seat.'

The woman nodded and sat down next to Seb, and across from

Merouac. 'Let me introduce myself, at least. My name's Garatrudie.'

'This is Seb, and I'm Merouac.'

'Ah, so that's the name they gave you. A right good one, too. And your sister?'

'Malaena.'

'Oh, yes. Perfect twin names.'

Seb cleared his throat. 'Garatrudie's a nice name too. You're from Meurre Fells, then?'

'Oh, yes, born and bred. I worked with the babies when I was younger, and then took over this bar some ten shades ago.'

'So you're saying you worked at an orphanage here, in Meurre Fells?' Seb continued.

'That's right. There was an orphanage at Ruptor Delle for a long time, and that's where I worked. Twenty shades, can you believe it? Four kids of my own, but I had my heart broken when my youngest died in my arms before he could crawl. Poor lungs, you see.'

'Oh, sorry to know that,' Seb said quietly.

Garatrudie reached patted his hand in acknowledgment. 'Thank you. Well, I knew I wouldn't have any more of my own, but I needed to be around babies, so I got myself a job where there were plenty.'

'But at Ruptor Delle?' Merouac asked loudly, then raised his hand to acknowledge he'd almost shouted it out.

'Aye, that's right, Ruptor Delle. It's not as bad a place as you might think. The grounds are enormous and the buildings are large. It feels quite peaceful out there much of the time. Orphanages here in Meurre Fells are often part of the prisons. They're big, they can take large numbers of babies. We had a whole wing on the ground floor for many years. It's not there anymore, though.'

'Well Garatrudie, Merouac, my boss here, well, he's from the Ingrue. Not Meurre Fells.'

'Ah, so that's where they took you in the end. Good on them.'

'Who took me? What are you talking about?'

'Well, we had so many of you for the first shade, and then you all started getting adopted out. Then, one day, about two shades after you all arrived, Janver and Elsie disappeared with the two of you, the dark-haired twins. We never saw or heard from them again.'

Merouac's heart started hammering, a rat-a-tat thump that unnerved him and made him put down his beer. 'You knew my parents?'

Seb looked quickly at Merouac. 'Your parents were called Janver and Elsie?'

Merouac nodded. 'Yes. Janver and Eloise, or Elsie for short.'

Even Seb was starting to look uncomfortable.

'They worked at the orphanage, of course,' explained Garatrudie. 'They were tired; there was always so much to do. I never knew why they just didn't come right out and ask to adopt you both. But no, they took off with you two in the middle of the night, never to return. I suppose they worried because they weren't high class, with lots of money – they might get turned down. And it's true, they probably would have. All the families that came by to adopt the babies paid a sum of money, you see. Kind of as a thank you to the prison for having taken care of them so far. And it just might have been a sum more money than your parents had between them.

'I think they had just fallen in love with the two of you. They likely just made the best choice they could. And it was a good one. You needed a family. Do you know you and your sister even used to cry in sync?'

Merouac shook his head. 'No, but it wouldn't surprise me if we had.'

'I suppose we were all just shocked at how it happened. But good that you ended up in the Ingrue. It's a good place to grow up. And they loved you so much, right from the beginning.'

Merouac felt Seb's cautious eyes on him as Garatrudie told her tale. It seemed incredible, and yet she didn't seem the kind to bother about making up stories for strangers. She seemed to care that she told Merouac something that was true.

As well as Seb's gaze, Merouac was aware that Garatrudie was also watching him for a reaction.

'It's true, then, is it?' she asked quietly. 'I just told you something that's come as a surprise. They never told you your birth story?'

Merouac paused. What was there to say? He didn't have enough information. He didn't really want to hear anymore, either. And yet on the other hand, his parents were gone. They had passed away many years ago, and if they had kept secrets, they had taken them with them.

'I never knew anything other than that I was born in the Ingrue.' he said simply.

Garatrudie looked as though she was about to say something else, but at that moment half a dozen new customers walked through the door, and then shortly after that, half a dozen more. And so it went on, until the bar was well and truly full, hot and sweaty.

Merouac and Seb took their leave after a time, and found their way back to the rooms they had booked into for the night.

Seb seemed to understand that Merouac didn't want to talk; they both retired with a brief goodnight, and Merouac went straight to bed, falling into a restless sleep that kept him tossing and turning until the early hours, after which he slept deeply and woke knowing that he needed to return and ask Garatrudie to tell him more.

'It was always cold there, you know. That was probably one of the hardest things', Garatrudie said as she put plates in front of Merouac, one after the other as if she thought the conversation would be easier, if it went down with eggs and fresh bread and good strong tea.

The public rooms had been closed when Merouac had gone to find Garatrudie, but she'd been out front washing the windows and had opened up for him, shooing him inside and pointing him to a stool at the end of the bar. He sat there while she made him tea, and then went out back to fire up her stoves to cook him breakfast.

'There was never enough heat. There was never enough food, either. It wasn't an easy place to work, that's for certain. And there were never enough staff working at any one time. Many got sick of the place and left after only working for a few months. Even the mills were thought to be easier places to work.'

Garatrudie watched Merouac eat, and seemed satisfied that her work in the kitchen was being well received.

'There were so many babies,' she continued. 'They just kept turning up. At first it was easier. But the babies just kept coming, and soon there were just too many of you. It was bedlam. We had the whole fifty of you arrive within a shade.'

Merouac put down his knife and fork. 'What is this arrival of so many children that you're talking about, Garatrudie?'

'Well, that's how you all came to us. You and your sister came towards the end. I remember the two of you were always pretty calm. But some of the babies were very fragile; they couldn't be consoled, or they took a very long time to settle. And we didn't have time. We just couldn't settle you all. Some of you just had to settle yourselves.

'I remember you because you were dark, and not many of the babies were dark. But we could never figure out how even though you were all pretty different in colouring and temperament, you all had these very similar birthmarks on your neck.'

Merouac found himself reaching up and brushing his neck with his finger, across the birthmark Garatrudie was referring to.

'But anyway, I digress. Janver and Elsie. Your parents. Or, I should say, the man and woman I worked with who *became* your folks. They were good people. They lasted much longer than most other folk I worked with. They worked hard and they never complained. And they had a lot of love to give.

'Word got out though, which was lucky, because we were all about to fall over. People were coming by to take you all off our hands. High society ladies from Banne who couldn't have children of their own came to adopt some of you. Some families from Augrelle who wanted another pair of hands to help on the farms.'

Garatrudie had made herself a mug of tea too, and stood stirring sugar into her brew, still deep in her reverie.

'At some point, the number of babies we had in our care began to dwindle. Most of you got adopted out. And then the deliveries stopped, just like that. The monks stopped coming and eventually things quietened down, back to the way it had been before. And then the orphanage shut up completely, about ten shades later.'

Merouac looked up sharply. 'The monks? What do you mean, the monks stopped coming?'

'Well, the monks were the ones who had brought you all to us.'

'Where were the monks from?'

'I don't really know, to tell you the truth. I would assume they came from the Remneur Ranges. I never asked and our bosses never said. But you weren't their kin, that was easy to see. None of you had their features. You were all pale skinned, even the two of you with your dark hair. Very fair skinned indeed.'

Merouac thought back to his time; with the Faurin in recent times, the trips to the mountains to seek green pala, to get guidance on frequency tunings and the work with the Intangien to build a frequency bridge – the very one that had helped the Helara to cross over and seek shelter in their planet's core.

Garatrudie continued, but not before looking at Merouac's empty plate. 'You want some more eggs? Plenty back there.'

Merouac pushed the plate away. 'No. But thank you, Garatrudie. It was nice of you to make breakfast for me.'

'Well, anyway,' she continued, taking the plates back out to the kitchen and returning to her tea. She stood on the other side of the bar and picked up a cloth and began wiping her shelves, almost as a distraction. 'Where were we?'

'The monks. Why on earth were the Faurin involved?'

'I have no idea. They wouldn't say. We asked them, of course. All they would say is that there were a hundred of you, all up. A hundred babies, and they had been charged with finding families for all of you. We were the biggest orphanage, and so we took the most. The other fifty were taken to other orphanages all around the continent, I believe.'

'A hundred children? How the damn would they have come across so many babies at the one time, with the same instructions, to find families for them all? What else?'

'Nothing. No instructions as to what to do with you, no special needs or things we had to do, other than make sure you were cared for and found homes for. That was it. It was all strange and quiet, really. They came, maybe a dozen times. They had you all bundled up well. It seemed like they had done what they could. You were all quiet in their arms, like you all felt alright. Safe, you know. Maybe that's why we didn't ask too many questions. It wasn't like you arrived damaged or in any danger. No, you came safe and calm.'

Merouac was shaking his head in disbelief. 'I still can't fathom how the Faurin would have anything to do with it.'

'Well, all I can say is that it was like they had been entrusted, you know? Like they had a job to do and they did it. We were told they were coming. To expect them and to anticipate that they would be bringing babies. And that's what they did. And then they were gone, and they never came back. Never sent word, asking which babies went with which families, or how long it took for them to all be adopted out. As far as I knew, we never saw or heard another thing at all.

'And my parents, they never wrote to you after they left?'

'No, nothing like that. What could they say, really? We knew what they'd most likely done, and why. Mostly, we wished them well.'

'What happened when you found us gone?'

'Well, there was a moment or two's scramble, but it was more the fact that we'd lost two good workers, really. No offense, you were beautiful babies, but babies, we had enough of. Workers were much harder to come by. We missed them a lot, and we also didn't worry about you two twins because despite the fact they pretty much kidnapped you, they were good folk. Their hearts were in the right place. You were going to be as safe with them as you would anywhere.'

13.

Merouac is called to Tenogru

'You in there, boss?' Seb poked his head around the door into Merouac's office. 'Got a runner here from Endren. Here to see you especially.'

Merouac looked up from his papers. After the return from Meurre Fells, he'd retreated to his office and had found the quiet made him feel better. He needed time to think, to synthesise all the new information coming at him.

'Right,' he said, standing up and pushing his work to one side. 'Outside?'

'Aye, in the main workshop. Bring him in, shall I?'

Merouac nodded and before he could move from behind his desk, a young man appeared, anxious to push a written note into his hand as fast has he could. 'Hi Merouac, I'm Pelly, this is from the

Leron Estate via Endren and Tielder asked you to go as a priority.' The boy's words were a blur; it seemed as though he was speaking faster than he'd ever spoken before.

Merouac took the note, glanced at Seb who gave an interested shrug, and opened it. On reading it, he frowned. 'Tenogru?'

Pelly nodded. 'Yes. You've been asked for. Tielder said to tell you that you were asked for by name. So not to hand it on to anyone else.'

'Tielder's got me working to a pretty tight schedule,' Merouac said. 'I've got to get these first five stages of the line down, and he wants me to head to the mountains? As in, today?'

Pelly's head bobbed up and down. 'Yes,' he said breathlessly.

'The note doesn't say why. Just that I need to attend,' Merouac said, mostly for Seb's take, leaning over his desk and passing him the note.

Seb looked at it more closely. 'Interesting. What does Lavilla Whelme want with you?'

'I have no idea at all. This is railroad business?' Merouac asked Pelly. Lavilla Whelme was the Governor of the Ingrue. 'If it's railroad business, there are others who could go,' Merouac said, when Pelly failed to provide an answer. 'But why on earth is Lavilla Whelme calling a council in the mountains, and on Tenogru, no less?' Even as he spoke the words, Merouac thought about his recent trips to the exact mountain being discussed.

Pelly shook his head to indicate he didn't know. Seb scratched his cheek with his pencil. 'Alright, son,' he said to Pelly. 'Tell Tielder we'll make it happen.'

Merouac raised his eyebrows as the boy nodded at them and flew out of the workshop as fast as his legs would take him, either hugely relieved to have done his duty or rushing to deliver the next note in his bag. Possibly both, Merouac mused.

'Since when does this kind of thing happen?' Merouac muttered as Seb handed him back the note.

'Well, that'd be the thing, boss,' Seb replied, almost apologetically. 'It doesn't happen. Ever. Which means it's likely non-negotiable. Why don't you get some things together? Harlin and I can look after Evra while you're gone.'

'I suppose I'd better head out,' Merouac agreed. 'Thanks, Seb. Maarte knows what it's all about. I'll take the buggy as far as East Suron and then catch one of the local trains north as far as I can to the base of the mountain.'

'Good plan,' Seb agreed. 'She's there ready to go and fuelled up, and we don't need her for a few days. Says here you'll be escorted up the mountain, so that's something. I guess Pelly will send word you're on your way, so your escorts will probably be expecting you at sunrise tomorrow.'

Tenogru was the fourth and most northern mountain of the Remneur Ranges. Something in him sensed a connection would make itself known soon enough, and with that, proof the call had nothing to do with railroad business at all.

But at this point, he couldn't make the connection at all.

ooo

Merouac felt heavy with fatigue. His leg and hip hurt. He trudged up the incline with effort. He hoped the trip wouldn't take too long – he had a railroad to get back to and he didn't want to be away from Evra for more than a day or two.

He felt lightheaded as they climbed higher. The two monks escorting him up the trail set down for regular breaks, but Merouac had still been using his crutches a few days ago; now his leg was throbbing. He knew his limp was becoming visible.

Nevertheless, it was good to be back in the mountains. The Faurin were farmers, among other things, and sold much of their produce at the markets at the southern end of the Ranges. They were famous for their tea, and many of the trails they climbed offered views of the tea plantations that covered the eastern sides of all four mountains. While the western slopes were buffetted by ocean winds, the eastern slopes were well protected and provided the right altitude and climate for the tea he and Evra drank most days, the marla tea that was simple, sweet and strong. He could see Faurin bent over in the fields – it wasn't the right time for harvest, he assumed, but there would be more than enough to do keeping the plants growing.

As they climbed, he began to send out feelers. It was time to connect with his sister again, across the dimensions, across space and time, to get some sense from her if what Garatrudie had told him was real.

There was so much to try and understand. He and Malaena, two of a hundred babies suddenly up for adoption across the continent? Where had they all come from, and how had they all come so close together, to send all the orphanages across San Aurelle into such a spin. And apart from that, the idea that they were not blood kindred with the man and woman they had always known as their mother and father? How was it even possible they could have been raised in an orphanage for the first years of their lives, and never known of it?

His call to Malaena did not go unheard. His sense of her was growing stronger. He could feel her presence even as he put one foot in front of the other, progressing up the trail to what the Faurin called their Original Monastery.

He replayed for her the experience of meeting Garatrudie and the conversations that had followed. Malaena seemed to listen, absorb and consider it. Then, she responded in kind, sharing one of her own memories – but an early memory from childhood, hazy, murky and somewhat nonsensical.

Perhaps it was because Merouac was struggling up the side of a mountain to meet with a Governor he had never met before, on a topic he hadn't yet been informed about. He didn't have the energy to focus singularly on the connection with his sibling and understand the feelings and images she was sharing.

As far as he could interpret it, his twin sister was telling him she remembered an arrival in a mountainous country. They were brought here, to Ahm, from across the realms, and deposited here. They were not natives of the planet; rather, gifted *to* the planet.

'Here?' he asked her. 'As in, here in the Remneur Ranges? That doesn't make any sense either.'

Malaena continued to share her hazy memory with him. They were perhaps a shade old. The twins were not the only ones to have arrived somewhere new. There were discussions about what would be done. Arguments, even. And then they were transported again, a long descent from the mountain peaks, always when it was dark, always guided by the two moons.

And that was it. His sister's memory faded away.

And then, too, he felt Malaena fade away as well. The connection was broken and he was alone again.

It didn't make a lot of sense. And yet Merouac wondered if that was a comfort in some way, since so much of what was happening didn't make any sense anyway.

They climbed further. Having started at dawn, and rested at intervals along the way, Merouac guessed they were more than halfway up the side of the mountain.

He thought about the time he had been here most recently, and what he had first learned about the Faurin fighter ranks, the Intangien. The reason the Intangien training grounds were based on Tenogru was because many of the royal family of Faurin trained as Intangien, and in fact led the ranks.

He and his small group had come to the Remenur Ranges seeking permission to take away some green pala stone, to help with their frequency tunings. And in doing so, he had come here to Tenogru and spent time with Qualan, who helped Merouac understand more about the Intangien.

In fact, it was not Qualan they had come to see but Kultan, the next in line to become ruler. That was the tradition. Because pala stone was largely found in the Remnur Ranges, and considered the sacred gemstone of the Faurin, permission had to be sought to take any of it away.

But Kultan was still young and had not been initially inclined to meet with Merouac at all. Even then, Merouac had felt some sympathy for the boy, who seemed alone in the world. Many of his family were dead – his grandfather and brother killed in an avalanche, and his father also seemed to have come to misadventure in the mountains early in the boy's life. And so there were no rulers to guide the young man and show him the way, only a guardian to care and train him, amid the other extended family and Intangien who lived on Tenogru.

Qualan, quiet and magnanimous with a broad face and generous smile, had invited Merouac to sit with him. 'We are fighters and farmers here in the Remneur,' he said with a twinkle in his eye. 'That's what we say to ourselves, even though it's mostly farming across the four ranges, these days. But the Intangien are special. They are the true fighters, and they use a technique we cultivated right here, on Tenogru. The Intangien transitions through different mental states in order to arrive at the optimum combat state. This ideal state is one where he can leave his body, shift his sensory capabilities into the aether around him in order to see wider, deeper, and further.'

Merouac remembered he had stared at the monk blankly, not understanding any of it.

Qualan patiently explained. 'The warrior will begin to warm up first. To tread the ground. And then he will shout his warrior cry. It is a stomp, a roar, a shout. At this point he will not look at the enemy. The Intangien warrior, as he descends into the Maoulfi state, looks only inside himself. He imagines thunder and rhythm, he imagines finding his own signature sound deep inside his belly. That is the first step to begin the descent into the Maoulfi state. He then drinks balche.'

'Balche?' Merouac had asked.

'It is a drink made from the grasses of the fields. It is not essential, but can be used to bring on a light fever, which the warrior feels heating his limbs, shutting down his day senses, his rational thinking. Many use it once just to learn the process and then do not need it again. The important thing is the shutting down of daylight thoughts. The Intangien do not allow themselves to be guided by good sense or logic. They shut down those senses and strive for something deeper.

'It is only then that a slower pulse comes to the fore and it is accompanied by a change in presence. the non-body is activated. One eye opens, one closes. The body pulsates, the Maoulfi awakens and begins to read the air, sending information back to the warrior's body.'

Merouac shook his head. 'I still don't understand. Tell me what the non-body is. How does it work?'

Qualan nodded. 'It is an etheric body, which acts a little like a sieve, or a drift net. It allows the energy of the body to be displaced, to appear in one dimension while physically disappearing in another. That is why the combat technique is so unique. No one else has learned how to do it. But it offers something else as well. The non-body can be cast out more deeply into other realms, capturing the information that streams through the universe.'

Merouac and his group had eventually met with Kultan and left the mountains with enough green pala to amplify their tuning efforts. And they had practised descending into the Maoulfi state. Or, at least, Heyla had made them try it, and had even created her own mix of balche to speed up the process. Heyla, the gypsy trader

Evra had befriended all on her own, had become a unique part of their group, pushing them to test and experiment and test again, to get a better understanding of how frequency tunings could work. And it had been enough to get the ball rolling. To make contact with the strange creatures they had come to know as the Helara. And to find out what they needed, and how to help them. It scared Merouac to think how very thin the veil really was.

At some point past the middle of the day, the climb became more challenging, as the altitude thinned the air. Merouac was breathing heavily. A dizzy spell came over him. He stood up and then stumbled.

'Merouac.'

The call came from above him somewhere. He stood up, looked to follow it and went dizzy again. He stumbled sideways, steadied himself and waited for his vision to clear.

'Merouac. Are you alright?'

The sound of a horse and rider came closer. Merouac grinned. 'Kultan.'

He heard the young Faurin dismount, say a few quick words to the monks escorting him. Moments later Kultan was moving him off the path, to sit a moment on an outcrop of rocks. 'You don't look very good, Merouac.'

Merouac snorted. 'Tell me about it. Where did you come from?'

'I've been riding further up the mountain. Come, you can ride the rest of the way on Oor.'

Merouac, his sight clearing again, looked at the speckled white horse a few feet away, his long neck stretched downwards to allow him to gently pull a few tufts of grass into his mouth.

'I think I'll take you up on that. I assume I won't get thrown off this time?' Merouac said lightly, referring to the last time Kultan had offered him a steed.

Kultan grinned and directed him to the right side of the horse so he could put his strong leg in the rope stirrup to get astride the horse. 'You'll be safe on Oor,' he said.

Astride Kultan's horse, Merouac started to feel himself again. Kultan walked beside the horse, guiding him up the path. The young monk, who had seemed impetuous and indignant when Merouac first met him, now seemed much more thoughtful and quiet. He methodically pushed vines away from the trail as they made their way through the dense forest foliage of the middle alps.

From time to time, Kultan would allow Oor to slow down and stop to drink from the water bag Kultan had slung over his shoulder. It allowed Merouac time to glimpse through the trees to the thickly forested lowlands below, and occasionally catch sight of the three other great peaks of the Remneur Ranges to the south: Aicatra, Chapatreau and Tattembru.

Merouac knew there to be around two hundred family lineages in the Remneur Ranges. Villages with family collectives were spread out over the other peaks and valleys. Tenogru was the quiet mountain reserved for the Remneur's royal family and Pilgrimage Paths.

By late afternoon, they had come close to reaching their destination. They came off the trail into an open field. At the highest end of the field they could see the stone arches of the Original Monastery.

Before them lay paved paths weaving around fenced areas containing a range of clucking and tuttering animals, from cheeknets to chickens and farnell. Beyond that, the temple compound was a complex of long, low buildings set deep into the side of the final peak of the mountain. The winding paths were paved with circular, flat charcoal coloured stones.

'We are here,' announced Kultan. 'You will be received in the East Hall. You can see them there, ready to greet you and feed you.'

Merouac slid off Oor. 'Thanks for coming to get me, Kultan. Will I see you inside?'

Kultan nodded. 'Yes, you might,' he said, and with a small smile, led Oor away into the fading light.

14.

Tor climbs Tenogru

Tor was tense and silent as he climbed the mountain, behind the ever-fussing Gartounne.

The party was small. It included only him, Gartounne, and a group of Faurin guides assisting them to make the journey up to the heights of Tenogru.

The Faurin monks had been quietly assembled, waiting for them. They had been silent as they presented Gartounne with a chair to sit in, to be carried up the mountain. Gartounne had given them all another black look before allowing himself to be seated. Four monks surrounded him, as if he were royalty, two to carry the chair and two flanking him on either side.

The path they trod was a simple dirt track, with symmetrical fans of deep green foliage on either side of them. In the middle of the day, the trees were still and the birds were quiet.

A cantankerous Gartounne could be heard ahead, shouting and complaining about the discomfort and the appalling rudeness of the situation. But the call to come had been non-negotiable. Gartounne, despite his age, was still officially Governor and governors were not allowed to send proxies.

The Faurin guides walked ahead on bare feet along paths winding through the deep forest, quietly and without fuss, sometimes murmuring between themselves and occasionally walking back among the group to check on them and indicate the way ahead, with small smiles or nods, but few words.

Tenogru was the highest of the four peaks. For the most part of the year its tip was invisible, the top third of the mountain hidden amid the clouds and cloaked in mist.

They left the west side alone and instead navigated around the eastern base. The western slopes were frighteningly steep. The goats loved them but herding families that chose to let their goats loose on the western slope of Tenogru had to be happy for those goats to make their own way back in their own good time, for in most parts the face of the mountain was so sheer, and the buffetting wind so overpowering, that neither adult nor child had much hope of sticking to the mountain.

The eastern slope, while still challenging, was much kinder. One could escape the winds there, and the rocky crags and leaning limbs of hyrea trees offered helpful branches for those who roamed across, up and down its incline, hunting game or collecting nuts, berries and an array of leaves, fronds, fruits and plants.

Even as a child, Tor had felt bereft and anxious in the dense growth of the forests and rainforests the Faurin lived in. He had hated constantly walking among dangling vines that brushed against your skin, leaving trails of dew; there was always dew, moisture in the air. He hated the dripping of it from everywhere, everywhere moisture, and when it was hot, it was like a clinging, suffocating blanket. He hated the feel of dirt under his feet. Before he was five shades old, he had developed the habit of fashioning protection for his feet, wrapping leaves around them so they stayed clean.

But of course his parents had laughed at him. No one wore shoes in the Remneur. The Faurin all developed tough feet that could handle running through the mountains. All the Faurin except Tor, that was. His feet stayed sensitive. He learned to run, but it never stopped hurting, never became comfortable, never slipped his mind as a concern. It was always a concern.

His eyes, too, felt as though they were always burning. He had detested the smoke from the wooden cooking fires that were tended in every family hearth. They sent smoke spirals up from the forested lowlands to the canopied highlands, and while the smells of cooking were pleasant enough, the smoke itself sent Tor's eyes watering. He cursed the small children sent on errands, running over the well-worn paths, ducking under greenery and pushing ropes of vine aside to deliver food cooked on those same fires to relatives or friends living in different parts of the mountain.

He reflected on his similar hatred of monkeys. He dreaded seeing the trail of a meribaun, or the flash of an emeret in the trees. Monkeys in the mountains weren't afraid of dropping from the branches directly onto your shoulder, to claw any food that might be making its way from your hand to your mouth as you walked.

Then there were mite-monkeys and akra-tails that were bold enough to chase you from behind and leap onto your back in cheeky greeting, only to clamber up over your shoulders and head, to latch on to the closest vine or branch above your head. They did this, Tor was sure, just for a laugh, and Tor did not like to be the butt of anyone's joke, especially monkeys.

Tor's distaste for mountain life didn't end there. He hated the mosquitoes and the undergrowth with its creepers, roots and insects. Higher up, the mountain peaks simply made him dizzy.

15.
First meetings on Tenogru

Merouac was ensconced in a room of his own, somewhere on the first floor of the Hall, eating fresh bread and some of the Remneur's cheeses and drinking marla tea. He stretched his legs out in front of him, massaging his left thigh, and listened to the sounds around him.

He could hear the bells sounding over on Aicatra; he knew they rang out across the mountains at the same time in the evening every day, a signal that the day was done and it was time for the Faurin to retreat to their villages and homes. There were voices moving up and down the hall outside; Merouac assumed more people were arriving for the meeting. He still had no idea why he had been summoned or who had received a similar summons. He should have asked Kultan more questions, he reflected as he finished his tea.

He was starting to consider the low bed, with its woven rugs for covers, waiting in the corner of the room, when he heard a rap on the door. He sighed. That was a shame. Surely it was time to call it a night. He considered ignoring the knock. But the rapping was loud and insistent.

'Merouac! Merouac, are you in there?'

Merouac rose, walked over to the door and opened it. On seeing the owner of the voice he let out a surprised laugh. 'Heyla, it is you! I thought I recognised the voice. How the damn are you here, though?'

Heyla, tall and tanned, laughed at Merouac's surprise.

Merouac hugged the woman and then held her at arms length. 'Is all this your doing?' he asked suspiciously.

'It might be,' she said merrily.

Heyla looked well, Merouac thought. He walked over to the bed and lowered himself onto it and indicated the chair was free for Heyla to sit in. 'Tell me everything. Tell me why I'm here. Why you're here.'

'It's happening, Merouac,' Heyla said. 'We're building momentum.'

She looked happy, he thought to himself. It wasn't that he didn't think she was capable of it, but Heyla was someone he considered to have a significant chip on her shoulder. She was sharp, perceptive, independent and her piercing grey eyes cut through almost every type of falsity. And yet, ironically, when he'd met her, she'd been travelling with a group of Ayuherica gypsies, determined to be one of them, and sell her wares at market, pretending she wasn't the sister of the Suroni Governor-in-Waiting, Sanat Leron.

'What kind of momentum? I thought you went back north after we settled the Helara,' Merouac said.

'I did. I found my sisters. But I couldn't stay with them,' Heyla said. 'It felt like everything was suddenly different.' Heyla paused and gave him a look. 'They are still my family, Merouac. I know you think it's strange, but the Ayuherica are my people now.'

Merouac held up his hands in defence. 'I didn't say otherwise,' he said. 'But you're right, I probably don't quite understand it. Keep going.'

Heyla gave her long sandy hair a flick, a habit Merouac had noticed from the first time they had met. There was something defiant in it. And she was defiant, he knew that from experience. He noted some grey streaks mixed with the other blonde and light-brown strands of hair. He'd never asked Heyla how old she was; he guessed a little older than he; possibly forty-two or forty-three shades.

'Well, I just felt the need to return to Suron.'

'Back to your original family, then?' Merouac asked solemnly, trying not to smile.

'Yes, as a matter of fact.'

'You went back to the Leron Estate? I thought you had sworn never to return.'

'I did swear that, but that was before I became aware I am the aunt of an extraordinary child. A creature who knows how to communicate beyond the realm,' Heyla replied. 'I have a responsibility to that child, now. That changes everything.'

'Yes, I guess it does,' mused Merouac. Heyla was talking about Ophrin, of course, the son of her brother, Sanat Leron; the very child who had first understood that the Helara's planetary ecosystem had been about to implode.

Heyla stood up from her chair and started pacing around the room. She had never been good at sitting for long periods of time, or containing her kinetic energy in any other way for more than a few moments.

'Well, I won't tell you everything, but in summary I'm pleased I went. I not only got the chance to see Delsaine, and spend time with Ophrin, but being at the Estate allowed me to make a very interesting connection. A new friend, if you will.'

'Let me guess. Lavilla Whelme?'

'Exactly,' said Heyla, still pacing excitedly. 'We talked.'

For a moment she stopped pacing. 'We talked about everything, Merouac. About what happened with the dust storms. The planet in the sky. The idea that the shield might be down.'

'How on earth did you manage to do that so quickly?' Merouac asked, impressed.

'I managed it, largely because my family are idiots,' Heyla said with relish. 'Lavilla was refused an audience with my father, would you believe it? Her people found some activity going on in the grid, went looking for answers and were told my father sanctioned it. He's denying it, but he also refused to meet with her, possibly just out of spite, knowing him. Can you imagine one Governor refusing to meet another who had gone to the trouble of coming in person? It was extraordinarily rude.

'I found her there, waiting in the reception lounge with her people. I listened to what she was dealing with and organised for her to meet directly with Tor Anale, who should know of any activity down in the grid that Lavilla could have mentioned.

'In any event, I had him summoned under the pretense it was my brother he was coming to see. Of course it wasn't. Sanat's too deep in discussions with his own team about how to leverage the railroad to make a bid for Federation, with Suron taking the role of Head State. You don't even want to know about the tedious meetings I sat in on about that.

'Well, Tor literally fled when he saw it was Lavilla and myself he was to meet. He's always been shady, but I've never seen him look so guilty. We figured he was involved somehow but then he wouldn't talk either, after that.'

'Tor Anale, down in the grid?' asked Merouac. 'Heyla, we've been down there again, too. We came to the same conclusion, that whoever was down there, using the generator, was probably trying to do the same thing we were – experiment with frequency tunings to test if the shield is really down or not. But Tor Anale?'

'Well, that's essentially why we're here,' Heyla explained. 'Lavilla was so furious at her treatment that she's called everyone here under one of the rules of the Separation Act. Basically, any Governor can use the law to call an extraordinary council if they feel the need to. And every other Governor is committed to supporting it by attending in person.'

'You mean Gartounne Leron got called up?' Merouac whistled.

'He most certainly did. He arrived kicking and screaming mind you, earlier today, despite being carried the whole way. Tor Anale, too.'

'Huh,' Merouac said. 'This feels like a big meeting. Why am I here, though?'

'Well, like I said, Lavilla and I really talked. The more I talked to her, the more I began to trust her. It's an excellent feeling, to be in the presence of someone who is actually a leader, a woman leader, I should say,' Heyla continued. 'My father certainly has no leadership talent, but Sanat is charismatic and visionary in his way, so I suppose I can't take that away from him. But Lavilla is something else entirely.'

'So you got talking to Lavilla. What did you tell her about me, specifically?'

'That you were a talented metalsmith. And you were capable of the art of tuning metal. I also told her you are in contact with your sister, who has travelled beyond the walls of the world, and you are responsible for effecting the transfer of an alien intelligence into our realm, thereby proving the shield is well and truly thinning, if not down completely.'

'So this meeting is not about anything to do with the railroads, then?' Merouac ascertained. He felt a sense of unease at the thought of officially discussing anything else with a governor like Lavilla Whelme.

'No. It is not,' Heyla confirmed. 'It is, firstly, about what has been going on down in the grid. And then, possibly other items for discussion to do with the shield. The council will convene tomorrow, if you haven't already been told. But tonight, you meet Lavilla. She has questions.'

'I'm sure she does,' retorted Merouac.

A short time later, Merouac found himself sitting opposite Lavilla Whelme at a long wooden table in another quiet room overlooking the mountains, just down the hallway from the rooms they had been settled into.

At the end of the table, two of the governor's assistants were discreetly seated. Merouac had nodded to them on arrival, but they had only given a fleeting acknowledgement, allowing Heyla to focus the introductions between Merouac and the most powerful woman in the Ingrue.

Helya herself was now standing next to the table, as ever, unable to sit down, more content to pace the small corners of the room as she allowed everyone to settle in.

The Governor of the Ingrue had been waiting for them in the room. She was tall and slender in build, entirely different to the average Ingruan, who tended towards a blockier, stout build. This of course, was because she was not Ingruan herself – a rare thing indeed for a Governor. She had long brown hair and inquisitive brown eyes.

Women, when all was said and done, ran the Ingrue. They sat their broad bodies deep in the seats of power at every turn – within the unions, in the turns of government that switched every five shades, in the industry of the metal houses and everywhere else that mattered. And yet their leader was not Ingruan.

Where did all the men go, many asked. They were tolerated; Ingruan women had no beef with men in general. They were simply, for the most part, outside the focus of the red-blooded, strong hearted, loud and lusty she-folk that ran the country.

The Ingrue was the industrial heart of the continent. It had been that way even back in the times when San Aurelle was a single federated country. The Ingrue, the only part of the continent that mined, processed and refined base molta, had always been responsible for the generation and distribution of hahma current, the energy source that powered the continent.

The other countries paid handsomely for the supply distributed to them through the grid.

Many men of the Ingrue laboured in the sprawling molta refineries dotted up and down the Ingrue. Their strong, robust and compact bodies were capable of handling the gritty heat. But many more worked underground, maintaining the hahma grid.

It was the main reason the Ingrue could seem so bereft of male adults – the large majority were spread out on assignment maintaining the grid, moving from one section to the next, often doing circles and twists along long stretches underground, surfacing here and there to enjoy weeks off at a time in any country they happen to be in, sometimes only returning home once a shade.

The Ingrue was a vast place, and it was also Merouac's supposed birthplace, and where he and Malaena had grown up with their supposed parents.

The country itself was famous for its twin cities that sat on opposing sides of the Broad, the stained brown river that divided the northern and southern cities, and the unknowable stretches of emptiness dotted with many townships in the middle of nowhere and specked with hahma plants, steel mills and metal working houses.

The Ingruans had always been tribal. Long before anyone could remember, family and history and clans and unions were the most important thing in the industrial townships that dotted the country, but never more fiercely did tribal connectivity reign than in the twin cities. And as the two cities had grown, neither would concede giving the other side control over something it could control just as easily on their own side, there was two of everything, in particular, two power plants.

Lavilla had been brought in to lead the twin cities ten shades earlier; long after Merouac had left to complete his apprenticeships in the outposts of the highly regarded Ingruan metalsmithing houses that were dotted all over the continent.

At the time, no one had been able to come to an agreement on how the Governor would be chosen, and how it could ever be fair to choose an impartial leader not beholden to either city. Lavilla had been recruited from Banne Country in the north and was known to run a tight administration, and her people were mostly good. Her background was in running large operations in the Banne ports, the largest international port across the whole continent.

Lavilla Welme was known as many things. Thoughtful and moderate, but also shrewd and a good negotiator. She was, most of all, known as fair. She governed from a place of balance that Ingruans simply found hard to access amid their deeply felt emotions and loyalties.

She worked long hours on her barge, which was the central meeting point for many of the meetings her Government hosted. She also took meetings with any Ingruan who asked for it, as long as there was good reason. She saw mill workers. Factory chiefs. She met with hahmatricians, the ones who monitored the pulse of the hahma current driving through the grid to each of the countries the Ingrue serviced, which was, in fact, all of them. Power was the Ingrue's biggest calling card, so wherever a decision was needed, or a crisis required resolution, Lavilla was called upon to resolve it. Which she always did, efficiently, matter of factly, without fuss or drama or the laying of blame in any direction. Lavilla wasn't a technical expert in the matters of hahma flow, although, after ten shades as the Governor of the Ingrue, she was close.

Lavilla Whelme was a woman who knew where her knowledge stopped and when to call in specialists. The Ingrue didn't need another expert in hahma power.

Merouac reached his arms forward to shake hers, with the formal Ingruan greeting.

'I see your Big Hunger, your Big Thirst and your Big Heart, my friend.' He spoke somewhat awkwardly. It seemed odd to use the word friend for the governer, but it was the way the greeting went.

Lavilla gave a small smile, accepted the greeting and replied, 'And I recognise and celebrate it in you also.'

Merouac looked at Heyla, but she waved his imminent words away, dismissing any need for an explanation of the greeting.

Lavilla noted Heyla's decision to keep standing and turned to Merouac across the table.

'Tell me about yourself, Merouac. I have heard a lot from Heyla, and there are quite specific things I'm hoping you can help me understand. But first, tell me about this rare art of tuning metal that you have.'

Merouac was thoughtful for a moment. 'When I was at Endren, I had men working three different rotations. I often stayed late in case anything needed my attention on the afternoon shift.

'Then, when the night shifts started calling me out more frequently, I suppose my sleep patterns got a bit disrupted. I started waking up often, and if I had nothing to do and couldn't get back to sleep, I just started coming down to the workshops anyway, and working on my sculptures.'

'So you never set out intending to create tuned pieces?'

'I had no idea that I *could*. Of course, we've all heard rumours over the years that it was possible. But I'd never really paid them much attention, and certainly I never had any idea I could do such a thing.'

'Evra did, though,' Heyla said, wandering over to the large window.

'Your niece,' Lavilla said. Clearly Heyla had already shared this part of the story as well.

'Well, yes. It does seem that way. I don't know that she knew anything about tuned metal especially, but as soon as she came to live with me she was curious about them, always wanting to get to them, play with them, hold them. And then, when we met Heyla, it was one of the first things she did, almost as if she needed to show them to someone who knew what to do with them. I certainly have no idea how my niece had any sense of the metal being tuned, or what gave her the idea of showing Heyla.'

'She's special,' Heyla said matter of factly.

'What did you use for your sculptures, Merouac?' Lavilla asked.

'Whatever was on the scrap pile. Sheet cut-offs, round bar. Bits of steel, copper, magnatite – whatever we needed for the railroad and anything else you might find in a metalsmithing shop, that's what I used.'

'And absolutely no plan to do anything with them?'

He shook his head. 'Only to quiet my mind. It was Heyla who took them and ran with them, so to speak.' Heyla snorted, turning back to the table, arms still crossed.

'Tell me what you did with them, Heyla.'

'I knew what they were, right from the beginning. I also know that the people who understand the potential of tuned metal better than me only travel and trade via market routes.'

'Fringe dwellers,' Lavilla smiled.

'I call them the ones who hold a wider and wilder interpretation around life on the planet of Ahm and the universe they existed within,' retorted Heyla. 'In this instance, I went to a trader in Tustennuit I know well. He held the sculptures in his hands. He felt the spark, also.'

Merouac found himself looking at one woman, then the other. Looking at them, he was struck by their similarities. Heyla was tall, her skin tanned and brown from all her days walking under a hot sun. Her face was freckled. And of course, those grey eyes, the signature trait of Leron's first family. She wore her long sandy hair out, flicking it from time to time, otherwise weaving things into it: fabric, leather, flowers, whatever she felt like on the day. Lavilla was also tall, a brunette, also with long hair, but worn as a simple, straight braid at the back and then twisted underneath. But it was the energy they both had that struck him. Both women were so strong in their intent and their personality. And they were both looking for answers and a way forward. It was a good partnership, he reflected.

'Tell me about the charging process,' Lavilla said.

'It turns out hahma current is a more complex proposition than I knew,' admitted Merouac. 'The Faurin have explained to us it isn't just a source of power but it's a carrier wave for charge particles.'

'What particles are we talking about?' Lavilla questioned.

'Particles that originate from other realms and dimensions, but which can attach to hahma current and find their way into our own realm, our own reality. Our bodies can recognise these particles and can also learn to digest the information they contain.'

Lavilla was quiet for a moment. Then, she leaned across the table looking at Merouac with a searching gaze. 'Merouac, Heyla and I spoke for a long time when I was in Suron. I know a lot from those conversations about you, and your sister, and what you and Heyla were trying to do with the first frequency tunings you tried to do before the dust storms. But let me ask you these questions directly. First, do you really believe the shield is down? And second, do you really believe you were able to use a frequency bridge to transfer an alien race into the space below the caves, below the hahma grid?'

Merouac's answer was simple. 'Yes,' he said.

16.
The Group Convenes

The next morning, the first meeting of the group convened under Lavilla's direction. A Faurin monk who had brought Merouac his dinner the night before had knocked on his door earlier. The older man, with an array of scarves and beads around his neck, had nodded kindly to Merouac and shuffled into the room with bread, cheese, ale and fresh water. He had told Merouac they would recieve another knock on their doors in a short time, a signal they were to join Lavilla for her meeting.

When the call had come, the hallway had suddenly seemed crowded with others being called from their rooms and escorted along the corridor, past the smaller room he and Heyla had met Lavilla in the previous night, to a large room filled with natural light streaming in from the wide windows that looked out onto the ranges. Merouac breathed in the fresh air, glad to have the sight of the ranges so close, for a meeting that already seemed tense and filled with individuals whose social rank far outweighed his own.

Lavilla was standing in the middle of the room, with a concentrated look on her face. She wore an earthy brown pant suit and her long brown hair was plaited and fixed high on her head. At the back of the room, several of her assistants moved quietly.

She beckoned for Merouac and the others to take the chairs that had been placed in a circle around her.

One person was already seated. Merouac blinked but otherwise tried not to show any surprise at seeing Gartounne Leron. Two men stood behind him, officials of sorts, Merouac mused, or perhaps caretakers. The grey Leron eyes were unmistakable; in this case Gartounne's eyes watered and the skin around his nose and mouth glistened. He looked far too sick to be out of bed, and yet, as Heyla had pointed out, if her father was well enough to hold on to the governorship, years after he should have handed it over to his son, then he shouldn't have a problem with actually doing the work.

As everyone else moved to find a seat, Lavilla nodded at each of them.

When everyone was seated, she spoke. 'Welcome. Most of you, of course, know each other. But let me make clear, for everyone, my knowledge of you, and clarify for everyone in the room, my relationship with each of you.' Lavilla's voice was firm and it was clear she would be brokering no foolishness.

'Gartounne Leron.' Lavilla spoke his name but the old man refused to look at her, staring ahead. Lavilla continued. 'I recognise you and I welcome you as the Governor of Suron. I'm aware you're not well. And you're here because I demanded it and not because you thought you should be.'

Still Gartounne said nothing.

'Over the time of my governorship of the Ingrue, we have rarely had the need to meet, to work together, or to achieve anything out of the ordinary. And when there has been that need, such as the return to considerations of Federation, and working together rather than apart, those discussions have been led with your son, Sanat. And that is as it should be; Sanat is a leader in his own right, and as Governor-in-Waiting, it's good to see him initating his own projects such as the Transcontinental Railroad.'

Gartounne rolled his eyes, which caused an immediate response from Heyla, who had placed herself to Merouac's left. 'Don't do that, old man,' Heyla said sharply. Heyla's commanding voice created a new ripple of awareness across the room that that there were in fact two members of the Suron royal family: Gartounne as Governor and Heyla, daughter of the Governor, powerful in her own individual right but with no formal inheritance to the line of power as it currently stood.

Gartounne glared at her, sighed and refolded his pale hands in his lap, then turned his head, beckoning to one of his aids. The aid nodded and brought forward another blanket, which was placed for Gartounne over his lap.

'It's cold in here,' Gartounne said.

'It's quite warm, actually,' Heyla countered.

Lavilla cleared her throat and continued.

'Gartounne. As you, and many others would be aware, after the dust storms that covered the country, there has been a lot of activity down in the grid. People from all across the continent seemed to have an idea it would be safer to seek shelter there. The amount of activity has meant my people have to work extra hard to keep the grid clear. Extra patrols have been present, and as a result, we found a section of the grid under Suron that was closed off. This is the issue I came to discuss with you not very long ago. That is not acceptable.'

'It's incredibly rude, is what it is,' Heyla said, eyes narrowed, to her father. 'If you can't represent Suron to visiting officials, and especially a fellow governor, then your time is up.'

'You don't get a say in any of this,' Gartounne snarled at his daughter.

Heyla let out a peal of laughter. 'Oh, is that right, old man? Let me guess, because I'm a woman?'

'You don't get a say because you walked out twenty shades ago. You're not a Leroni anymore. You're nothing.' Merouac watched in fascination as Gartounne's face started to darken.

'It doesn't work like that,' Heyla retorted.

Gartounne snorted and looked at Heyla with cold irritation.

Merouac glanced sideways at Heyla. It was striking how different they both were, both carrying the genetic trait of the grey eyes, but Heyla wild with energy and intelligence, Gartounne sour and weighed down with bitterness and contempt.

Lavilla held up her hand. 'Heyla,' she started, reminding the room that she was still only at the point of introductions. 'I recognise you as the daughter of the Governor of Suron. I also recognise you as the one Leroni who agreed to meet with me at the estate during my visit.'

'She had no right,' Sanat barked.

'I have every right,' Heyla said calmly, leaning back. 'And what a good thing it was. And, in fact, a very good series of conversations have been had since. Your loss, and your stupidity.'

'Shut your …' Gartounne roared, spit flying from his mouth.

'No, don't go any further, Gartounne,' Lavilla warned, raising a hand. 'Heyla's right. I had a very insightful conversation with her during my visit, which is also part of the reason for our meeting here, and the reason for Merouac Dane to be here as well.'

As Lavilla looked to Merouac, all other eyes in the room followed her. 'Merouac Dane. Metalsmith and head of the East-West line and the associated sub-camp for the Transcontinental Railroad.'

As Merouac nodded and thanked Lavilla for the invitation, he saw Gartounne frown. 'Why do we …' he started, but was both interrupted by his own coughing fit and Lavilla's firm hand signalling him not to interrupt her introductions.

'Kultan,' Lavilla said, acknowledging the young Faurin who had come in last. Merouac turned around in surprise and smiled at him. 'Kultan kindly allowed me to host this gathering here, on Tenogru, the home of the Faurin Royal family. As you know, Kultan is in training to become the leader of his people, once he reaches the age of twenty-five.' Kultan still looked young, Merouac thought to himself.

'Qualan,' Lavilla continued, smiling at the older man seated next to Kultan. Merouac smiled at him also.

And then, last but not least, Tor Anale. 'Tor, I recognise you as one of the many who leave the Faurin mountains to help train the Suron army. Unlike most who simply do four shades of service and then return to the mountains, you stayed. You have worked your way up, under Gartounne, to lead the Suron military and logistics for the railroads, and you report directly to Gartounne Leron.'

The group swivelled to look to Tor, who sat in shrinking isolation on the other side of the circle. Merouac knew him from interactions at the logistics supply camp, and from his reputation as a man of quirks, one of which was his penchant for dressing in military whites as a rule. And here he was, in his whites that were now rather marked from the journey up the side of the moutain. Tor looked small, pale and unhappy to be here. He, too, said nothing in response to Lavilla's introduction.

'Tor, you also refused to talk with Heyla and I when you were asked to join us,' Lavilla said, giving the small man a hard look. Tor shook his head but said nothing, as though he was quietly willing himself to disappear completely.

'Alright, I think I've set the scene for you,' Lavilla said, crossing her arms and pacing from one side of the circle to the other, then moving out of the circle completely to walk towards the windows. She seemed to take strength from the fresh light and air and turned back with an intense look of complete focus.

The group, now seated, looked around expectantly.

'So, let's get started,' the governor said. 'You all know who I am. You also know I've called on a part of San Aurelle's agreement, the agreement between the seven countries that was signed as part of the Separation Act. It's never been invoked before, so you can understand that this is important.'

The room was quiet.

'The first purpose of this meeting is to understand what's been going on down in the grid. As you are all aware, the grid falls under my purview. Only me and my people have the right to be down there. And yet it seems much is going on, and I have brought you all here to better understand it, and ensure you are all aware, as well.'

Merouac felt strangely nervous.

'Let's just step back a moment and consider this situation. Every country across San Aurelle agreed, as part of the Separation Act, that the grid would be the one thing that stayed fully complete across the continent. It didn't make any sense to carve up such a complex thing with the demarcation lines of each country. In addition, the Ingrue agreed that each country could send us its molta, which we would refine, for a cost of course, and send back through the grid for each country to use its hahma power as it wished.'

Lavilla looked around the room. 'Any questions so far?' There was a general shaking of heads around the room, apart from Gartounne and Tor, who were still.

She continued. 'The grid is old, it's complex, and none of you have any reason to be there, for any purpose. And so of course it was surprising to come across a Suroni military presence, guarding access to certain tunnels and patrolling sections of the grid night and day. Anyone trying to close off a section of the grid, without explanation, is unacceptable. And to have our investigation held up with lies and misdirection has simply confounded the issue. But for it to be endorsed and approved by a Governor? That causes me serious question.'

Lavilla faced Gartounne. 'I'd like you to explain this to me,

Gartounne.'

'I don't know anything about this,' snapped Gartounne. 'Well, I didn't until a few days ago. It's got nothing to do with me.'

'You're the Governor,' replied Lavilla calmly. 'It's part of your job to know. I'm afraid it's got everything to do with you.'

Gartounne glared at the woman through watery eyes. 'The way I govern is clearly different.'

'How so?' Lavilla prompted. 'And why don't you also share what you found out a few days ago, then?'

Gartounne ignored the first part of the question and went straight to the second. 'That Tor, foolish as he is, has been using a section of the grid for unapproved purposes.' The old man cast a derisive look across the room at Tor Anale has he spoke.

'What purposes would that be?' Lavilla asked.

'Why don't you ask him? He's right there. I've been kept in the dark about it,' Gartounne retorted.

Lavilla turned to Tor. 'Well?'

Tor was white in the face. Sweat tricked down the sides of his cheeks. He looked furiously ahead, not meeting the gaze of Lavilla or anyone else in the room. 'Conducting scientific experiments,' he said, as if speaking any words at all was hard.

'Experiments? What kind of experiments does the Suron military need to do that are so secretive they need to be done in the grid?'

Tor looked at Lavilla suspiciously, and then covered up his response, forming a smooth face of no emotion. 'We don't have to explain ourselves to any other country. I also don't believe the grid should be off limits. But if that is to be imposed, I will move my operation.'

'I'd like to understand more of this operation, please, Tor,' Lavilla said.

'It wasn't anything to do with the military, was it?' Merouac voiced slowly. He had spoken aloud, meaning to only think it, but it was clear and apparent the room had listened. The words of Mingus and Jan started ringing in his ears. *If this generator is already tuned to L7, then maybe someone else has had the same idea we had. Could it possibly be Tor who had been down in the grid, trying to tune metal?*

'Its not relevant. It's none of anyone's business if it had anything to do with Suron military operations. As long as I agree to vacate the grid, then it shouldn't matter and we can all go home. Isn't that the case?' Tor asked.

'Far from it, I'm afraid,' Lavilla stated.

'Were you trying to tune metal, by any chance?' Merouac heard himself say. Lavilla had told them little the night before about what topics would be raised in the meeting, only that she wanted to test if he should be there and, after their conversation, had decided that he should be. Maybe Lavilla had succeeded in connecting the dots better than anyone else had.

The room turned to look at him.

Tor Anale started at Merouac and went white as a sheet. 'What did you say?'

'I just wondered if that's what your experiments were about. We've been down in the grid also. We found a generator tuned to L7. That's what you need to try frequency tunings.'

'You took my generator?' Tor jumped up. 'You're the one? You thief. Thief!' he shouted, pointing at Merouac.

'Sit down,' Lavilla ordered.

'Well, well,' Heyla grinned.

Tor sat down, red-faced. He continued to look at Merouac with incredulity. 'What do you know about tuning metal?'

'He's a metalsmith,' Heyla said.

Tor shook his head, deathly white. 'That doesn't mean anything.'

'In this instance it does,' Heyla argued. 'Merouac is the one metalsmith on the continent who can actually tune metal.'

Lavilla sighed. She looked at Heyla with a mix of patience and frustration. 'I was going to hold off on that particular part of the conversation, but since we're here, let's go ahead. Were you trying to experiment with frequency tunings down in the grid, Tor? Is that why the area was sectioned off?'

Tor was flushed. He looked to Merouac, and then to Gartounne.

'Don't look at me,' the old man said. 'You're on your own.'

Tor looked for all intents as if he didn't know what to do or say. He seemed well and truly stumped. He simply stared at Merouac, his mouth opening and shutting.

'Did you have any luck with it?' Merouac asked.

'Of course he didn't,' Gartounne shouted. 'What a spectacular waste of time this conversation is. Lavilla, you better have something bigger than this to have pulled me here. Get on with it.'

Lavilla continued to gaze at Tor intently. 'Yes, I think I agree with you, Gartounne. Let's move on.'

Lavilla moved out of the circle and motioned to her people who stood at the back of the room, as if having anticipated this moment. She gave them a nod, and the three of them quietly made their way out of the room.

Merouac noticed with interest that Lavilla's support team were not Ingruans; they would have been immediately recognisable with their shocks of orange hair. He was Ingruan, and his and Malaena's jet-black hair had always set them apart from their childhood friends.

He had black hair, he repeated to himself. He and his twin sister were from the Ingrue, where everyone was freckled and pale and genetically disposed to any array of orange coloured hair – from a light golden colour to deep rusty red. But always, always orange. And yet theirs was black. He put the thought aside, and with it, all the words that had run over his head and through his body when Garatrudie had told him he and Malaena were adopted.

Lavilla had opened the door to the meeting room. 'I've asked two more people to join us. Kii and Afourla, please come in.'

One of the monks standing near the door opened it, allowing two figures to come in. Two men entered. The older man was tall and reed thin, with silvery grey hair in a long plait down his back. The younger man wore a mask across a full half of his face, hiding one eye and one full side of his face. His hair was long also, but black.

Tor gasped and stood up.

Gartounne did a double take. 'That's not possible,' the old man stuttered, looking first to Lavilla, then Tor, then the two newcomers again. Then he looked at Tor with new suspicion. 'Tor,' he roared. 'What the damn is going on?'

Merouac even heard Heyla beside him draw in a sharp breath. 'Afourla? Kii?' she asked in wonder. Heyla stood up immediately and crossed the room to where the two Faurin stood at the door. She drew the younger Faurin into an embrace. Kii hugged her back with a gentle smile.

Tor's fists were clenched at his sides. 'What?' he whispered. 'How …'

'How did they get here?' Lavilla asked the question for him.

'How are they alive is the question we need to answer first, Lavilla,' Heyla said, looking upset and confused.

'It's not possible,' Gartounne stated. He blinked as if he thought he was seeing things.

'Your vision is quite fine,' said the silver-haired Faurin from where he stood at the doorway. 'It's really us.' Hearing the man talk for the first time was strange; he had a light, lilting voice that seemed to perfectly accompany his lean and angular frame.

Tor started to talk but Lavilla held up a hand. 'No, Tor, not yet. I want to hear from Gartounne first. Why isn't it possible this could be the leader of the Faurin, and his grandson?'

'They're dead, that's why,' Gartounne said, staring at the two suspiciously, as if his eyes were deceiving him.

'You had no idea at all that they were still alive?' Lavilla pressed.

Gartounne's look darkened. 'Neither of these two, supposedly, made it out alive from an avalanche in the ranges over a shade ago. What else is there to know?'

Suddenly, Gartounne and Heyla were both asking rapid-fire

questions. Merouac realised that theirs were the only faces registering surprise, shock and disbelief. Qualan and Kultan were expressionless, which Merouac thought was odd. Although, if Lavilla had already consulted with them about convening the meeting, they must have been made aware their family members were alive, and not at all dead.

Merouac thought back to what he himself knew about the situation in the mountains. The Faurin of the Remneur Ranges were led by their royal family, the head of whom acted in the role of what the other countries across San Aurelle called Governor.

The Faurin, although known to have an alliance with Suron, mostly kept to their traditional mountain ways. They traded, but not in great volumes across the continent. They traded livestock, tea and food goods, and mostly from the markets at the very southern tips of the ranges.

Merouac had really only been to Tenogru for the first time when he and Heyla had come to request green pala. Heyla had seemed to be on good terms with the Faurin, knew members of the royal family, and had explained the decorum required in regards to green pala. You had to journey to the ranges, climb the heights of Tenogru, and ask the permission of the royal family to take the stone out of the ranges.

Merouac had been surprised at the formalities, and annoyed when, after their journey, Kultan had refused them. Qualan had been helpful, encouraging Merouac to be patient and give Kultan enough time and space to reconsider.

It had been Qualan who had explained that Kultan was troubled and having a hard time learning how to be a leader with neither his father or grandfather present. It was a lot for a young man to have on his shoulders.

Merouac glanced at Kultan again, to see if he could find any glimmer of emotion that would indicate pleasure and relief his grandfather was alive, could take his place once again at the head of the family, and relieve Kultan of the need to step into the leadership role before the rightful age of twenty-five shades. What had been the situation, then, when it was revealed, Merouac wondered. Had there been tears and joy? But Kultan, for the time being, showed only a reserved face.

'Alright, let me just confirm and clarify to ensure everyone in the room has the same information,' said Lavilla.

Lavilla turned back to the two newcomers and invited them to come into the room. Her helpers had brought out new chairs, and the two Faurin walked through the room to sit down.

'Tor, sit down. You, too, Heyla,' Lavilla instructed.

'Afourla,' she said to the silver-haired man. I recognise you as Head of the royal family of the Faurin of the Remneur Ranges.' Afourla nodded.

Afourla, imposingly tall, seemed elongated even seated. His long body was draped in dark green flowing garments. He crossed his long legs and then crossed his hands on top of one knee and sat back, taking in the group. He scanned Merouac, and then startled. He focused his gaze on the metalsmith with a quizzical look, as if he wanted to say something, then reconsidered.

'And Kii, I recognise you. Grandson of Afourla, and twin brother to Kultan.' Kii also nodded to Lavilla and to all in the room.

'You are probably all aware that both Kii and Afourla went missing and were presumed dead, well over a shade ago. And yet these were the two men I found imprisoned in the hahma grid just a few days ago.'

Silence, and then a roar from Gartounne as he swivelled fully around to face Tor. 'What?' he screamed at Tor. 'What is she talking about?'

Everyone will now be quiet,' Lavilla said. 'I'm going to tell you the story of how I found these two men. And then you're all going to give me the information that will help me make sense of this impossible situation. Am I clear?'

The group nodded.

Lavilla turned to Tor. 'Tor, please explain to me and the group what we're looking at here. These two men have been kept prisoner down in the grid. They were taken, pulled away from their lives and their families. A lie was concocted as to their death. And they have been here, underground, guarded and kept, without light, without anything much other than basic food and water, it seems. Cruel punishment for any being, let alone the leader of your own country and his grandson.'

Tor flinched, and then looked stubbornly first at Gartounne and then Lavilla. 'I have nothing to say to this. Nothing to say at all.'

Lavilla stood up. 'Enough, Tor. Under the Separation Act there are still national laws that mean I can imprison anyone, anywhere across the continent, if a breach of the agreement occurs. I don't need to ask anyone. And keeping people against their will, in what amounts to an underground dungeon, fits the bill nicely. Start talking or I'll take things into my own hands, Tor.'

Tor looked to Gartounne. 'Talk,' the Governor said with a snarl. He looked ready to jump out of his seat at any moment, although Tor knew that physically he couldn't.

Tor turned to face Gartounne directly. 'You told me to stop the issues in the mountains.'

Gartounne did a double take. 'You're accusing me of what, exactly?'

'You told me to sort Afourla out, quite specifically. You said you'd had enough and you'd leave it in my hands.'

'No!' Gartounne screeched. 'I told you to get your people to stop spreading rumours that the shield was down. I said nothing of imprisoning anyone.' The old man was sweating profusely and one of his helpers leaned in with a cloth, presumably for Gartounne to wipe his face. He pushed it away roughly. The helper, surprised, stepped quickly back.

'You told me to sort it out,' Tor said adamantly.

'Sort what out?' Lavilla intercepted.

Gartounne coughed a deep, hacking cough, which took seemingly endless moments to ease. He looked intensely aggravated. He turned back and called for the cloth that he had only moments ago pushed away, and coughed once again into it, before wiping down his face.

He motioned at Afourla. Merouac noted that they were probably of a similar age, although Afourla certainly seemed to have aged better. 'Afourla insisted on turning up regularly to my offices to tell me the shield was fading. It's been his regular act since we were both young men. Over time I've grown tired of hearing it, because of course it is the ultimate foolishness. Wanting me to do something about it. Me, a governor. It doesn't matter what our grandparents thought.'

'What did they think?' Lavilla said, looking quickly back between the two old men. Both Gartuonne and Afourla ignored the question, focusing only on each other.

'You refused to listen,' Afourla spoke. 'All those years.'

'Any sensible person knows that all talk of the shield dissipating is pure fiction,' Gartounne continued. 'Tor might have been working for me, but he is Faurin and I told him to go and sort his people out.'

'So you're saying Afourla had been trying to tell you something was going on with the shield? And you ignored him? Then told your lackey to sort him out?' Heyla asked with incredulity. 'Even I wouldn't have guessed that.'

'I've made many attempts,' Afourla answered when Gartounne remained silent.

'Gartounne – is this true?' Lavilla probed.

'Correct,' snarled Gartounne with contempt. 'The shield is the shield. Any discussion of it thinning is utter nonsense. I won't be a part of it.'

Heyla snorted. The room turned to her. 'Apologies,' she said, standing up. 'I laugh because my father has made it his business to turn away from everything optimistic, sensible, hopeful. Everything that represents change and evolution, he has fought. We hear word the shield may be down, and it gets ignored? Old man, you're turning down the chance to explore life beyond the very walls of the world?' Heyla vented her words in frustration, striding down the length of the room and back.

She returned to face her father from across the room. 'Part of your basic job as Governor, surely, is the business of listening to what other leaders across the continent have to say. And what, you took it on yourself to make a decision that you're not even qualified to make?'

'I may not be qualified, but we have a shield survey team. Or, at least, we did. Tor got rid of them, I recently discovered. In any event, my opinion stands. The shield is the shield. It isn't going anywhere.'

'The survey team were never looking for the right thing in the first place', said Afourla. 'It doesn't make any difference that Tor disposed of them. There was a misunderstanding.'

'What kind of misunderstanding?' asked Lavilla.

Everyone in the room looked back to Afourla expectantly.

'The shield survey team was only ever monitoring the seventh layers of the hahma spectrum,' explained Afourla impatiently. 'That's because when the visitors told us all that time ago that the shield was thinning, our grandfathers agreed to maintain a survey of the seventh layer to see what changes were occurring.'

'Grandfathers?' Lavilla tested.

'Yes. This was an agreement between Suron and the Remneur Ranges, back in a better time when we were still able to cooperate productively.'

'What?' Heyla cried out, at almost the exact same time. 'Old man, this goes back that far, and you've still kept your mouth shut?'

Gartounne gave his daughter a belligerent glare. 'That's my right and my privilege.'

'Maarte help us', said Heyla in exasperated frustration.

Merouac noted that Lavilla looked just as unimpressed as Heyla, if not more so.

Afourla continued. 'That was a long time ago. But they came again. And when they did, the visitors spoke with me. I was the one that received them, and I'm the one who learned that there is an eighth layer of current that was never understood and as a result, had never detected.'

'An eighth layer of hahma current?' Merouac found himself asking. His mind started racing with the possibilities at the very idea.

'When did the visitors return, Afourla? asked Heyla, eyebrows knotted.

'When I was twenty-five shades old. They told me that they wanted to clarify our understanding of the shield.'

'It took them all that time to figure out we hadn't quite understood?' Lavilla asked.

'Maybe they thought we'd figure it out. But we didn't.' Afourla said with a wave of his hand.

Lavilla sat back and crossed her lean arms in front of her chest.

'So, the Remneur Ranges and Suron have been holding information about the shield thinning for over a centennal. But between the disagreements about the validity of the information and what to do about it, and the confusion about the information that the visitors shared with you, we've essentially gotten nowhere. Is that right?' Lavilla asked.

Afourla stopped short. 'No', he said abruptly. 'That's not right at all. But let me finish.'

'Can you explain the eighth layer of the hahma spectrum to us, Afourla?' Merouac heard himself interjecting.

Heyla turned to him and nodded in support of his question. He noticed Tor and Afourla both giving him further odd looks, but Afourla shrugged and indicated that he would explain.

'Yes. Well, as I said, when the visitors first told us the shield was dissipating, we thought they meant the seventh layer of hahma current. But there was no change in the L7 current at all. No ripples, no variations. It continued to do what it has always done, continuing to reinforce the lower hahma layers.

When the visitors returned, they explained that the eighth layer of the spectrum is only partially made up of hahma, which is why no-one had detected it previously. It also contains imote. And over time, the amount of hahma in this outer layer has been reducing, and the amount of imote has been increasing. This is the change in energy structure that the visitors have always been referring to.'

'And that translates to the shield thinning,' Merouac said quietly.

Lavilla took the reins of the conversation again. 'And Afourla, you provided this new information to Gartuonne? That's what he means by inferring you've been pestering him all these years?'

'Exactly', said Afourla with a cold stare at Gartounne.

Lavilla turned to Gartounne. 'So, Afourla came to you with crucial information about the shield. And you chose to believe it was all a lie?'

'I know it is.'

'How so?'

'As I said. Shields don't change. It's just common sense. The Faurin were just causing mischief and looking to scare people. I'm sure that even in the time of our grandfathers, the Faurin just managed to tell a good story. None of it was ever true, I'm sure of it.' Gartounne was grim as he stared back at Afourla.

'So you told Tor to take care of it?' asked Lavilla. 'Just to stop Afourla from trying to tell you what you didn't want to hear?'

The room swung round to Tor. Tor was as white as his uniform. 'You implied,' Tor insisted. 'You told me to do what I needed to do. And you told me there would be a reward. And there was.'

'And what was the reward, Tor?' asked Lavilla.

Tor was silent.

The room waited.

'There was no reward!' shouted Gartounne. 'Nothing. It's a lie.'

'Head of the Buntans,' Tor said quietly, still staring at Gartounne.

'Head of what?' Lavilla asked, looking confused.

'When I first came to Suron, I was a trainer in the army,' said Tor. 'When I started working for Gartounne, promotions were offered. First, head of one of the Buntans, or the training houses. There are four in Suron city, in different quarters. Then, when they were all merged into one, I was offered the role. My understanding at the time was it was conditional on sorting Afourla out.'

'And so you decided to imprison your royal family, to shut them up and pretend they had been killed? And you felt you had Gartounne's support?' Lavilla pressed.

'Yes. He didn't want to know the details. I knew that. But he wanted someone who listened to him, who understood what he needed. A son who heeded his direction, since the other one didn't.'

Lavilla stepped closer to Tor. 'So, what you're saying is that the shield really is down.'

'Of course it's down,' Tor shrieked.

'It's been fading for a hundred and fifty shades,' Afourla said more calmly. 'In another fifty shades, it will have dissipated completely.'

17.
High Country

Tor stabbed a finger at Afourla. 'He's no leader,' he said in a shrill voice. 'He's been out to get me since I was six shades old. He's kept me from things.'

Merouac thought Tor might actually choke on his rage, his fury. A vein pulsed visibly on his forehead. Beads of sweat had gathered at his temples.

'What are you talking about, Tor?' Lavilla questioned.

'I asked and asked. I asked to become Intangien. I asked to join the elite training groups. The answer was always no.'

'Faurin children try out to join the Intangien ranks when they are six shades old,' Kultan explained for Lavilla. It was the first time Kultan had spoken, and the group looked at him. The young man had stood up and walked towards the windows. His gaze was difficult to interpret, half sullen, half thoughtful. But no surprise had registered, Merouac realised.

No shock at seeing his twin brother and his grandfather. There had been no reunion to speak of; the family members had not raced across the room to embrace each other. It was getting stranger by the moment, he thought. He glanced at Heyla, and she, too, looked like she was trying to put pieces together that didn't yet fit.

'Most children don't make it,' Afourla retorted. 'You've been carrying that grudge all this time? That's what took you to stand by the side of a Governor not even of your own people?'

'Gartounne gave me a place. I have done the things asked of me, as a person loyal to his leader. And he wanted you silenced,' Tor replied.

'And taking them down into the grid and keeping them locked up was the answer?' Lavilla asked.

'I thought it would make them talk to me.'

'About what?'

'About the fact that the shield is thinning. Afourla could have assisted me with my frequency tuning experiments. This knowledge is based on Intangien skills of moving through space and dimensions. But he and Kii stayed silent. Insubordinate. I threatened ongoing imprisonment and reduced light. Still, they refused to assist.'

'Afourla, how did you know the shield was down?' Lavilla challenged.

'We've known for a long time.'

'Yes, but how, exactly, did you come across that knowledge, Afourla?' Lavilla continued.

Gartounne looked around the group and sighed. He sat down, fingers still working the beads around his neck.

'Alright, I'll start from the beginning. That is to say, the time when the Faurin first started receiving visitors from beyond the shield.'

Lavilla leaned forward in her seat. 'Who were these visitors? And when did they come?'

'They first appeared to us one hundred and fifty shades ago', Gartounne replied. 'They explained that they were able to make themselves known to us at that time because the shield had started to thin. The shield wasn't down, so to speak, and it isn't down now. But it has been thinning over time, since they first appeared. And it will continue to thin until we get to the point where it has completely dissipated.'

Merouac saw Lavilla's posture stiffen. Likely, she was trying to remain patient and calm, even in the face of the news that the Faurin had been holding on to this information for longer than anyone had imagined.

'Where did they come from, these visitors?' Lavilla asked.

'We don't know as much as we would like to.' replied Afourla. 'They wanted it that way. And of course, for the first visits, all that time ago, we are relying on records and the stories that have been passed down through my family line since then.'

'Well, what do you know?' Lavilla asked.

'We know that the visitors first appeared just near here, on Tenogru. There were only three of them, and they came three times. They explained that they had been able to make the transition into Ahm because our planetary shield was thinning.'

'What did they look like? And how did they act?' Heyla asked, also now leaning forward in her chair, her gaze skeptical and intrigued at the same time. 'And what did they want, most importantly?'

'We understood that they were tall. That they looked normal enough.' Afourla replied. 'They came at night, wore long cloaks and did not stay for very long.'

The room was intensely quiet. Merouac barely dared to breathe.

Afourla continued. 'And to answer your other question, they didn't want anything. They came to offer insights. They showed us the art of transitioning in and out of frequencies for moments at a time. This is how the Intangien first attained the knowledge of their craft.'

'The Intangien skills came from another realm?' Heyla murmured, sitting up straighter. She glanced over at Lavilla. 'That makes sense, actually.'

'Wherever they came from, your country certainly benefitted from those exact skills', Afourla said, directing a glare first at Gartounne, then at Heyla. 'San Aurelle's other states would have succeeded in tearing Suron to the ground during the Separation Wars if the Intangien had not come to your defence.'

Merouac glanced around the room as Afourla paused and surveyed them all, as if wondering how much of a history lesson those in the room required. He felt sure that no-one there needed reminding that the dismantling of San Aurelle's federation model had happened because Suron, as head state, had started to demand more tax from the other states than any of them had thought was reasonable.

Heyla took a breath. 'This is true', she said, directing a nod to her father Gartounne, who glared sourly back at her.

'Suron was saved because the Intangien helped to protect the perimeter of the city,' Heyla continued. 'And their skills in combat were a big part of that, including the ability to transition in and out of physical space, which no-one has ever really understood and most likely tried to forget about.'

Lavilla turned around to Heyla. 'Explain it to me, then. I represent one of those states that did, at the time, try to overthrow Suron city. I'm not sure that Ingruans were ever really clear on the skill sets you're talking about that were used to defend Suron city.'

Heyla looked to Kultan, 'May I?' she asked.

Kultan nodded.

'The Intangien skills are based on traditional hand-to-hand combat but there is one difference – the Intangien have the ability to move in and out of space,' explained Heyla.

'So, in a combat scenario, their enemy may lose sight of them for a short period of time. The Intangien used this skill to thoroughly confuse those they were fighting at the perimeter of Suron city, and as such, were able to win the battle, if not the war.'

Lavilla's eyebrows were raised high, but she listened and then remained quiet for several moments. Then, she continued. 'Alright. So now, what I believe you're saying, Afourla, is that those skills of being able to disappear, and then reappear moments later, were taught to your people, specifically the Intangien, by these visitors?'

'That's right,' said Afourla. 'All Intangien training has been based on the knowledge that was given to use a hundred and fifty shades ago.'

'And you told Gartounne of this, as a reason for believing that the shield was thinning?'

'We did.'

'And what about Tor, when he asked you about the shield. Did you share this information with him?'

'I did not.'

'Even when you were imprisoned, he kept asking you and you refused to provide any information?'

'He was keeping us captive. Why would we share anything with someone who had decided to lock us up? No. We said no and we stuck to that for an entire shade. We told Tor nothing, and it made him angrier and angrier.'

'It wasn't supposed to be for long,' Tor muttered.

Lavilla turned to Tor. 'What do you mean by that?'

Tor looked deeply aggravated. 'It was temporary. I didn't plan on keeping them for long. But they weren't cooperating. Then the avalanche occurred.'

'So Afourla and Kii were nowhere to be found when the avalanche happened,' Heyla commented.

'People drew their own conclusions,' Lavilla finished.

Tor nodded.

Lavilla sighed. 'I don't think it's an excuse, Tor. You could have corrected the situation earlier.' The Governor paused, as if she was trying to find the most productive way to progress the conversation. She turned to Kultan. 'You knew your grandfather and brother were safe? How many others?'

'Yes, I knew. All the royal family knows.'

Lavilla turned back to Afourla. 'Tor is Faurin. One of your own people. If he was asking about the shield, why would you have been so obstructive? What made you feel this was your information to keep secret, Afourla? My sentiment is that this should have been shared as broadly as possible.'

'Tor needs to learn his place,' Afourla replied.

'Why would that matter, considering how important this is?' Lavilla asked.

'I think you're overlooking what he did,' Afourla shouted. 'He imprisoned me, the head of the royal family of the Remneur Ranges. Kii and I were left down there for an entire shade, with no light, no decent food, no way to exercise and no contact with our people. And our people were left without a leader. I don't owe him anything.'

'You go too far, grandfather,' Kultan said from where he still stood at the windows. His back to the group, he looked out to the mountain ranges.

Confused silence fell over the group.

'This debacle is just turning into a family drama,' said Gartounne, folding his blanket on his lap. 'You don't need me here for it. I'd like to leave.'

'Absolutely not,' said Lavilla calmly.

Kultan walked over to Afourla and sat down next to him.

'Grandfather, Lavilla has brought everyone here so that she can understand the situation. She is a leader and so are you. You are supposed to be *our* leader. You owe it to everyone here to understand.'

'I owe it to everyone here? I don't even know everyone here,' Afourla snapped.

'Well, I do,' Kultan replied calmly. He turned and looked at the people in the room, first motioning to Heyla. 'Heyla is Gartounne's daughter. She's come to the mountains often.'

'And in any event, Afourla, we've met,' Heyla added. 'You know me from the entire shade I spent in the mountains.'

Lavilla turned to Heyla. 'You lived in the Remneur?'

'Yes. The Faurin and the Suroni have a partnership, but it's a patriarchy,' Heyla said dryly, sending Gartounne a disapproving glare. Gartounne pulled out a damp-looking kerchief and blew his nose loudly in response.

'The sons of each royal family are paired together,' Heyla continued. 'This is so when they come of age they can continue the partnership we've had since the Separation Wars. And that meant that my brother got to spend every summerial in the mountains. I never got that opportunity.'

'Patriarchal leadership,' Lavilla mused. 'Gartounne, we must have you to the Ingrue sometime. You'll see how well we do with a country almost completely run by women.' Lavilla gave Heyla the glimmer of a wry smile.

Gartounne gave Lavilla a withering stare and said nothing.

Kultan nodded and then inclined his head in Merouac's direction. 'Merouac is a metalsmith. I think Lavilla has brought him here because he's the first metalsmith we know of to have been able to create a frequency bridge. He asked the Faurin for green pala to assist his experiments and I agreed. He can tell you about it later.'

'You've succeeded tuning metal?' Tor said in a hoarse whisper, looking at Merouac in disbelief.

Merouac looked at the short man who seemed to be alternating violently between flushing red and turning a desperately pale white. Sweat was streaming down from his brow in rivulets now.

Afourla was also staring at Merouac, and there it was again, a seemingly startled look that made Merouac feel as if Afourla was seeing something that surprised him. He looked as if he was wanting to say something directly to Merouac, then decided not to.

'But you know what I'm talking about.' Kultan continued talking to his grandfather. 'You were never really imprisoned, and you need to explain that to everyone, right here and now. And if you don't, I will.'

'I think you should hold your tongue,' Afourla said to Kultan with a note of danger in his eyes.

'No,' said Kultan slowly. 'I will not.'

'I think you should think long and hard about what you say next,' Afourla warned.

'I already have,' Kultan said. 'I've been quiet this whole time. Since the avalanche. I've listened. Followed instructions. Learned how to be a leader.'

'You're not here to be a leader in this meeting,' Afourla replied.

Kultan continued. 'I disagree.'

Merouac felt proud of what he was seeing playing out in the room. Kultan, who had been teetering between boyhood and manhood, was becoming a leader.

'Go on, Kultan,' Kii said softly, from the other side of Afourla. Afourla whipped around to glare at his other grandson. 'Not you, too.'

'If Kultan thinks it's the right thing to do, then I'm alright with it,' Kii said with gentle equanimity. 'We need to take the right approach for everyone. And this isn't it. You need to be truthful, Grandfather.'

Afourla narrowed his eyes, glaring at his grandson. Merouac sensed him calculating the situation. Across the room, Tor was looking horrified.

After what seemed a very long moment indeed, Afourla shrugged his shoulders and let out a breath. He was silent for some moments. A dark look had collected on his face; he hadn't anticipated being pushed into this corner by his own grandson, that was clear. Afourla glared at Tor, and finally, spoke.

'I let you think you had us imprisoned,' he admitted. 'But it's possible I exaggerated our situation.'

'*What?*' Tor and Lavilla both asked in chorus.

'Well, this is taking a new and interesting turn,' Gartounne said dryly. 'Perhaps I'll stay after all.'

Lavilla rubbed a hand across her brow. 'What are you saying, Afourla? You told the men who found you, and then you told me, that you and Kii had been kept underground for a full shade. Please explain what you mean.'

'We did say that,' Afourla confirmed. 'But from a certain perspective, you could also say that we have been able to come and go at our own will.'

'Afourla,' Lavilla said raising her voice. 'Stop obfuscating.'

Tor was once again going white. 'Have my men been letting you out of that cell? Is that what's happened? Who betrayed me? And what did you offer, to make my own men turn on me?'

'Think about it, Tor,' Afourla said shortly.

Tor seemed to once again choke on his words; he didn't seem able to process what Afourla was implying.

Afourla pursed his lips and then tossed out, 'We departed through shifting vibrations and moving across frequencies.'

Tor looked shocked. 'No, you didn't,' he said. 'You can't have.'

'Why couldn't we, Tor?'

Silence.

Afourla continued, seemingly relishing the fact he now had everyone's full attention. The room was completely silent.

'We moved from the frequency of the cell, to the frequency we have called High Country. We have established it as our new home. Many of the royal family have now migrated there.'

'Impossible,' Tor said, although it was clear he didn't believe that.

Afourla rolled his eyes and stood up, brushing down the necklaces that rested on his chest and smoothed out the fabric of his long tunic as he walked to the other side of the room. 'These are the skills you have so desperately been trying to find out more about, Tor. I find it ironic that you didn't even have a sense of us coming and going and that made me more aware of the danger of having to explain it to anyone who didn't have a natural sense of it.'

Lavilla held up her hands to call for a pause. 'Alright, you've lost the rest of us, Afourla. Please explain what you mean.'

'What I'm telling Tor is we didn't talk to any of his men and we made no offers to have a way of coming and going from our detainment. We didn't need to. No doors needed to be opened at all. We used Intangien methods, the exact same methods he locked us up to find out more about.'

'Liar!' Tor shrieked. 'You're lying. Every time I came to question you, you were there. Every time my men checked on you, you were there. It's not possible you were …'

'Tor, you of all people should know the skills of the Intangien. You've been asking to train with us since you were a child. You know that these skills exist, and that we have mastered them. Why did you not think we could, and would, use them? Tor was silent. Merouac thought that he looked quite honestly and profoundly shocked.

Afourla continued. 'We didn't go near the entrance. We touched no doors and fiddled with no locks. We spoke to no guards and so no one in your command betrayed you, Tor. You just weren't smart.'

Afourla looked around the group. 'What Kultan seems desperate for you all to understand is that we've learned to use Intangien skills in a new way. We didn't just jump in and out of a frequency, to disappear and challenge our opponents, as Intangien do in combat. We created a frequency bridge and took ourselves out of that ridiculous cell every so often.'

Then Gartounne hacked a loud gurgling phlegmy cough and wiped his damp kerchief across his face. 'What absolute garbage,' he said. There wasn't anyone in the room who didn't hear the new tone of uncertainty that had entered the old man's voice.

'We've been establishing another frequency for the purpose of habitation. It's enabled Kii and I to travel back and forth, despite being imprisoned,' said Afourla.

'So let me get this straight,' said an enraged Tor. 'All this time, you've been doing exactly what I thought we *should* be doing, doing exactly what I asked for your help to do.' Tor's rage was palpable.

'You didn't ask,' Afourla retorted. 'You demanded that I tell you. And, as I said, it's my decision as to who is inducted into this knowledge.'

'Why is it your decision?' Lavilla asked. 'What gives you the right to withhold it in such a way, especially if that someone is, like Tor, one of your own?'

'In the spirit of partnership, I attempted several times to share what we were learning about the shield with the Governor of Suron, the old man sitting right here in front of us.'

Gartounne snorted. 'All lies,' he argued.

'Alright,' said Lavilla. 'Clearly, engaging Gartounne didn't work, but what else did you try? Did you just decide to keep this information to simply a few members of your own royal family? Do the rest of your people know?'

Gartounne was silent.

'Let me get this straight,' Heyla interjected in amazement. 'You knew the shield was thinning. You and your family have migrated to an entirely different frequency. And you haven't even told the rest of the Faurin?'

'Not much has been explained,' Kultan said, looking at his grandfather as if challenging him to say otherwise.

'So nothing has really been shared,' Lavilla surmised. 'And your plight, as you explained it to me, is an untruth. Tell me, Afourla, what and where, exactly, is High Country?'

18.
Journey to High Country

It was dawn and the rocky beach at the base of Tenogru was cool. The party had descended the eastern side of the mountain at first light.

Afourla had refused to talk any further about High Country; he had insisted the only way to move forward was for them all to see it for themselves. That morning they had commenced the journey, following Afourla's directions in order to proceed to the promised destination, the frequency the Faurin royal family had discovered and partially migrated to. The place Afourla and Kii and been able to come and go from during their time imprisoned by Tor Anale and his military guard down in the power grid.

The wind was sharp and biting, buffetting up against the high mountain cliff and giving water birds like the orange-winged crite and the blue magans powerful air currents to glide on. The mood of the party was tense; Lavilla had demanded details of their destination, the route they would take and the process for getting there, how long they would stay and what they would see. But Afourla had answered very few of those questions, merely indicating that the visit may take a day or two, or perhaps more.

Merouac had noticed Lavilla's patience being tested, but the two leaders had seemingly reached an impasse. Somewhat reluctantly, Lavilla had agreed to proceed on very little information indeed.

Over the course of their early morning rise and journey down the mountain in the half-light, Merouac and Heyla had been talking quickly and quietly, to try and put the pieces of the puzzle together as they were becoming clearer.

'I never thought to ask why Tenogru had been so quiet when we visited,' Heyla had murmured, her long limbs more easily navigating the steep path than Merouac's, who felt every step in his hips. Heyla clambered down the rocky path a stretch and then would turn and look back up for him, tossing her long hair, waiting impatiently for him to catch up, sometimes taking a step back towards him to share her fast-moving thoughts more quietly. 'It sounds like most of the royal Faurin family are already over there. I thought they must have all just been out and about, or on the training fields. Now it makes more sense.'

'So Kultan's parents? What was the story they told about them, to make everyone believe they had also disappeared?'

'That story, unlike Tor's accidental myth-making, has been told for longer. Possibly for as long as ten shades. But very similar, that they'd been on a trip right up to the top of Tenogru, way past the Original Monastery, had been caught in bad weather and had never returned,' Heyla said, reaching out an arm for Merouac to lean on and help him take some of the weight off his leg.

'So it looks like your old man isn't as evil as you thought,' Merouac said, breathing harder than he would have liked as they navigated the path.

'He's certainly looking foolish right now,' Heyla agreed, watching the others in the party behind them. They had managed, with Heyla's fast pace, to keep ahead of the group, giving them more freedom to talk. 'I trust Lavilla gave him a good talking to after we left the room and he'll do the right thing, although my father and doing the right thing have never gone hand in hand before now.'

'You think he'll hand over the governship to your brother?'

'Hopefully he won't have a choice,' Heyla replied. 'And what do you think about Tor Anale?'

Merouac shook his head, offering Heyla something that sat somewhere between a grimace and a smile. 'Who would have thought the head of the Suroni military had an interest in tuning metal. Mingus and Jan were onto it though, I can tell you.'

'Mingus and Jan?' Heyla stopped again, waiting for Merouac to catch up.

'A couple of my men. I've bought them into a bit of a closer circle. Explained a few more things to them. I've been thinking I need a few more in the workshop who understand what's going on.'

Heyla smiled and patted Merouac on the shoulder as he caught up. 'Well, look at you. That's quite a big step, I imagine. Well done and I agree. We need people who know more, as long as you trust them.'

Merouac twisted to follow Heyla's gaze to those coming behind them and saw Tor Anale trailing far behind the mid-section of the group, a dark and introspective look on his face. 'He looks lost,' he commented.

'Well, he pretty much is,' Heyla reflected. 'Gartounne's not with him. Lavilla's on to him. Afourla's got something against him. I'm not sure he's really got a friend in the group at all. Although Kultan's done the right thing by him. I'm not sure how I feel,' Heyla said.

'Well, Tor's experiments are what's landed me in hot water with the railroad,' Merouac said. 'But at least we know the who and the how and the why. I can get things back on track and clear my name hopefully at some point.'

'What, by telling your bosses all this?'

'No, not quite. But at least I know what made the trains derail, and it's got nothing to do with the metalwork, as it was claimed to. I'll be able to sort it out.'

'You still care about a career with the railroad, even with all this happening?'

'I've got a kid to take care of,' retorted Merouac. 'But actually, it's not that simple. I think they're connected.'

'The metal working part of it?'

Merouac nodded. 'And I've been connecting with Malaena. It doesn't happen any one way in particular, but it's happening more and more.'

Heyla turned around and looked at him searchingly. 'Ah. Now this is getting interesting. Tell me about how you're connecting with your sister across the realms.'

'She's told me, in various ways, pretty much what Afourla is backing up,' Merouac explained. 'That Ahm is reaching its new level of maturity. It's shedding its own frequency protective layer. It probably makes sense, if that's the case, that Afourla's found a way to move in and out of realms for more than a few moments at a time.'

Heyla looked ready to ask more questions when Afourla and Kii caught up with them. 'This way,' Afourla stated, directing them down an offshoot of the path. The incline grew steeper and it took all Merouac's concentration to get down the final stretch to the beach.

Twelve Intangien monks, led by Kultan, were working quietly and without fuss at the water's edge. They were embedding long ceremonial poles of varying heights in the sand. The poles were covered in intricate designs and Merouac saw that each one had several areas where green pala stone had been embedded in the wood.

The monks ranged from young boys still in their teens, to young women at the height of their strength, to older monks who were sinewy and supple in their movements. They wore flowing pants of a coarse, woven fabric that ended halfway down their calves, or long skirts that came down to just above their ankles. The top halves of their bodies were clad with deep red, brown and black sleeveless vests that left their strong arms free.

Around their necks they wore masses of beads, entangled fibres and glittering stones. On their heads, the Intangien wore more jewellery; in each case the design varied. From small ornamental heads to crown-like structures, they were crafted with metal and made wearable by wrappings, stitching, and other soft adornments.

Afourla joined them and started waving the rest of the group over to join him. They waited there as the others began to appear, first Lavilla, then Tor and six Faurin guides who would, they had been told, assist with the next step, a crossing over water.

When the group was standing in front of him, he pointed to the Intangien. 'They have begun the frequency tuning. This will allow us to take a journey across the water. I will take you to the place we now think of as an extension of the Remneur Ranges. The only difference is that it is not in the realm of Ahm.'

'How did you know to do this?' Heyla asked.

'This has taken us many shades,' Afourla replied. 'As you may or may not know, the problem with frequency bridges is that to make them work you need some kind of intelligence on the other side who want to participate in the bridge building. Otherwise, no bridge. We had to have help. We asked the visitors and they worked with us to find a frequency we could turn into a land of our own. They showed us the frequency we have called the High Country, and activated the frequency bridge so we could make the crossing. Some of us then migrated over there to maintain, and strengthen, the frequency bridge.'

'And so this is where our journey across water will take us?' Heyla asked.

'Yes,' said Afourla impatiently. 'Shall we begin?'

The group watched Afourla instruct the Intangien group who were already preparing the passage, moving closer to the water's edge.

Afourla had explained only moments earlier that this was part of the preparation. In this instance Merouac felt a step ahead of the others in the group, as perhaps Heyla did; they had been here before with Kultan. He remembered the first time he had seen an Intangien group assemble for this kind of purpose.

As the Intangien chanted, Merouac observed Afourla moving quickly around the six canoes with wide, flat bottoms that would take them over. He was fussing over a large pile of leaves, which the assisting monks were bundling into nets in the rear of the boats.

'What are the leaves for?' Merouac asked but got no answer.

With the Intangien having progressed their chanting and movements, the tuning process had begun. The light was becoming cloudy, and a mist had started to roll in. Afourla motioned to Kii, who nodded and indicated that the group should start to get onto the boats, four per boat, two of the group and two Faurin per canoe.

Lavilla was assisted onto the first boat, with Kultan leaving his Intangien group to continue their work without him and taking position behind her. Heyla was helped into the next boat, and chose her seat closer to the back end. Merouac stepped on board after her, moving to the front of the canoe and taking care not to disturb its balance as he sat.

Tor and Kii were helped into the third canoe and Afourla hopped into the final one. The Intangien stepped up their chanting.

The group fell completely quiet as they started moving out, the occasional spray of foam and salt water finding its way onto their respective faces and bodies. It didn't take long for Merouac to feel damp.

Then, a shift in the air, a change in register of sorts. The Faurin continued to paddle expertly from the rear of the canoes, breaching the small waves of the shoreline and steering their small flotilla out towards open waters.

Almost immediately, the light shifted and became hazy. Merouac felt as if they had started moving through a thick soup of flittering, glittering flares of illumination. They shimmered in the aether and then went dark, appearing here and there around them.

It wasn't just the light that was changing. The air itself seemed thicker, denser, weightier, as they were embedded in a mass more like water than air.

Heyla murmured from behind him, 'It's an island ahead, can you see it?'

Beyond the mist, Merouac could see the faint outline of an island ahead of them, although he felt certain it had not been visible from the shore. From afar, the island glowed with five shimmering tiers of colour.

The atmosphere was darkening and a pulsing sensation rippling through the air when Merouac felt a flash of dizziness. It started behind his eyes and roiled through his whole body. If he had been standing, he felt sure he would have toppled over. He blinked, shook his head and gripped the edge of the canoe.

His vision cleared and he dipped his hand into the cool water, feeling momentarily better before another wave of nausea buckled through him.

He leaned over the side of the canoe. His face burned with heat. He heard a roaring in his ears, which then travelled through his chest to his stomach and down his legs.

He felt a hand on his shoulder. 'Merouac?' It was Heyla.

He couldn't answer. His body felt like it was vibrating from the touch of some strange force, almost as if he'd been shot through with hahma current himself. He felt the air around him pulsing, the sense of sound breaking and bursting across the water.

'I'm not feeling so good,' he said. 'Something's happening.'

'Turn around,' ordered Heyla.

'What?' Merouac could hardly see, the dizziness was so overwhelming.

He felt Heyla place firm hands on his shoulders, as she directed him to swivel around in the canoe to face her and the rear of the boat.

'You're not looking so good, either,' he heard her say. He felt her cool hand on his forehead. 'What are you experiencing?'

Merouac was about to explain his symptoms – dizziness, nausea, a hot and cold flashing – but he couldn't get the words out. He leaned back over the side of the boat and retched.

'Afourla,' he heard Heyla shout. 'We've got a problem.' Further away, sounding very distant, Merouac heard Lavilla echo her. 'We've got a problem over here, too. Tor's having some kind of reaction. Afourla, do you know what this is about?'

Merouac heard Afourla calling out to the Faurin rowers in each boat, telling them to pick up speed. Spray off the oars sent salty showers over the boat and were a cool welcome for him as their rower followed instructions and picked up speed.

He felt the world fade around him. The thud of the canoe against sand nudged him out of his fugue. He felt Heyla's hands still firmly on his shoulders, keeping him from slumping and falling out of the the boat entirely. 'Get them out, and lay them down on the beach,' he heard Afourla order.

'What's happening?' he asked Heyla.

'I'm not sure,' she said briefly, and then before she could say another word two of the Faurin who had been on Afourla's boat were at the side of the canoe, thigh deep in water, pulling the canoe further up the beach and working to lift him out.

Merouac felt himself falling into darkness again, and the shuddering and shaking he'd experienced returned with a vengeance.

The Faurin helped Merouac out of the boat and laid him on the sand. 'Get the leaves,' Afourla was shouting somewhere overhead.

And then he blacked out entirely.

19.

Recovery on High Country

Merouac was dreaming. His head felt thick, and the dreams were at once heavy and far away, he was in and out of them without understanding the sequence between them. He tossed and turned, sweated and then fell into a new series of dreams.

He came close to waking, but couldn't quite open his eyes. He felt someone lift his head, hands gentle around the back of his neck. He felt a sweet, syrupy liquid touch his clips. He swallowed whatever it was that was being put to his lips and then slept again.

He came close to waking again, hours later, body pulsing, but his eyes still would not open and his body was vibrating. Almost like a machine, he felt his insides whirring and grinding and alive in a strange way they never had before. Was his body making a noise? And then there were the aches, some of them so strong he had to clench his teeth.

As sensation and awareness returned to his body, he realised the air was thick and the light dim. It was thick, still misty, and full of small illuminations that looked like hahma lights. They shimmered in the aether and then went dark, appearing here and there around them.

He saw Heyla, her long body stretched over a short box or a stool, leaning against the brush-leaved walls of the room. He looked around. The room was basic, a shelter with a roof made of a bamboo-like material. The floor was sandy.

Heyla opened her eyes as she heard him stirring.

'Alright?' Heyla asked, taking the cup from the matted table near his bed and offering it to him. He drank. His vision cleared.

'Where is this place?' he asked, indicating to the room itself.

'The infirmary. They've put us all in some kind of lodgings near here but away from the rest of the community, by the looks of it.'

'Did you feel anything coming over?'

'No, I didn't. It was surreal, but mostly because the light is so different. It makes you use your senses differently. And the air is thick, have you noticed? Like jelly, almost. It's dense, and you have to practise how you move through it. You'll notice it more when you start to move about. You know, that niece of yours is hardier than you think. She'll survive being away from you for a few more days.'

'What do you mean?'

'You've been calling out for Evra. Quite a bit. I think you need to let go of what happened down in the caves and move on. And besides that, she's a strong kid.'

'I know she is,' Merouac sighed.

Merouac sat back and looked around. There was a woman who looked like one of the Faurin from the Remneur Ranges working on a cloak in the corner. He wondered if she was there to keep an eye on him. There was another person, perhaps a nurse, moving in the background. Both wore some of the jewellery that many of the

Faurin wore every day, starting at the throat and going down to the waist – elements of metal, string, wire, green pala and another amythal – a glittering purple crystal.

'She's resilient. Malaena wouldn't want you to be this worried about the job she's given you, surely. But in any event, since you keep getting in the wars, I've asked for her to be brought over.'

Merouac sighed. 'Good. Thank you. Where are we, anyway – can you tell?'

'Well, it's an island, and not a very big one, so far as I can tell. A mile in diameter, perhaps. It didn't take us that long, when we were coming across the water. It was more the distraction of the two of you going to pieces on us.'

'Two of us?'

'You and Tor. Exactly the same reaction, almost at exactly the same time. Like you were in sync. But there were Faurin waiting for us on the beach, fully prepared. Like they had anticipated it would happen. They knew exactly what to do, and who to attend to. There's others here, too, I should say.'

'Others?'

'With the Faurin. Another kind. Another race, I think. I don't know yet. We haven't had the chance to ask many questions. But perhaps they've interbred. There are similarities, and some younger ones who look like a mix of both. These others are taller than anyone I've seen before. Very long necks, broad, quite refined looking, actually.'

'Interesting,' Merouac said, but felt a dizzy spell come over him, a nauseous wave that darkened his vision and made him gag.

'Its fascinating, marvellous, and I'm keen to explore. But I want to make sure you've adjusted, first. They tell me it should only take you the day. And we're getting a formal welcome from the Faurin – that has to happen first, apparently, before we can explore. Ah, and here is Afourla. Hello, Afourla.'

Merouac saw that Afourla came and was aware of Heyla leaving the room and Afourla settling beside him. Merouac noted through the dull light that Afourla himself also wore neck jewellery, the same as he always seemed to wear – a neck piece of corded metal twisting around small green gems – most likely pala – that started at his throat, with threads of more woven cords extending down to his waist.

'Why is the air so different?' he murmured, trying to swat away some of the low-lit glimmers that darted around him.

'This is a different place. The air and energy work differently. You're seeing and feeling the currents in the air that are normal here.'

'Tell me what happened on the journey over. Do I remember being covered in leaves, on the beach? And those were the leaves you had ensured we brought with us? You knew that this would happen?' Merouac clearly remembered the massive net of leaves being packed into the rear of one of the boats.

'I recognised you. I anticipated what might happen, and we made plans for it. Organic matter from the frequency of origin, such as those leaves, helps the equalisation process. All that's needed then is to give the bodies time to do the rest on their own, which they will do. You can see the main reaction has come and gone.'

Merouac blinked. In the half-light, there were small veins of illumination shooting through the air around him. 'What …'

Afourla followed his gaze. 'It's a heightened energetic environment. What you can see in the air are veins of energy. Communication is going on around us, made visible.'

Merouac was silent, absorbing Afourla's words and watching the air. 'Where is this place in the bigger scheme of things?'

Afourla shrugged. 'Not anywhere on the planet of Ahm, at the very least. But at most, not very far, I don't think. You saw an island appear when we were a way offshore. We have now travelled to that island. We named this place High Country. It is a realm all of its own and yet it is also simply an extension of the Remneur Ranges. This is the evidence that shows you the shield has been fading.'

Meroauc tried to sit up but was assaulted by a a sense of overwhelming fatigue. The Faurin nurse came over and pushed some pillows under his back, covered with what looked like a woven fabric made from grasses.

Merouac's body still felt fragile and tired. 'Where is everyone else?'

'Outside, around, waiting for you to rest and recover.'

'Why was it only Tor and me who had a reaction?'

Afourla was silent for a moment.

'What do you know, Afourla? What's going on?' Merouac's head hurt. His mouth felt dry and he looked around for the Faurin nurse, who saw his need and provided another kind of cool drink, which Merouac sipped gratefully.

Afourla started to talk. 'Starting about a hundred and fifty shades ago, there was a series of visits to the Faurin. This is what I told you all on Tenogru. I said there were three visits.'

Merouac nodded.

'In fact, there was a another visit that I have not yet mentioned.'

'When?'

'Forty shades ago. In the order of events, it was the third time they made themselves known to us. The fourth and final visit was when they showed us this place, High Country, a little over fifteen shades ago.'

Merouac felt an odd hot and cold flush sweep through his body. 'Keep going.'

'The third time they came, they told us they were bringing us a gift. That we needed to be ready to receive that gift. So, we gathered many of the royal family. And many of the Intangien. And we waited.

'We waited for two days, and then they returned at dusk on the third day. The gift was a hundred newborn babies, most only days old. All with different shades of hair, different shades of colours of skin from light to dark. But they all had the birthmark that you have. You had all been carefully swaddled. You were all peaceful. Most of you were sleeping.'

'Where the damn would they have been able to get a hundred children, and what happened to the parents?' Merouac asked, fatigued and confused.

'The visitors told us we must disperse this gift across the country.'

'But where had they come from?' Merouac asked.

'They told us it wasn't necessary for us to know. All we had to do was ensure the children were dispersed across the continent.'

The flushing Merouac felt lingered and his throat seemed to thicken. He sensed there was something in this story that related to him, and he also sensed he didn't want to know what it was.

'We were told the children were a gift to a realm that was growing up. That the shield was dissipating and that the children would know what to do.'

'What did you do?' asked Merouac.

'Of those children, all but one were delivered to an orphanage in Meurre Fells. One child was kept in the mountains, gifted to a family that could not have children of their own. That child was Tor Anale.'

Merouac swallowed. 'And the others?'

'Each one of us took a child. And over the next few days, we travelled down from the mountains across the country to every orphanage we knew of. We didn't ask for any updates once you had all been taken. We had been told it was unnecessary to involve ourselves any further.'

'So you're telling me I was gifted to the Faurin and you took me to an orphanage?' Merouac asked with gritted teeth, his vision swimming. How could it be that he was hearing another version of the same story that he'd heard only recently in Meurre Fells, but had never heard a whisper of, his whole life, until this point?

'Merouac, there was one thing all the children had in common. And that was a light brown birthmark on their neck. The same birthmark you have. You are one of the one hundred. And if you are, then your sister was, too.'

Merouac was silent. It didn't compute, and he didn't know how to respond to the words coming out of Afourla's mouth.

'I'm not an orphan,' said Merouac slowly, willing Afourla to stop, to walk away, to have never started this conversation. 'And neither was Malaena. My twin sister and I were born and raised in the Ingrue. My parents were factory workers.'

Merouac stopped speaking. He felt so tired.

Afourla looked at him. 'You need to rest,' he said.

Merouac was asleep before Afourla had left the room.

20.
Evra arrives

Evra clambered out of the boat and shrieked with delight when her feet hit the water. It reminded Merouac that he and his niece had never been so close to water that they could play in it, but it was clearly enormous fun now.

Merouac waded into the water and enveloped the child in a hug. She hugged him back, her small arms tight around his neck, before releasing herself from his embrace to splash her way over to Kultan, standing on the sand, who she also hugged.

Heyla was allowing herself to be aided off the boat; she also landed in the water with a splash. She also seemed to enjoy it. None of them had the chance to swim in the ocean since setting up the sub-camp. Few of the railroad lines other than some of the old Ingruan ones tracked close to the coast, but Heyla, with the time she spent at the Banne markets, possibly got more time in the water than he and Evra did.

'It's a bit dark,' Evra said said to Merouac. 'But we saw creatures the whole way here, didn't we Heyla?'

Evra had returned to his side and clasped her hand in his.

'All okay with the crossing? Where are Seb and Harlin?' he asked.

Heyla unpicked some of the beaded notches in her long hair, letting it loose and combing her hair through with her hands, and allowing droplets of moisture to fall off. 'Yes. We had a good trip. We made it back to the sub-camp quickly, and Seb and Harlin have come all the way back with us. They are back on the other side waiting. They thought you might prefer it if they came with Evra the whole way.'

'They did a tuning on the beach,' Evra announced emphatically. 'That's how we're here now.' She looked to Kultan. 'Like when you helped us before,' she explained.

Kultan nodded. 'And a frequency bridge. It needs to be strong for people to cross directly from one frequency to another.'

Evra nodded as well, as if for all the world, she, a child of five shades, knew exactly what he meant and it made perfect sense and didn't require any further questioning.

'Well, Kultan, what next?' Heyla asked, as the Faurin who had brought Heyla and Evra to the island prepared to bring the small watercraft further up the shore. She waved her thanks to them, and they nodded in acknowledgement.

'You have some time,' Kultan responded. 'My family will welcome the group later, they will cook our evening meal and host us this evening. But you could rest first.'

'Lead the way,' Heyla said approvingly.

Kultan eyed Merouac and Evra thoughtfully. 'I will take the two of you somewhere else,' he decided. 'You don't need to rest so much.'

Evra shook her head, agreeing with Kultan. No rest for her, Merouac surmised.

Moments later, with Kultan having returned from showing

Heyla the way back to their dormitory, Kultan was leading them down a path, explaining the terraces to Evra, who skipped along, still holding Merouac's hand, exclaiming at the low light, the sparkles and shapes that were faintly visible in the air, the sense of being nudged by thick parcels of air.

Evra moved from one side of the path to the other, untangling herself from Merouac to pluck Kultan's hand and hold it for a time, then releasing the young Faurin to run ahead and peek through the shrubs to the ground, then staring up at the higher trees and then settling back at Merouac's side, only to begin another variation of discoveries all over again.

It wasn't long before Kultan had led them off the beach, bypassed the dormitory and directed them to a small forest ahead of them that had a faintly luminous pink glow.

'I will leave you here,' Kultan said. 'It's just a pretty place. Take a look around. Don't go too much further. You can come back when you've had a look. I'm going to find my brother.'

Evra, who had started racing gleefully ahead, whipped around, returning to stand in front of Kultan. 'You have a brother?'

'Yes,' Kultan said solemnly. 'He's my twin brother, Kii.'

Evra grinned, looking at Merouac. 'You're a twin.'

'That's true', Meroac said.

'Can I meet him?'

'You'll meet him later today,' Kultan said.

Evra, satisfied, nodded and turned back to take Merouac's hand and lead him towards the forest.

'Thank you,' said Merouac to Kultan, who had already turned and was walking away. He raised his hand, but kept walking.

Merouac heard a shriek behind him and turned, racing towards Evra, aware that his heart had started pummelling in that small instant.

'What's happened?' he said, running to where she was standing.

She was frozen, but instead of their being anything wrong, she had a rapturous look on her face. On the ground, a very large, fat lizard sat, turquoise in colour, shimmering in the low light.

Evra crouched down to get a closer look and was in an instant on her knees, her face only inches away from the creature who seemed unsurprised and unphased at the attention. Before long, he waddled on, moving past Evra, and crossing the dirt path to a small cluster of orange ferns. He disappeared.

'Alright Ev, let's explore a bit and then we'll have a bit of a sit down and catch our breath, eh?' he suggested.

The small forest glen was startlingly beautiful and unique. Massive leafy fronds, a shade of pink Merouac had never seen in a tree before, pushed upwards from thick stumps of husky bark. He and Evra ran their hands over the bases of the trees, feeling the feathery texture of the bark. Other trees had fine, smooth and very tall and thin trunks, with curious markings on them. Looking closer, they saw one variation of the markings was the work of small critters eating their way through the bark.

'Evra, do you know what happened to me?' Merouac asked as casually as he could, as they explored the forest.

'Yes,' Evra said with a definitive nod. 'You got sick. You've been asleep. Heyla said I should come here because you wouldn't be home as quickly as you were supposed to.'

'I see. But do you know where we are?' Merouac tested gently.

Evra paused. 'High Country?'

'That's right. Well, that's good you know what happened. Did Heyla tell you there might be a reason why I got sick and most of the others didn't?' Merouac thought he might be pushing it with this last question, but his niece hadn't looked at all phased so far, so he continued.

Evra was still inspecting the trees, tracing the markings on the trunks with her small fingers and sticking her face as close as she possibly could to the trunks. 'You're like Mama,' she said, as if it was the simplest thing in the world. 'But you're better now, aren't you?'

'I'm not sure what I am,' Merouac sighed. 'But it's good to have you here, kid.'

ooo

After they had spent time in the pink forest, Merouac took Evra back to the long communal lodging hut where the group was housed. He had learned the lodgings were used by Faurin acolytes practising their skills in attuning to High Country. Some were coming back and forth regularly from the Remneur Ranges, those members of the royal family who had not yet migrated here.

Kultan had also told Merouac that the village was only a short walk away, around the headland beach where they had landed. There was a small community of Faurin on the island, all members of their extended royal family.

The infirmary, where Merouac and Tor had been initially taken, was in another small area up a way from shore, a cluster of huts and cabins that also worked as storage areas for one thing and another. The Faurin had decided early on that an isolation area was required as they learned about the frequency and put measures in to protect themselves as they went.

The long building had communal areas and small rooms containing space for two or three people to sleep on low beds. Even Evra, with her joyful noise and curious chatter, became weary from the trip she had made. He found a bed for her and let her sleep.

When the low light of High Country had faded to the hazy dusk of evening, Kultan appeared. The young man's appearance caused a whole new round of excited chatter from Evra, which continued as Kultan led them back down to the beach and along a sandy track around the base of the terraced hills that rose behind them.

Merouac was now feeling more himself. His enormous sense of fatigue had started to dissipate, and the worry that had been hanging over him had also lifted, with Evra close by. No matter how strange the experience they were having now, it was not much stranger than many of the other things that had been happening of late. Despite the rough voyage it seemed now almost worth it, considering what they were looking at around them.

What they were seeing and experiencing was proof the shield was down. The terrain was similar, but like the forest they had spent the afternoon in, the texture and detail of the plants and foliage was foreign. Alongside the bright vivid pink foliage of the trees they had just been exploring that afternoon, much of the other plant life glimmered with a silvery blue-green haze. It was not at all like the foliage of the Remneur Ranges, which was a deep, dark green that often turned black in areas of dense vegetation.

Merouac paused to look up behind them. Rising above them were the gentle slopes of the mountain, with four horizontal striations of colour, seeming to glow with different levels of luminosity in the dim light. The terraces shimmered gently, each level with a different, flickering hue. Looking at the low-lying vegetation around the path, that too was different. Rose-coloured lichen covered rocks. Even as he stopped and leaned down to touch the tough, prickly growth, he felt the air buffering around him, the clearest sign of all that they were somewhere different.

He stood again and felt afresh the frequent ripples of disturbance in the air, like flutters you could feel more than see. The frequency itself was being poked and prodded, it seemed, by other types of sentience on other frequencies close by.

Smells of cooking were in the air and made Merouac's stomach growl. Evra was skipping ahead, racing between Heyla and Kultan, the two from the group she knew, but also finding moments to walk with Lavilla. He saw that the Governor of the Ingrue was no more immune to Evra's young charms than any of the others – before long they were chatting like they had known each other forever.

Some of the members of the Faurin royal families were out and about. They had been told of the arrival of the group, and greeted the guests with smiles as Kultan led them into the village compound.

Many of them wore the head garments he saw on the Intangien monks who had assisted with their frequency tunings. Seemingly created with decorative metal filament, thin strands of silver were woven and threaded into different designs. Embedded in the strands of metal were small shards of stone; much of it looked to be green pala. Small dark shards made Merouac wonder if there was black pala embedded in them as well.

Merouac observed something else, as they stopped in the centre of the village compound, where a small woman and a collection of others behind her were waiting. Some of the individuals looked quite different. Even from afar, he could see that they were taller, with long necks, elongated bodies and features. He noticed that rather than calling out a greeting, many were simply nodding or smiling their welcomes.

It felt oddly quiet, even as more and more Faurin emerged from the village. His head clamoured with new questions: were they a different race, from another frequency – and did that mean there was even more crossover than just the Faurin migrating to another frequency? Had other races migrated here, to High Country?

Merouac felt Heyla give him a small jab with her elbow. She had appeared by his side quite suddenly. He looked at her and she, in turn, firmly directed her gaze to the small woman in front of them, who Kultan was introducing.

'Asta, my mother,' Kultan explained.

The small woman was beaming, radiating a warm affection that seemed starkly different from many of the other Faurin who had a loose, gestural openness but perhaps without the warmth that Asta had. Her hair was worn in long white braids. It looked as though she had dyed and cured fabrics and sewn them into her hair, in a similar fashion to what he had seen Heyla do from time to time. There were also painted glass baubles, tiny things that shimmered in the light and created a chiming sound when she moved.

'She welcomes you,' Kultan explained. 'Asta has been in training with our friends the Raja, who don't speak using words. She's just taking a moment to get her voice back.'

Asta hugged each of them one by one. After the greeting and welcome was complete, she pulled Kultan closer, rasping a few words into his ear, a small hand on her neck as she tried out her vocal cords; he had to stoop down to listen. Kultan nodded and stood up. 'My mother apologises and wants you to know that Afourla will not be joining us for the rest of your time here on High Country.'

Merouac noted that Heyla and Lavilla exchanged glances, but nodded politely.

'My father Telbe has also gone with him,' Kultan added. 'So Asta is your host tonight. And Kii and I will be your guides for the rest of the time.'

'Thank you, Kultan,' said Lavilla with a gentle smile. Lavilla had been quiet, but Merouac saw she was on high alert. She moved quickly to walk in step with Asta, who was leading them on a tour of the small village compound, asking questions and nodding as Kultan provided the answers.

Asta showed them the village; small as it was, it had been carefully planned and built. Huts sat positioned in two semi-circle arcs, three deep, all facing in towards a large, central, communal living area. Beyond the huts, more areas for eating, washing, storing, drying, sorting, playing, cooking. The commune seemed to unfold in sections and spaces of colour, smoke, scents and movement – not unlike the Faurin villages in the Remneur Ranges – but rather than rambling down a densely covered rainforest incline or terrace, this commune stretched down towards the shallow beaches.

Asta whispered sociably to the group, encouraging questions and touching each of them on their arms and hands as if she needed to feel their bodies to get a sense of them. Even with her light, enquiring touch Merouac sensed there was an undeniable strength and power in Asta; perhaps here at last was a leader that both Heyla and Lavilla could get on board with.

Asta stopped outside one of the rows of huts, reaching out a small hand to touch Kultan, letting him know that she was alright to talk. 'It only takes a while to get my voice back,' she explained. 'I have not spoken much at all this past shade. It was true. Asta's voice seemed to be gradually warming up, and she talked to them about the hand-painted, wooden totem-like poles at the front of each hut.

'See these markings? Each pole explains the family who lives here,' Asta explained. 'Huts are grouped by families and the markings are codes that show what their allocated duties are here on High Country. Each pole is different,' she continued. 'Feel them,' she invited, although Evra had required no such heeding – before Asta had even uttered the sentence she was beside the closest pole, trailing her hand over the wood with its carved details and sections of entangled metallic fibres enclosing more green pala stones.

'I would have thought you were a small enough community to not need codes like this,' Lavilla said. 'But they are very beautiful.' The Governor followed Evra's example, tracing her hand lightly over the carving.

Asta smiled. 'Perhaps you're right. We are a small community, and we are family. We mostly know what everyone else is doing. But it seems to help. It keeps us all in agreement.'

'So what does each post say?' Heyla asked.

'These numbers explain the family group and what they are responsible for and what level they are trained to go up to on High Country. If the sign has the number three, then the third level of the island's terraces is where their family group can go together without being accompanied by the Raja.'

'Who are the Raja?' asked Merouac, sensing he knew the answer to his question already. They were the strangers, the tall ones in the group he had seen from afar with the elevated necks and long features.

Asta listened to the question and touched Merouac's hand lightly. 'I am sorry, I have raced ahead and left things out. The Raja have been helping us learn more about the Broadsphere and document what we're learning. They've been with us for more than ten shades and are now our kindred and friends. Some of them have found mates, made families.'

'Where are they from?' Merouac asked.

'Elsewhere in the Broadsphere, originally. Another frequency. A few of them will join us later this evening. They wanted especially to meet the metalsmith who is one of the one hundred, and who already knows how to tune metal. There's more for you to know.'

Merouac nodded without knowing quite how to respond. Heyla gave him another nudge with her elbow, this time with a curious smile.

'So everyone here has specific duties?' Heyla asked, as Asta started walking, waving for them to follow her.

'Yes. Each level of the terraces on High Country you can see behind us need to be maintained and cared for. They are part of our life here. We are documenting what we experience here in detail. Each of the family groups has some responsibility for that. We also have makers – those who have responsibility for making our garments. We have teachers and caretakers, foragers and cooks. We have others who ensure the frequency passage between here and the Ranges is kept strong.'

Asta was waving them to a sandy stretch near the beach where a spread had been prepared. Large slabs of dark, shiny stone had been nestled into the ground to make a natural, low-lying table, and it was being covered with wooden platters of food. 'Please, sit,' she invited.

The group settled on the sand. 'Thank you for the invitation,' Lavilla said to Asta. 'It's an honour to be welcomed like this by you and your family.'

Asta's eyes twinkled. 'Let's eat,' she said. 'Please, help yourselves.'

The group passed around plates of smoked fish and salted clams, and deep red and brown root vegetables layered with dried seaweed.

'Why did you stop speaking?' Lavilla asked, after they had been quiet for a time, enjoying the fresh food.

'Ahm is one of the planets still using primarily vocal communication,' Asta explained. 'Here, and elsewhere beyond the shield, it is more important to understand and use energetic communication. That does not require you to talk, but to listen more deeply, using your whole body.'

'So you stopped talking in order to listen more?' Heyla asked, passing more roast vegetables to Merouac, who plucked a few off the platter for both him and Evra.

Asta considered the question. 'Yes. But also to listen in a new way. Deep listening is part of being part of the Broadsphere, and paying attention to those on other frequencies who may wish to communicate with us. Which, of course, is possible if we agreed to it. High Country is not like Ahm, so we must also learn to be different here.'

'So you can do things here that are not possible on Ahm?' tested Lavilla.

'Yes, but of course Ahm is changing, and so soon you will have a lot more contact with the Broadsphere. That is part of our work here, to understand what that means, and to be ready.'

'What do you mean when you say Ahm is changing? Are you talking about the shield?' Lavilla asked, her brows tightly knotted, as if she were doing her own kind of intense listening to get the facts straight.

'Well, yes,' said Asta, reaching for the larg urn of water in the centre of the makeshift table. 'Oh, thank you, Merouac,' she smiled when he lifted the urn and poured water into her wooden cup for her. 'Planets are living things. They have their own journeys to take as well. The shield is fading because Ahm is shedding its own protective layer.'

'And once the shield has completely gone?'

'Then Ahm will be part of the Broadsphere,' confirmed Asta in a matter-of-fact way. 'As we are here. And all lines of communication will be open.'

Asta smiled at two young Faurin who had arrived to clear plates. They returned moments later with new platters of berries, breads and cheeses. Then, she smiled again. Merouac followed her gaze to see Kii was approaching.

Two of the individuals, who Asta had been referring to as their friends the Raja, were walking with Kii towards them. Merouac felt strangely nervous at their appearance and wondered if his heart had just started beating faster. They moved slowly, as if they were marking a different kind of time. There was no rush and no fear. They walked as though walking was the act in and of itself, the end and the beginning, not a means to get to a destination but a powerful process in and of itself.

The two men were slow moving, graceful, each with a high mohawk of golden straw-like hair, and heavily decorated with neck jewels. The neck-ware was gnarled, twisted, fibrous, fragments of plant stems dried and interwoven with beads and fresh flowers, trussed with other leaves and organic material, and embedded with strange jewels that seemed to glow and fade, changing colours across a spectrum of blues to greens and then back to blues.

Evra didn't look the slightest bit perturbed – only excited that there were more people joining them.

Kii came over to him and Merouac got quickly to his feet to greet the newcomers.

'Merouac,' Kii said with a gentle smile. 'Our friends are very interested to meet you. This is Tundra and Elan.'

Merouac noded a greeting and then blinked. Was he imagining it, or was Tundra coming and going right before his eyes, vanishing and then swiftly reappearing, almost in the same breath? The person Kii had introduced as Tundra was massively tall with a tall, large body, long neck and what looked to be a slightly elongated skull.

Tundra inclined his head, made a small gesture and a bow.

'He greets you,' Kii translated. 'Tundra does not speak very much, and so I'll translate for him.'

'How do you know what he wants to say, then?' Merouac asked.

'I can see it, or sense it, in the atmosphere,' Kii explained.

Merouac watched in surprise as the Tundra gestured again, imparting information through the aether which Kii seemed to easily recieve and decipher.

Tundra then eased himself into a crouching position and cleared a patch of grass. He shook his head and determined it would not suit, and looked for a sandy patch. He moved over to another, more suitable, patch of ground and beckoned the other two to join him. He went through the same process of clearing the ground, and then used his fingers to trace lines into the sand. He was silent as he did so, but then looked at Kii expectantly, and Kii nodded.

'Tundra said you did the right thing with the race that was escaping their imploding planet. They are safe, and they will rest in the core of Ahm now. Tundra was just drawing a map for me, to show me where they are.'

Merouac felt a shock run through him. 'How does Tundra know about the Helara?' he asked Kii.

'There are things that can be seen in the energetic environment. He is able to perceive the place where the Helara now rest. It is under the power grid, deep below Suron. There is a cave network, and catacombs with very deep canyons. Below those canyons, this is where you found a place for the Helara to enter the core of the planet. It was the right thing to do,' Kii said, translating as he watched Tundra's fingers work in the sand.

After that, Tundra stood up and looked at Merouac reflectively, and offered him a deep smile.

'Thank you', Merouac said hoarsely, feeling his heart racing. His mouth felt completely dry.

Kii smiled again at Merouac as the Raja moved around the group, silently greeting the other guests and then receiving a fierce hug from Asta. 'How are you feeling, Merouac?'

'Alright, I guess,' Merouac smiled at Kultan's twin. Even though he had seen the two young men together a few times now, there was a lot to think about seeing them side by side, and Merouac was interested to see them together every time. Despite Kii's facial covering, which seemed to be protecting his right eye, there were many similarities, beyond their golden skin and tawny hair. Some of their gestures were almost identical: the way they moved their long arms and the way they spoke. But there were differences, as well. There was something more restless about Kultan, a sense of energy still finding its place and waiting to settle. Kii's movements were quieter, more assured.

Merouac noted Evra sidling up to Kii and tapping him on his side. As Kii crouched down to talk to the child, Merouac rolled his eyes, which Heyla saw and grinned at. No one was safe from Evra's insatiable curiosity, although Kii didn't seem to mind. He allowed Evra to trace her fingers over the mask that covered half of his face, and settled down to sit with the child as she asked him questions about the creatures, plants and flowers they had come across earlier that afternoon.

'Asta, another question for you, and perhaps the Raja as well,' Lavilla said, nodding her head at the two tall men who had now sat down with them around the table.

'What have you discovered here, so far?'

Asta clapped her hands together. 'What a wonderful question.' She gave Lavilla a warm, appreciative look, and laughed out loud at Kii and Kultan's faces. 'My sons both look troubled at this question, for different reasons, I think. But you are here, and I will tell you what I wish. And that is to say that we are simply starting to know of many more differing kinds of life.'

'Here, on High Country?' asked Merouac.

'Yes. In the frequency of this island, High Country, we have created small variations, slight adjustments to the frequency so that each of the terraces you see behind us is tuned differently. Each tuned environment is different. Each has different possibilities and potential. And so every day, we are exploring what that means. We have been here fifteen shades and we are only just scratching the surface.'

'And you plan to stay here for good?' Heyla asked.

'Yes. As soon as we found this place, we immediately felt at home there. It was a gift. The greatest gift. We knew straight away this place was very precious.'

Asta smiled at her two sons. Kii returned her smile but Merouac noticed that Kultan continued to look troubled. Asta continued, 'We love the Remneur. But High Country feels like coming home. And as we establish the frequency further, we become more rooted in this place. We will stay.'

Tundra, listening to the back and forth of question and answer, directed his gaze to Kii, who found the right interpretation and spoke on his behalf. 'And, because things are changing in any event,' Kii said.

Tundra nodded. 'It is time,' he seemed to be saying.

It wasn't until later that night that Merouac wondered how he'd had a sense of what Tundra had been communicating, since in fact, he hadn't spoken a word. Perhaps it was what Afourla had been saying; the air on High Country was so thick with information, it seeped right into your skin.

21.
Adjusting to High Country

The guest compound was quiet when Kultan arrived. Merouac had been sitting outside taking in the atmosphere. The dim light and air took some getting used to and seemed to shift and move around him.

'A familiar face,' Merouac said with a smile.

'You are feeling better, I suppose, with your niece here?'

'Yes. I worry whenever I don't have her close by.'

'I understand. And last night, meeting my family …' Kultan trailed off dubiously.

'They are very nice, Kultan.' Sensing the young Faurin's discomfort, Merouac changed the subject. 'Tell me, how long are the days here?'

'Much the same. It's just that the light is lower. But that helps you see the things that are different. If the light was brighter it would be harder to see and sense them.'

Merouac reached a hand up and felt the air shifting and nudging around it, a gentle pressure prodding his skin first here, then there, then fading away.

'Are you ready for a walk? I'm here to take you up to the first terrace.'

'Up yonder?'

'Yes. It's time to start your training.'

'Only me?'

'For the moment.'

'Yes, I think I'm ready. And Evra has taken Heyla down to the pink forest so she's taken care of. But tell me, why only me? Is it because of what happened on the way over?'

Kultan walked over to a grassy mound near the bench and plucked a long-plumed stem of a plant, broke it in two and put the lower part of the stem in his mouth, chewing it thoughtfully.

'So you know some things now. Afourla came and sat with you, didn't he?'

'Well yes, but I was tired and delirious. I'm not sure I got all the detail, or that I completely believe it, to be honest.'

'He told you about the visitors bringing children?'

'Yes.'

'And you know that you are one of the one hundred?'

'Yes. Did you know that before? When we met for the first time?'

Kultan shrugged. 'Not really. But it didn't surprise me. We're training you because of that and because you have already shown that you are using your gift, tuning metal. So, yes, it's just you we will train.'

'What about Tor? Isn't he also one of the one hundred?'

'Yes. But he has left High Country, now.'

'What? How has he already left? If he's anything like me, he's still recovering.'

'You ask too many questions,' Kultan said. He looked at Merouac's bare feet and put down the knapsack he had been carrying. 'Try these,' he suggested, pulling out and handing him a pair of tough-woven thongs. 'Your other shoes are not right for High Country. They are still in the infirmary with your clothes. You can pick them up when you are ready to leave.'

Merouac stood up, slipped the thongs on, and nodded. They were the final piece to his mountain attire; the nurse had changed his clothes when he was in the infirmary and he now wore Faurin pants and a sleeveless vest, which somehow felt coarse and soft at the same time. 'Alright. Ready when you are.'

Kultan led them along a dirt path, away from the accommodation building and towards the rising terraces.

As they walked, Merouac felt the air buffering around him, like a gentle but inconsistent breeze that had parcels of condensed air bumping into him every so often. 'These elements … Can everyone see and feel them?'

'Yes. Everyone can see and feel them. But the skill is about knowing how to connect with them and unlock the information inside.'

'And how do you do that?'

'It depends.'

'On what?'

'On how skilled you are at energetic communication. People on Ahm are not skilled at it. You can learn over time but you won't see it all to start with.'

'What about you? Can you see everything?'

'Not everything. My brother is blind in one eye and yet he can see almost everything. We have different ways of sensing things. He is in his element here, and he has focused on learning how to see and feel here since he was young.'

'You mentioned we're heading towards a gate?' Merouac asked.

'Yes. High Country is set to five frequencies. There isn't much difference, just variations. The gates set the frequency for each level of the island. You have to pass through the gate to enter each of the terraces.'

'So the ground level?' Merouac questioned

'That is the base frequency of High Country. Then there are three terraces above. We are going to the first one.'

'What about the fifth?

'That is not for you. Many of the Faurin living here do not even go up that high,' Kultan replied. 'We call it the frequency highway. It would overpower you, if you were to go there without being fully trained and prepared for it.'

Kultan forged ahead, and soon the path widened even more, and then came to an end. 'This way', the young Faurin beckoned, leading Merouac to a cluster of low brambly trees. There was a small path, partially hidden, that wound its way around the trees and then led to a small grassy space – and beyond that, was the first gate.

Merouac stopped in surprise and admiration. It was a real gate, over six feet high, and ornate in its creation. It was made from garganta steel, rolled and forged and set by hand, with artisan embellishments like the signature motifs that came out of the southern metal shops in the Ingrue.

Merouac whistled. It was a craftsman's gate. Made by someone similar to himself. He walked over to it. 'Really? A metal gate, here on the side of the mountain? This is what sets the tuning?'

Kultan had slyly been watching Merouac's face when the gate had become visible. 'I thought you would like it. Yes. There is a workshop up on third terrace. The Raja are going to help train you there.'

'Ah, interesting. When?'

Kultan frowned. One thing at a time, I think. Here, I will open the gate.'

'Alright. But Kultan, before I forget, what happened to Tor?'

'Merouac, nothing has happened to Tor. But you should slow down your questions,' Kultan scolded. 'Come through.' He opened the gate and directed Merouac to pass through in front of him.

The gate led them towards another rocky path, and that path led them to the terraced area of the side of the mountain, with tiers of descending beds of flowers, plants and vegetables. The slope was gentle enough that you could walk down through the plant beds, and so that's what Merouac did. He stood and looked out down to the lowest level of High Country below them, to the gently glowing terraces above them and then out to the ocean that surrounded them. Kultan walked down the slope to join him, pausing to kick some soil back into the plant bed it had escaped from.

'So, if I were to set out across the water?' Merouac asked.

'It depends.'

'So, if we didn't create a frequency bridge back to Ahm, we could end up anywhere?'

'Or nowhere,' Kultan replied.

Further up the slope, the cleared hillside gave way to trees with a soft, blue-green carpet covering their bases, climbing their trunks as if to give layers of coverage and protection.

Stepping into the shade of the trees reduced the light even further, and Merouac noticed the blue tinge was in the air, as well as casting a tint on the plants, the ground and the trees.

Just ahead, beyond the outstretched limbs of a thin tree, hovered the oddest-looking creature Merouac had ever seen. It looked like a cross between a flower and a butterfly. Each part of its body glowed separately, distinctly. It wheeled backwards and forwards, often not looking like it was going anywhere in particular. It seemed to notice Merouac's gaze, fluttered its wings and disappeared.

'It's a hummer,' Kultan said. 'There are lots of them around.

Different ones at each different level. We think they move between frequencies as well. That's why they appear and then disappear. We think they follow a feeding trail across dimensions.'

'Do they communicate with you?'

'I don't think so. But even those Faurin who live here all the time do not understand everything about how this realm works.'

A moment later, the hummer flickered back into sight, taking a moment to right itself before continuing on its way, deeper into the forest.

'This is as far as we go today,' Kultan said. 'This is as much training as you are allowed, at least until tomorrow. We are just allowing your body to start getting used to the differences on all the different terraces.'

'That's fine by me', Merouac said, seeing a thick tree stump and wandering over to it, leaning against it. He crossed his arms over his chest and leaned back, staring at the hummers and their erratic, jerking movements in and out of time and space.

'So the difference between the lowest level of High Country and this first terrace is the plants and things like hummers? What else?' Merouac probed.

'That's it, really,' said Kultan. 'It's only a very gentle adjustment, as most of the Faurin come up to this level to manage the gardens. But it's enough of a difference to see the blue tint and be present with the hummers when they appear.'

'Can we keep walking?'

'Yes. There is the track. If you are not feeling too tired, we can walk all the way around the hill and we'll arrive back at the gate soon enough.'

As they walked, Merouac asked if he could resume his questions. Kultan nodded. 'Alright. Yes, ask what you want to.'

'Well, let's see. Firstly, who else has this happened to? Who else had the same experience as Tor and I did, when they came over to High Country?'

'No one,' said Kultan.

'Then how did you all know to have the leaves ready for me?'

'Afourla knew who you were. He saw your scar. It's what you all have. All one hundred children have exactly the same scar.'

Merouac felt the front of his neck where the small scar was. 'You know, on Tenogru, I thought Afourla looked at me strangely. I suppose he knew then, didn't he? As soon as he saw me.'

'It seems that way,' said Kultan vaguely.

'And so all the Faurin know about the one hundred children?'

'It's the royal family's knowledge to keep because we had the duty of finding homes for you.'

'But what about the rest of the Faurin?' Merouac probed. 'What about the rest of the people in the mountains? Do they know?'

Kultan shook his head. 'It wasn't thought to be necessary to tell everyone.'

'So the rest of your people don't know anything of the visitors?'

'You misunderstand. All the Faurin know of the visitors. They know the visitors gave us the skills our Intangien fighters now use. They don't know about the one hundred children.'

'So how do you feel about it? Understanding that there are a hundred people like me out there. Who you say are not from Ahm at all. Born somewhere else entirely.'

'I don't know,' Kultan said.

'What about your mother and father, Kultan? Where do they stand?'

'They fall in line. They follow Afourla, and they have led the community here since Afourla and Kii were detained by Tor. And they believe everything is as it should be. They feel their role is here. I have their blessing to stay on Tenogru and lead the people. But how can I?'

'How long until you are officially made leader?'

'I have six shades until I turn twenty-five. That is the traditional age for leadership to be handed down.'

'And between now and then?'

'Qualan remains my tutor and guide.'

Kultan was thoughtful and they walked quietly for a time.

'Where is Qualan, anyway?' asked Merouac.

'He comes back and forth. He'll be here soon. He knows that you're all here.'

'So what about Tor?'

'Tor is like you. I think my grandfather has been fearful of that, even though he personally brought Tor to a family in the mountains. And so now Tor is very angry. He feels he has been left out in the cold. He has returned home to the village of his childhood.'

Merouac was quiet again. They walked slowly.

'But how did Kii and Afourla even pull it off? How were they able to cross back and forth from Ahm to here, without the Intangien to assist with a frequency bridge?'

'Out of everyone, Afourla has the most skill. He is advanced enough to be able to create a vibratory match from this side, from High Country, and that created the bridge.'

Merouac shook his head, only partially understanding. 'But how did they never get found out? How did no one discover they weren't in their cells?'

'I don't know. The guards might not have been paying very much attention. Tor was visiting them less frequently because he wasn't getting the information he wanted.'

'And so you have been able to see both of them whenever you wanted to?'

'Occasionally. I don't come here very often though. Sometimes I am just told that they have been and gone again.'

They had arrived back at the gate. 'We'll leave now,' Kultan said.

Back at the guest dormitory, he gave Merouac a wave and kept walking. Merouac smiled at the young man's understated way of saying goodbye. 'See you tomorrow,' he called out.

Kultan raised his arm in acknowledgment. He didn't look back.

Merouac shrugged and wondered where Heyla and his niece might be.

22.
Training

'So, another day of training?' Merouac asked, as Kultan approached the next day.

'Yes. I am taking you up to the second terrace today. Kii will meet us there. Are you ready?'

'Yes, I think so,' replied Merouac. Heyla had taken Evra down to the beach to explore, Lavilla was still at the village commune and it seemed that all was clear for him to depart.

'What's our focus for today?' he asked, as they began the walk up the mountain paths.

The lower light levels of High Country seemed to make the green of the trees and plants more vibrant. Beneath the layers of lush vegetation, the undergrowth was glowing.

Kultan said, 'Your training today is about listening. Kii is better at this, on High Country at least, so he will train you today. There is the gate, just a little further up. We'll keep going and then rest there while we wait for my brother.'

'Listening?' Merouac asked as they made their way up the last stretch of the incline and then both sat and took in the view.

'Yes. Kii is very good at it.'

'Because of his eye?'

'Yes, probably. It helped him to develop his other senses. And he has just been here more often, for longer. He has practised for many shades with Afourla. But he always had a good way with it.'

They passed through the first gate and Merouac felt the change more clearly than he had the previous day. They stopped for a few moments, and he enjoyed the view down over the terrace below and down to the beach, the same thoughts occuring to him as the day before, about the shift in time and space that meant simply getting on a boat and heading in the direction from which they had come would not necessarily lead them back to Ahm.

Below them, the lower terrace gardens and vegetable patches were partially visible through the gaps in the forest coverage of the incline. Large fruit palms stuck up above the lower growth, waving in a gentle breeze.

'This way,' Kultan said, leading Merouac though the forest growth higher up on the incline. The path was rocky and narrow, and soon became steep. Merouac's leg was improved but he noticed the young Faurin was watching him carefully. 'You think I'm going to go into shock again?' he asked jokingly.

Kultan shrugged and looked embarrassed.

At the gate to the second terrace, Merouac felt another shift in the elevation and atmosphere. On this terrace, there were no gardens of vegetable patches; instead, the grass was high and deep. When he adjusted his gaze to look further, the air itself had a mauve tinge to it.

'The air looks purple,' Merouc commented.

'Yes,' Kultan replied. 'Every level of the terraces has a different tuning, and so the colours shift as well. You would have seen that when you were coming across the water, I think.'

'You're right,' Meroauc murmured. 'I had forgotten I'd seen that.' From the water, before Merouac had faded, the island certainly had looked to have five tiers of colour. Merouac reached his arm out into the air but the soft and gentle mauve was something you couldn't feel or capture close up.

'Kii is going to help you practise the Maoulfi state.'

'Ah, my old friend. The Maoulfi state,' Merouac grinned.

Kultan scowled, but there was a grin underneath the scowl, shyly wanting to emerge. When Merouac had first come to the mountains asking for green pala, Kultan had taken him out to the fields, ostensibly to experience the Maoulfi state, with the additional support of their herbal drink that amplified the experience. It had not been a good start to their relationship, even though Merouac had learned a lot from the experience.

'Kii will also take you to see the Raja tomorrow. You will enjoy it.'

'They're the ones who helped set up the gates at each of the different levels?'

'Yes. They are far more experienced. They are usually with us whenever we go above the third elevation.'

Moments later Kii appeared on the path in front of them; Merouac realised he must have gone ahead before them into the second terrace of High Country. He smiled at Merouac and his brother as he approached.

'I will leave you,' Kultan said, and turned, in his quick fashion, started back down the path, offering Merouac his usual back-hand wave.

'Your brother tells me the lesson today is about the Maoulfi state,' Merouac said.

Kii laughed. 'Yes, but it is not a punishment, as you make it sound. Come over here and I will show you your task for today.'

Kii led Merouac deeper into the terrace, across areas of dense vegetation and continuing low light that showcased the flickering around them, tiny shimmering seeds of energy that moved and sparked, burning then fading to appear again a moment later, somewhere else.

'Here. Do you see these piles?'

Kii had led them to a clearing. The ground was grassy, but the grass was short, as though it had been clipped, and around them were benches as though the space had been purpose-built for the Faurin to simply come and sit and take in the colour and energy whenever they wanted.

'These piles are for you.'

Merouac found himself staring at three large piles of wood. 'To do what with, exactly.'

'Well, it depends. I know you are still recovering, and you hurt your leg before you came here, so you're not in the ideal shape for the way we would normally do this exercise.'

'Which is what?'

'Moving wood from one place to another.'

'You want me to move this wood? Where will I be moving it to?'

'As I said, it depends on how you are feeling.'

Merouac considered the question. 'I'm alright to walk a bit more. I can move this wood if you need me to.'

Kii shook his head. 'No, I don't *need* you to. It's simply an exercise. If you are feeling up to it, I would like you to start moving these piles over to the small hut just around the turn. It is a very easy and natural way for you to descend into the Maoulfi state without overthinking it.'

'And I want to do that because?' prompted Merouac, half jokingly.

'The Maoulfi state is about listening. It is the deepest state of listening that can be achieved. And when you listen that deeply, to all the sounds our ears cannot hear, it is like having a map that guides you to other places. If you listen with your whole body, the frequency landscape opens up. If you can shut down your thinking, and descend, descend, descend, you find the waves. The waves of different frequencies. And you can find your way to other places. And you can start to exist for longer amounts of time in those other spaces. And that is what we are here to do.'

Merouac had not noticed that the path continued to fold around the side of the hill. He followed the path and noticed there was a small wooden hut to the right of the path, perched a little higher up the terrace's side. It held only a bench, as if it had been fashioned as another place to look out, this time over the terraces and the ocean below and hazy skies around them that disappeared into cloud. It was something Merouac had noticed. The visibility across water and skies faded quickly, as if the frequency of High Country was only dense enough to create this living ecosystem as far as a certain point, and then just faded into nothing. Surreal only just started to describe it.

Returning to the place where Kii was standing, Merouac pointed to the three piles, all with small pieces of wood no larger than his hand, piled up as high as his waist. 'So I'm moving one of these piles?'

'All three, if you can,' Kii said.

'How long do I have?'

'There isn't any time limit. And I will ask you not to talk, or look around, as you do this. Simply focus on picking up one piece, moving it to the hut, and create the new piles there. Whatever you hear, listen but don't look. Whatever you think you see out of the corner of your eye, take note but do not look up from your task.'

Merouac felt a sense of what Kii wanted. He nodded. 'Alright', he said. He took a breath, walked over to the first pile, plucked a piece off the top. It was no more than twenty strides to the hut. He placed the wood down on the ground next to the wooden construct and returned.

Kii had seated himself on one of the benches nearby. He looked out towards the ocean, seeming to have retreated into his own revery, and so Merouac picked up another piece of wood, and repeated the activity. By the time the first pile had been moved completely to the hut, he was sweating and his side was starting to ache. Kii was unmoving.

Merouac wiped his face with his arm and stared at the second pile. Was something supposed to have happened yet? He couldn't tell. He continued.

The second pile took longer and the morning seemed to stretch out before him. The light seemed to increase and then fade again. Hummers moved around him, but as instructed, he didn't avert his gaze from the wood and his task.

What seemed a long time later, the second pile had been completely moved.

Kii was now standing farther down the terrace. He paid no regard to Merouac, asked no questions about how he was feeling or if he wanted to stop. Merouac did, at that point, wish to stop. His leg was well and truly sore, he felt tired, and not at all sure that anything had shifted. He swore under his breath. Perhaps the third pile would work its magic.

As he worked, he let his mind drift. He thought of Malaena. His sister's true gift, in Merouac's own mind, was telling stories.

Ever since they had been children, she had always been full of stories, tales of what the world could be. She had never been fooled by other people's thoughts and limitations. She and Heyla would have been great friends, he reflected.

They both had a reservoir of stories that never seemed to run dry. A story for every occasion. In Heyla's case, it was a story for everything she sold at market. A beautiful song she could sing about where the object had come from, what its intent was for itself, the life it wanted to live as that object in search for the perfect owner.

Merouac had an instinctive distrust of gypsy traders. But he'd listened to Heyla singing at market and had been impressed at the ingenuity and the uniqueness of every story she sang and how connected they were to every single object she sold, whether it was a vase or a bowl. Even the smallest things had their own story. And he knew Evra was completely fascinated by each and every one of those stories.

Perhaps it was the reason Evra had bonded so quickly with Heyla – she had delighted in every single story Heyla told, in the same way she would have delighted in every story her mother had told her.

Merouac wondered now if Malaena had been using more than just her imagination. He wondered if the stories had really come from elsewhere, from beyond the walls of the world. Perhaps the connection to the stories led to a more powerful connection to those places and spaces; perhaps the storytelling was the firing up of a connection across frequencies that allowed a physical bridge to be built, and had allowed her, fully and physically, to step over it.

As far as Merouac understood it, there were several ways to enter the Maoulfi state, which was essentially a trance state. Through concentrated movement and dance, like the Intangien. Through drinking Balche, which locked down your rational thinking. Or by being in a space that was being tuned to other-world frequencies, with a tuned metal perimeter. Which is where he came in. And of course, you could combine the three to enter the state more easily. He, Heyla and Hieime had previously entered the state by drinking balche and sitting inside a tuned metal perimeter.

He wondered how Malaena had managed it. And then he thought about the experience of terror. Of absolute fear, and the state of heightened awareness it catapulted a body into. He knew that Malaena had felt some of that the night she had been stranded on the face of a cliff at the age of thirteen shades. He had certainly felt it, the night he thought he had lost Evra. And so he wondered if that was another way you could enter the state, in extreme states of awareness. He was sure Malaena had made her very first steps across the walls of the world on that cliff face as she waited to be found and rescued. And he felt sure the first time he had reconnected with her had been the night Evra had fallen into the chasm, and he had never felt such terror in all his life. So possibly, there was something in that as well.

An age later, Merouac had completed his task. But the air was still. He had not needed to keep his eyes on the wood and only the wood – there hadn't been any distractions in the end to ignore.

He was confounded. Was this how he was supposed to enter the Maoulfi state, this heightened state of listening, hearing and sensing?

Moments later, Kii appeared, serene. 'Let's return to the ground level and let you rest, shall we? You did well today. Your lesson is finished.'

Merouac frowned. 'Nothing happened, Kii. I don't understand what the lesson was.'

Kii smiled his kind smile. 'It takes its own time,' he said.

They made their way down the path, through the second, beautifully sculpted metal gate, through the gardens of the first terrace and then back down to the foot of the hills of High Country.

'So I wasn't supposed to connect with everything else you say is around us here?' Merouac probed on their descent.

'Who's to say you didn't?' Kii countered. 'Perhaps some part of you connected and another part of you didn't.'

'I don't think I felt, heard or saw anything,' Merouac said.

'It doesn't matter. You can sleep on it. We'll go up again tomorrow.'

'So you and Tor are kindred,' Kii commented as they walked towards the guest dormitories, having completed their descent down the terraces. 'How are you feeling about that, and all that my grandfather has told you?'

'It makes no sense to me. But having said that, I've mostly been focused on getting back on my feet,' Merouac replied.

'Did you know that Lavilla has accepted my mother's invitation to stay with her in the village for a few nights and asked to spend time with my family?'

'Ah. I had wondered.'

'She is a good leader, I think,' Kii said with equanimity.

'Agreed,' Merouac replied. He thought of Afourla, Kii and Kultan's family, the sense of a tug-of-war that was going on between those who were here and those still in the mountains, knowing of High Country and its existence, and then also those in the mountains who knew nothing more except that many of the royal family had somehow disappeared.

'Are you close with your grandfather, Kii?'

Kii nodded. 'Yes. I was born different, I suppose,' he said, touching the shield that covered half his face with his fingers. 'Afourla was always protective of me for that reason.'

'How did it happen, if you don't mind me asking?'

'I was born this way. I suppose it's made it easier, since I never knew any different.'

'I would think you still might have had challenges though,' Merouac reflected. Kii didn't respond. Merouac hoped he hadn't offended the young man. 'Although perhaps it helps you live here successfully?'

'I think so, yes.'

'What about Kultan? Does he do well here?'

'Kultan is different. He is the first-born twin and he wants a lot for our people. He doesn't understand Afourla, but he has Qualan, who he is close with.'

'And Qualan will continue to be Kultan's guardian until he is twenty-five shades old? That seems a long time for a young man to have a guardian.'

'I hadn't thought about it like that,' Kii said, helping Merouac navigate a rocky area on the final stretch of the path. 'Kultan has his heart and soul in the mountains. He wants his family all together, but all together over there, not here. It is a hard situation. I try and keep both sides peaceful.'

ooo

Late that night Merouac lay wide awake, unable to fall asleep.

He could hear Evra breathing evenly nearby, and further down, Heyla seemed still as well. It wasn't unusual; in fact, it had become the habit of these past shades for him to feel alert around this time. It was what had started his habit of getting up, heading back to the workshop and working on his sculptures.

He knew the feeling well enough to know that sleep wouldn't come till much later. Often it was closer to dawn when he was able to drift off, grabbing a few precious hours before being jolted into the day. He thought he could still see his way around if he were to go outside. And no one had told him he couldn't return by himself to the second terrace.

Quietly, he dressed and moved out of the dormitory, into the night. All was still around him. He started walking up to the first terrace in the near-dark, passing through the first gate and stopping for a time to enjoy the sense of being up and about when no one else was around. This was always the time of day he found he could think, make sense of things, hear his own thoughts.

The air felt alive, and in a sense, he knew it was. It was exactly what the Faurin had said; the air around them was full of energy trying to connect with his senses – and yet as far as he understood, he'd need to find a way to the Maoulfi state before he could actually tune into any of it.

He kept walking, made his way slowly through the second gate, and walked over to the small hut. His three piles of wood stood in the night, quietly, untouched since he had placed them there earlier that day.

He looked back in the direction he had come. Twenty paces back. He walked over to where the piles had originally been positioned. It might be different at this time of night, he thought. Before he'd really thought too much more about it, he found himself returning to the stacks. He picked up one piece of wood from the pile closest to the shack. He felt his left thigh, rubbing it in a way that had become so habitual in the past weeks. There was a slight twinge of an ache, but nothing more. Then, he felt his whole body flush, a wave of something that at first felt like heat, then static. It faded.

He slowly made his way back and forth, moving one piece of wood after another, all back to the location of the original piles.

It was different, he realised. He felt more alive and the air around him pressed and pushed into different parts of his body more firmly, as if someone was digging an elbow into his side, or pressing his face with a finger.

He kept going. Back and forth, one piece of wood travelling with him each time.

Gradually, the first pile disappeared from its position near the hut, and reappeared where Kii had originally assembled it. He was feeling lighter, somehow. Perhaps it was returning to his habit of being active at this time of night; it was a comfort, something that felt normal after days of astonishing sensations and events.

And, he thought, it was at this hour that the Top Hats had started appearing to him, all those many months earlier, deep in the nights back at Endren, in the workshops where his time was his own. Even when he was called down by the night shift to attend to some issue or other, it was usually resolved quickly, and then he had the rest of the deep night hours to simply be alone, not needing to worry about schedules or the needs of his men. And then, when Evra arrived, he had picked her up and carried her to the workshops and she slept on, unworried, in the corner, as he worked.

There was something about that zone of quiet concentration. It was always somewhere in the middle of those quiet moments where the blue light of the Top Hats had started to appear at the edge of his gaze. It had always been hard to see the things directly in his sight; they shifted and moved and always seemed hazy and insubstantial. He wondered if, in those moments, he had drifted into the Maoulfi state without realising it.

He kept working. The surges of static came and went, heating his body, and then leaving, giving him a sense that his whole body was buzzing, vibrating. He kept moving, concentrating only on the wood. And things started to shift, but not in the way he had anticipated.

Soon, two piles had been moved and Merouac was starting to feel a welcome feeling of tiredness. He contemplated leaving the last pile of wood for the morning but kept moving instead. Then, something sounded.

He looked up. Nothing. Had anything made a noise at all? He felt sure he had heard something. All was still. What was it that he thought he had heard? Like someone or something was crashing through the trees, perhaps. He shook his head. Nothing unusual stirred, the flickering lights continued and below he could see hummers and their fluorescent markings shimmering in the trees.

Then he realised. He hadn't heard it. He'd *felt* it.

He closed his eyes, tried to make his way to the place the Faurin called the Maoulfi state. Kii had wanted him to find a place of deep listening. And perhaps what he was just starting to understand was, that you could listen with all your body, and feel sound in other ways than just noise.

After a time, he opened his eyes again and saw spheres hovering in the air, full of something he couldn't quite comprehend.

Reaching out to touch them, they felt full and weighty and yet his hand could partially pass through them. They were not solid, and yet they were full. Like bubbles being blown by some invisible child, they formed and hung in the atmosphere.

They grew larger, then fuzzier, then collapsed from their own weight, dripping a strange sentience that dispersed back into the atmosphere. Often, they formed again straight away, the same spheres, the same size and colour, the same weight, only to burst and disperse once again.

Some of the smaller ones were only as large as his hand. Others, twice the size. And then hovering at greater height, larger spheres his whole body could have walked through. They shifted and mutated, formed and faded, pulsed and glowed. They were magical.

'This is different,' he said out loud, and grinned.

23.
The Maoulfi State

The path up to the third altitude was covered with a pale purple moss creeping up around the large, slate-coloured stepping stones. Over the path, large palms hung overhead and, beneath them, more of the long, pale-stemmed, pole-like trees Merouac had first seen in the pink forest glen with Evra.

'What's our plan for today, Kultan?' Merouac asked.

'You are with Kii and the Raja today.'

'Ah, good.

At the third terrace, Kii greeted them with a broad, genuine smile. 'I hear you returned to the terraces last night, Merouac. How did you find the experience?'

'Satisfying,' Merouac said. It was true. He was glad to have found a way into the Maoulfi state that was more akin to the ways he worked, late at night, in his studio.

'That's good to hear.' Kii stepped aside, and beckoned for Merouac to follow him. Kultan gave his usual brief farewell and disappeared swiftly and without a sound, back down the paths towards the beach.

'Our friends the Raja are very interested to show you their ways of making tuned gates, to connect one frequency to another. They see a great future for you, Merouac, if you continue to do these things back on Ahm. Come, Tundra waits for you.'

Tundra, the very tall person Merouac had met at the family's welcome dinner, was standing in front of a small shack Kii had guided him to. His his impressive height, terribly long neck, arched skull shape and large eyes, reminded Merouac that he was in new territory in more ways than one. Tundra greeted him silently.

Despite the soundless greeting, Merouac had a sense of calm, a sense that the air was enriched and alive with energy and sentience.

Merouac turned to Kii. 'I have some questions I'd like to ask Tundra,' he said. 'How is the best way?'

Kii nodded approvingly. 'You can ask him and I will respond, based on my understanding of what he shares with me.'

'So you'll hear Tundra respond by listening in the Maoulfi state?'

'You are learning swiftly, Merouac,' Kii smiled.

'Alright. Could you ask Tundra why the Raja are here, on High Country?'

'I can answer that without needing any more information from our friends here,' Kii said, nodding in shared understanding at Tundra. 'They have already shared with us that they are here help. They say they have more knowledge than us, and the ability to move between frequencies is only new to us, and not them.'

Merouac nodded.

'It is a tradition,' Kii continued. 'Tundra wants me to tell you that whenever a planet awakens, whenever their shield starts to dissipate, energies from other realms will come and offer assistance. That is what the Raja are doing for us.'

'Tell me again how you and Tundra are communicating?'

'The Raja have told us we are one of the only planets still to use our voices as the primary method of communicating. They do not speak very much, because they now use energy to communicate. While we experiment, and descend into the Maoulfi state for moments at a time, they exist in this deeper state continually. So they can see it all in the air around us. Your words don't just come out of your voice, they emanate from your body as energy particles into the air. Tundra is reading the air.'

'Do they speak at all? Can they even, if they want to? Or have their communication skills completely changed?'

Kii checked with Tundra. 'It is their choice not to use their voices. If they had to, Tundra said they still could.'

'And they have the same understanding of the Maoulfi state?'

'Yes, it is the same. The deeper state of awareness where you are thinking less and being in your body more. It gives your body the power to interact with the energy it senses. It is a state where you are porous, open.'

Merouac nodded his understanding.

Kii motioned to Tundra, and Merouac observed them in a kind of energy exchange he could only partially sense.

Kii, after a few moments, nodded swiftly again, confident that he understood Tundra's intent.

'Tundra wants to help you take more skills back with you, when you return,' Kii said. 'He thinks it is important that you, in particular, are learning and becoming more confident. Your work is important, and Tundra can show you more about tuning metal gates to ensure you affix a frequency to the gate effectively.'

Merouac was touched. 'I'd appreciate that,' he said.

'There is more, and it is just for you to remember. It relates to the race that you call the Helara, who you have given shelter to below the caves under Suron.'

'Alright,' Merouac said.

'Tundra says that it is good you have started to utilise L7. The Helara detected Ahm's transmission signal as L7, and so they made a great effort to migrate there, to escape the destruction of their habitat. But it will have cost them dearly. And that is why you are right in your sensing that they will not reappear for some time. Migrating frequencies on a mass scale is very hard, and they may have mapped across extensive frequency variations. Their old world may have existed on a vastly different frequency and, if so, it would have been even harder. Here in High Country, we are doing things gradually. We are bringing people over a few at a time. And when your group came over, you and Tor felt the shock of it, even though High Country is very close, in both distance and frequency range. The disturbance is only gentle for most.'

'So we are right to let them rest,' Merouac said. 'I thought as much, but I'm glad to hear that's the right approach.' Merouac looked up at Tundra. 'Thank you', he said. Tundra nodded slowly, and then turned to open the door to the hut.

'This is the forge,' Kii said. 'We will be making a gate, and we will see what you tune.'

Merouac stepped inside and was surprised to see a full working forge and metalsmithing set-up, although of course they must have been using this to create the gates he had passed through on each level of the island. He simply hadn't considered where their workshop was.

Kii, standing at the doorway, was once again in conversation with Tundra, although Merouac could only tell because Tundra was facing Kii and Kii had the glazed look on his face Merouac had come to know as deep listening.

'There is more', Kii confirmed. 'Tundra has one last thing to tell you for today, while the forge warms up. And that is that *the metal is not the magic.*' Kii was more focused now than Merouac had ever seen him, as though it were taking some effort to translate this part of the message. But the young Faurin continued regardless. 'Tundra wants you to know it is merely a carrier of the energy you create, and which the pala stone also magnifies and strengthens. Tundra tells me that you have a kaleidoscope-like ability. You will be able to connect and tune into many different frequencies. That is your endowment and why you were gifted to the planet. To help those of Ahm learn how to use such a gift.'

Merouac didn't know what to say, so he simply nodded once more to Tundra, who gave him a brief smile and then signalled that the forge was ready.

Merouac looked at the table in front of him, laid out with all the tools and materials to build a gate.

He thought back to the first gate he had tuned, and it had almost felt strange to return to his craft after the pressures of the railroad where he'd done everything *but* work metal. Since they'd settled Bitroux, he'd established his teams, worked on schedules, fought for resources, negotiated deliveries, and built his shed and the huts on the hill. He'd tried to take care of Evra, he'd kept up with all the orders and instructions coming up from Endren. He'd tried to help the families of his small team get settled and make the sub-camp friendly and hospitable and safe. But working metal? It had been the last thing he'd had time for, and he'd only gotten back on the tools when they decided to venture into the first of their experiments in tuning metal.

Back when Heyla had first encouraged him to start using his ability, she had accused him of stalling unnecessarily, practical and as blunt as ever.

'There is nothing to fear,' she'd said. 'Things are strange when they are not familiar. You will become confident soon enough.'

Heyla had continued her rapid-fire assault. 'Let me ask you another question then,' she had said. 'What happens if we do not take this path?'

'Which path would that be?'

'The path that is opening up in front of us. The path of new possibilities.'

'Everything goes back to the way it used to be?' Merouac had suggested.

But now, with the chance to learn more about the craft from Tundra, he was glad things hadn't gone back to the way they used to be.

He and Tundra donned the gear Kii had lain out for them.

'There is another thing,' Kii said, laughing at Merouac's face. 'Don't look so alarmed. Tundra is just pleased to have the time with you, and he has a lot to say.'

Merouac placed the protective apron over his head and fastened it behind his back. 'Go ahead,' he said, this time to both of them. 'I'm hear to listen and I appreciate having the opportunity to hear Tundra's wise words.'

'Alright,' said Kii, proffering some well-worn gloves to Merouac. 'It is just a reminder that when you return to Ahm, and start creating more gates, you do not have to work on every element. You just need to do enough to set the metal alive with the frequency. So it just has to be a few components of the gate. Tundra is going to work with you to create a gate frame today, and you will create the small elements that create the tuning. But only a few pieces are required.'

'Understood,' Merouac said, lowering his protective goggles over his eyes.

They started by creating the outer shape of the gate, a rectangle with a circular section rounding out the top. A range of saw-horses and clamps were set up to support the creation of the frame, and Tundra and Merouac set the frame in place to allow the welding to begin in earnest.

The first few welds were tac welds to hold the structure in place, to be ground away later. They helped with keeping the steel bars together after the clamps were removed. The sparks were bright, a fusion of light, energy and hahma current – flickering out from the metal as Merouac coaxed and welded the structure into form. The metal turned molten under the heat of Merouac's tools, burning a simmering golden orange. The colour was lively, and even brighter than normal in the soft light of High Country terrain seeping through the large workshop windows.

The rat-a-tat clicking of the welder on the metal, as the sparks flew, was a hum so familiar to Merouac that it felt like the blood coursing through his veins – a constant thing that was present more often than not, somewhere in the workshop, nearby, or further into the general workshop floors. Even if it had not been him working the metal, the sounds of it were part of the structure of his working life, grounding him in the every day. Now, it brought him home to the familiar and the everyday.

Tundra indicated that Merouac should start considering his tuned elements and so he quickly sketched out several different circle and scroll motifs.

Merouac worked with the others in the creation of the frame, flipping the structure over as they moved to firm up the outer structure.

Then Tundra stood back and allowed Merouac to focus on the crafting of the scrolls. Tundra had guided him to consider that two dozen scrolls would be an excellent amount to aim for, and ideally, all twenty-four scrolls would be created in the one session, to ensure he was transmuting the same energetic signature into each one, another consideration in consolidating the frequency setting. And then that would be all that was required to hold the frequency he attuned the gate to.

After cutting over thirty lengths of metal, Merouac begun to work the ends of the bars to enable them to fit into the scrolling jig, the ends of each rod still burning a dull orange after being pulled from the forge, ready for Merouac to work. He was the only one to handle the rods, and so had placed over a dozen into the fire to ensure they could all be pulled and worked quickly once he had his process sorted. It usually took two or three scrolls before Merouac found his momentum; after that, he was able to get into a rhythm and lose himself in concentration and the step-by-step process of creating the scrolls, making the hot metal curve this way and that.

As he worked, Merouac was aware of the air shifting and moving around him, becoming more active. It was as though the pulsing air contained not just information, but hints of context, breaking through into his consciousness. Not just the what, but the why. Not just the fact that the universe was coming to life around him, but the why, because that had been the journey he had been heading towards all his life.

Here and there, sound and vibration melded and merged, broke and burst around him. Sequences of other types of language pulsed, stopped and pulsed once again.

Standing over the jig, Merouac worked to create double scrolls with each piece of metal, working quickly to ensure the metal stayed maleable as he worked. The scroll curved one way and then reversed to curve the other, emerging from the jig a fully finished piece of tuned metal, infused with Merouac's energy and whichever frequency he was attuning to as he deepened into the Maoulfi state.

Again, he remembered his sister's words. *It's like you use your whole body to hear. Like it's a sieve. Somehow you start listening to the air and somehow you start to understand things. I don't know how else to explain it.* And that was exactly how it felt now. Deep in concentration, the gate coming into formation as he and Tundra worked on their various sections, he felt fragments of sentience, hearing them come closer, fragments of a conversation he was tuning into and possibly even participating in. Was his whole body being reformed as he worked, new pathways becoming alive in some way? It seemed entirely plausible the whole point of this process, the arriving on High Country, the experience of crossing dimensions, was for him to understand that somehow their bodies, perhaps his in particular, was capable of an entirely new kind of understanding.

Tapping and adjusting the metal to keep the scroll balanced and aligned, he moved the jig to feed in the metal to create the scrolling effect.

Merouac started to perceive new energies around him, but they did not appear in any kind of visible way. It all seemed to be something that could just as easily be happening in his imagination. He imagined one body, then two, standing nearby. He imagined they were inquisitive, curious. Small, perhaps standing only as tall as the distance between the ground and his knee, but they were hovering at different heights, hanging here and there in the ether around him. He imagined they were reaching out to him.

Merouac flipped the bars before him, remembering one of the things Kii had encouraged him to do when walking wood from one side of the terrace to other, was to let the world shift around him without paying it too much attention. And so, he continued to work.

He thought back to how the approach had worked the first time, when Hieime had been with him on the hill behind the shacks, telling him how he should approach building the first tuned gate of his life, when they had been trying to connect with the Helara, the pale planet looking fragile, but still intact, above them.

Merouac had fitted pieces of forged round bar onto a loose structure. He'd then laid it out on his bench and tightened each piece with the support framework. When all the individual components were set firmly against each other, he'd begun winding the lever that would hold everything tightly together for welding. He turned on the joining welder and pressed the machine head's tip to where the joints needed to come together. He'd been wildly unsure of what they were all doing, what they were even thinking they could achieve, but he knew how to work metal and so that's what he had continued to do.

The metal had glowed red and then cooled again. When the entire structure was complete, he and Hieime had inserted the last piece of the circuit and set the generator to start pumping L7 current through it. It had been Hieime's reckoning the gate would charge the other poles connected through the hahma circuit and allow a new frequency to come into being.

Now, Merouac wondered how Hieime had even known so much that he had been able to instruct him.

Merouac looked to both Tundra and Kii. They gave no signal of having felt the creatures Merouac sensed around him. He wondered if it was he, as creator of the tuned frequency, who got the first insights, and as the tuning became stronger, the others would feel it, too. It seemed logical, if any of this could in any way be considered logical. For now, they were absorbed in their own activities, contributing to the air of intense focus in the small workshop, and so he continued with his scrolls.

He started creating the same kind of scrolls from the other end, finishing the rod with two double scrolls ready to fit into the overall structure of the gate. This would be the key gate, the one that created the frequency field and that the hahma currents were attached to, and sent around the circuit of the frequency tuning. When the scrolls were finished, Merouac plunged them into the nearby buckets of hot water, to seal the work, cool the metal and at the same time, he had learned, would seal the frequency that had been tuned to the metal. The metal hissed and smoked as it met the cool of the water. When the metal had hardened and turned from a dull burning orange to grey-black, he pulled out the scrolls and set them to fully harden.

The scrolls were fitted deftly by Tundra into the borders of the gate, repeating outwards from the centre in both directions, to create a mirrored effect, perfectly identical and balanced on each side of the centre. The gate was set, completed and ready to be integrated into a powered energetic circuit, like all the other key gates that set the frequency for each terrace. This was to be a small circuit, only ten feet in diameter, and simply for he, Tundra and Kii to see what Merouac had tuned.

He and Tundra carried the gate outside and connected it to the small circuit Kii had erected. Even before the gate was set, Merouac knew a tuning of sorts had occurred. He felt the familiar shift in the air, a rising of the hair on his skin, goosebumps and a change in the air that couldn't be described by any words he knew.

Tundra and Kii looked at him. Kii beamed. Tundra bowed in acknowledgement.

Flashes of yellow and blue became more prominent in the air around him. A chirping, like birdsong, rose in the air. His heart hammered inside his chest, but then steadied as he saw how calm Kii and Tundra were. The air was shifting and moving and now felt like he was being nudged by something with a curious energy with a light touch.

Whoever they were, the creatures around them had come because he tuned them. Tuned into them. Made contact, invited them to connect and appear and communicate with him.

Now, all that was required was that he understood them.

Keep listening, Tundra told him.

Merouac looked at the tall man, standing a few yards away, nodding in his direction with approval.

Then, of course Merouac realised Tundra had not spoken a word. And yet he had heard him as loud and clear as he'd ever heard anyone in his life.

24.
Discussion with Lavilla

The day after Merouac's experience tuning his gate on the terraces, Lavilla returned from her stay with Asta and the royal family, and announced it was time to depart; they would be escorted back to the Remenur Ranges later that day, through the same kind of frequency crossing that had brought them over.

'Merouac, can we walk together?' the governor asked.

They walked slowly towards the pink forest, Evra running ahead of them and shouting out as she investigated one plant or curious insect after another. 'I hope you won't suffer on the journey back,' she said. 'But the Faurin have made accommodations, just in case.'

'At least I know it won't last. I guess it's a little like sea-sickness,' Merouac considered.

'I'm not sure it's like sea-sickness at all,' Lavilla retorted. 'To me, it's a reminder we have so much more to learn and understand about who you are.'

'Fair enough,' he replied.

'Merouac, there is something else I want to talk to you about.'

'Ask away.'

'I want to ask you to tell me exactly what happened with the transfer of the Helara. It was originally my intention to have this as part of our discussion up on Tenogru. But, of course, things took one surprising turn after the other and in the end, it didn't feel like the right time.'

He nodded. 'I thought as much. And yes, we should talk about it. What did Heyla tell you originally?'

'She told me the main points, in her words. But I want to hear the main points again, in your words. It doesn't matter if there is overlap.'

Merouac nodded. 'Alright. Well, I suppose you could say it started with Hieime. He's a gem man, trades right across the continent. Travels from one town to the next. I met him by chance at the markets up north and found out he knew a bit about tuning metal. I invited him back to Bitroux to help me and Heyla with our experiments.'

Lavilla nodded and thanked Evra who had spun back to place a flower she plucked from the edge of the footpath into her hand.

'He's a good man. I trusted and liked him immediately. Unfortunately, he's also a bit of a ladies' man. And it seemed that during his travels, he met the wife of Sanat Leron. They were having an affair. Still might be, I don't know. I don't think I want to. But anyway, that's how we met Delsaine. I was dead against her coming out to the camp, but she wanted to be with him and he didn't have a problem with it, and when she came, she brought her son, Ophrin.' Merouac shook his head. 'It is strange, actually.'

'How so?' asked Lavilla. They had stopped at the edge of the forest and, rather than entering the shady interior, walked down towards the sandy beach instead, following Evra who had darted down towards the water.

'Well, Ophrin doesn't talk much, but he can scream and yell without any trouble. But Hieime was very good with him, in fact. I wondered if that was why Delsaine came; he just seemed to have a way with the child. Calmed him right down.'

'Sanat Leron's child?'

'Exactly. It was problematic, of course. Anyway, Delsaine was sitting nearby with Ophrin when we did some of our first tuning experiments; this was when the Helara had started to come through. They were making contact, but we couldn't understand what they were saying. Then, out of nowhere, there was this young boy, and he helped me connect the dots between the dust storms, the planet, the fact that frequency tunings seemed to be activating and indicating that the shield was down.'

'How did he do that?' Heyla asked.

'He spoke with the Helara,' Merouac said, still feeling a sense of awe when he remembered the moment Ophrin turned to them all and said just one word.

'"Boom" was the word he used,' Merouac explained. 'And then somehow it all made sense. I knew that Ophrin was trying to tell us, in his limited words, that the Helara's planet was about to implode. That they needed safe harbour. And that we could offer it.'

'And you felt no sense there would be danger in this kind of activity?'

Merouac turned to Lavilla, but she held up her hands calmly. 'I'm honestly asking you, Merouac. I'm not judging. But the decision you made was a very big one. It needs serious thought, as to how we move forward. I want to know what you were feeling at the time, and if you felt coerced or forced to act in any way.'

Merouac felt his face flushing. 'No, I didn't,' he replied. 'But I understand what you're saying. All I can tell you is that there were so many events that led to us finding that space below the grid, deep down in the cave system. I truly felt like I'd been guided down there for a purpose, and that purpose was to bring the Helara there.'

'This is when Evra fell?'

Merouac nodded; he had shared with her his experience with the Top Hats the morning they had left Tenogru for High Country. 'I can't explain it, really. I knew, with absolute certainty, that the space could harbour the Helara without any knowledge of who they were, where they had come from, or how their planet had been able to so suddenly, and shockingly, make an appearance in their night sky. In the moment, it had seemed perfectly sensible.'

'Alright,' said Lavilla. 'Then what?'

'Well, Kultan brought his Intangien team down to the caves to help. Delsaine and Ophrin came down as well; I thought since Ophrin had been the one to communicate with them, he would help again. We built the frequency bridge, using the generator Tor had brought down here for his own experiments.'

At that, Lavilla tut-tutted and shook her head, giving Merouac a wry smile.

'They came thick and fast after that,' Merouac said. 'Everyone felt them; no one knew how many. Just that they had come, they were grateful, they understood where to go, and knew that after they had made the transfer, the space would close up around them and allow them protected space to recover. And I knew that nothing else was required; we just needed to let them settle. I knew that they would go into hibernation, but I also can't tell you how I knew that.'

'And that's it?' Lavilla asked.

'That's it,' Merouac said.

'I guess that's a start,' Lavilla concurred. 'Thank you, Merouac. Are you ready to return?'

'It feels like time,' Merouac said.

25.
Return

The school was being built. Twenty men from Merouac's workshops turned up on their days off, families in tow, to assist. Picnics were laid out in the open areas near the stores for all to share. The buildings were going up quickly. Laughter and conversation was loud and fast during the breaks when tea and biscuits were served, and some stayed after the work finished to talk and enjoy a few drinks together before calling it a day.

The school would have a main hall and an annexe for different activities or groups. It would allow up to fifty young children to attend, more than enough for their needs. Having said that, Merouac pondered as the buildings went up, it was possible numbers could jump up a lot when they were at full capacity. With the clearing for the East-West line complete, work on building the tracks was moving into full swing and the workers' camp would start expanding week by week. But those numbers would ebb and flow; soon enough most of the families in the camp would move on to wherever the railroad work went, and they would return to being a smaller camp.

Merouac was taking a break from the hot sun in the shade of the rest area, sitting on one of the tree stumps that were used for seats and affectionately known as tubbies. Tubbies were dragged around the area to wherever the men felt like sitting, mostly where there was shade, and often when it was time for a smoke and a break. They were solid and comfortable enough, and were found at nearly every workers' camp Merouac had ever come across. Wood was largely brought in already cut and ready, but every so often a new pile of tubbies arrived, a throwaway and goodwill gesture from the mills, he supposed, which didn't need the cut bases of the trees they milled, but knew their popularity as seats. Although, now the mills were under pressure to keep up with the railroad and the wood was coming from across the oceans, tubbies might soon be in shorter supply.

Just as he was downing his mug of water, he saw a familiar body walking into the camp. Mostly, in fact, it was the head of golden hair Merouac recognised, even from a distance.

He stood up. 'Hieime,' he called out. He noted that Seb had heard and looked over in the direction of the newcomer, who looked to be alone, and was distinctive in his cream linen trousers and thick hair that seemed to catch the light from every direction possible.

The man heard Merouac's shout, waved and turned to walk in his direction.

'Well,' said Merouac with a grin, walking forward and extending his hand. Hieime closed the distance quickly and shook Merouac's hand with warm affection.

'Merouac,' he said. 'Here you are. What's the building going up? All hands on deck, eh?'

'It's been a while,' said Merouac to Hieime.

'It certainly has. I went to ground for a bit. Make things a bit easier for Delsaine, you know. And, of course, get out of the way of the storms. But things seem to be getting back to normal now, I'd say.' Hieime continued to look with interest at the school building going up, and the workers and families shouting to one another with various directives and demands.

'I hope so,' Merouac agreed.

'How's your young one?' Hieime asked, scanning the area for Evra, grinning when he saw her standing off to the side of the build, with Harlin's hand on her shoulder, the two of them gazing skyward as six men worked to set the rafters in place.

'Pretty good, all told. This is a school we're building, to keep all the kids safe and learning. She's decided she'll be supervising all efforts, as you can well see. Originally, my agreement with the powers that be was that I'd get the first five sections of the East-West built, and they would build me a school. But it seems we've been given the funds early.'

Hieime nodded. 'Excellent. So does that mean that the camp will stay established for some time to come?'

'Looks that way. Hieime, do you remember my second in charge, Seb?'

Seb had wandered over and now gave a nod and extended his hand to the visitor. Hieime gripped Seb's hand for a good shake and offered a sparkling grin. 'Well met,' he said to Seb.

'What brings you to our neck of the woods?' asked Seb with genuine curiosity. 'Trading nearby?'

'I guess I'm always trading nearby, so to speak. I'm always on the move, and I come by these parts often. In fact I was just thinking I must tick off every town in the continent at least once an annalshade. But no, actually, I came with a word for Merouac, this time. Something I thought you might like to know about.'

Seb was gracious and knew when to mind his own business; he

gave Hieime a wave and wandered off towards the building activity, signalling that he was free to lend a hand.

Merouac noted that Salvette was also working nearby, collecting the cut-offs of the timbers used in the frame of the school buildings, and piling them ready for repurposing. He, too, was watching Evra observe the buildings going up. Merouac called out and beckoned him to come over.

'Salvette, this is Hieime. Thought you might like to be introduced. A friend of this railroad camp, that's for sure. Hieime, Salvette here is Evra's dad, come to give us a hand on the railroad and get to know his daughter a bit better at the same time.'

'Well, very pleased to meet you,' Hieime said.

Salvette, the more awkward and unrefined of the two, bobbed his head. 'Aye,' he said, his eyes flicking back quickly to Merouac, as if to check how he was required to act in this situation. 'Anything else, Merouac?' he asked.

'Nope, just an introduction, that's all.'

Salvette nodded gravely at the two of them and shuffled back to his pile of wood. At least Harlin had sorted him out with some better fitting clothes, Merouac thought to himself. Bit by bit, the man seemed to be pulling himself together. He seemed clean, largely well intended, if still a little slow and clumsy on his feet. But progress, certainly.

'Well, I thought you might like to know there's white pala about,' said Hieime, taking Merouac's arm and drawing him closer so he could speak quietly. 'A pair of miners got out with a catch. I got a part of it, through means we won't discuss right now. I wanted you to have it. If you weren't already well aware, as I'm sure you are, it's the most powerful gemstone on the continent when it comes to amplifying tunings.'

Merouac's eyebrows shot upwards as Hieime proceeded to pull out a bundle of cloth from his trouser pockets, slowly and carefully unwrapping the layers to reveal the sharp and gleaming contours of the rare, and immensely valuable, white pala.

As soon as he saw that Merouac had seen and noted the stone, he folded it back into its wrappings and handed Merouac the bundle. 'Here you go,' Hieime said. 'Use it to amplify your tunings.'

'I don't know what to say, Hieime,' Merouac said truthfully.

'Well, it's powerful, and rare, so do keep it safe. But I thought you were the right person to have it, and use it for the best purpose possible. There's a few pieces floating around, but the other piece I'm aware of has been snapped up on the black market, and I have no idea who the buyer was.'

Merouac nodded. 'There was a game, I suppose.'

'There was. Out in the depths of the Southern Ingrue. Quite the event, more players than ever, I heard. Made me think that there could be more than one party looking to see beyond the walls of the world, if you know what I mean.'

'I know for a fact there is,' Merouac replied dryly. 'Just wait till you hear the details.'

Hieime grinned. 'Glad my instincts are still good, then.'

'Your instincts are right on. But I hadn't thought about how many more there might be out there. Not that it's a bad thing, though. There should be more people trying to figure out this puzzle.'

Hieime shugged, untying his scarf and correcting it, to cover his neck in a broader fashion. 'Possibly,' he agreed.

'But this pala, Hieime, why not keep it? I know how rare this stone is. Sell it for yourself, retire! It must be worth a fortune.' The weight of it in Merouac's hand was more than it should have been, a sincere and powerful weight like a marble of some kind, instead of a gem forged from minerals, sand and heat.

Out of the corner of his eye, Merouac noted that Salvette had stopped working and was standing quite still. Clearly, he was paying attention to what Hieime had been saying.

Hieime continued talking. 'No, it's something worth using, and worth using well. Consider me an investor in whatever it is we're doing. It's more valuable and important we get a handle on how much the shield has thinned and what we're capable of doing, if we try. I'll be coming and going, but I want to be a part of it, even though I think I've got some catching up to do.'

'Yes, you do need an update,' Merouac acknowledged. 'Why don't you stay a while, so I can tell you all the latest?'

'Tempting, but I won't, at least not today. But I'll be back, in a while. Count on it.'

Merouac closed his hands around the cloth, folded the outer layer over one more time and placed the bundle in his own trouser pocket. He reached out to shake Hieime's hand once more. 'Thankyou for trusting me with the stone. And I hope we see you again soon.'

'Indeed you will,' Hieime said, glancing out one more time over the camp, turning on his heels and setting out in the direction he'd come. He offered a final wave and flashing smile to Merouac, and a nod to Salvette, who was still standing nearby.

Merouac stood for a moment, feeling the stone heavy and powerful in his pocket. Then, taking in Salvette's still stance, called out, 'Alright there, Salvette?'

'Aye, alright,' Salvette replied with a quick nod. He turned slowly back to his work, as if intending to return to it, and then stood still again, as if half-way through a thought with two possible options or outcomes. But then Evra's father shook his head, decided on one of those options and returned to his wood pile.

26.
Horizons

Merouac was still working when he heard a screech from Evra.

He looked up to see his niece running towards the road, where two women had entered the gates of the sub-camp. Two tall, impressive figures Merouac new well. Heyla and Lavilla.

The child flung herself into Heyla's long-limbed embrace and he could hear peals of laughter drift towards him. He stood and stretched his back, and walked towards the two women, who looked relaxed and pleased to see him.

'We come with baking intentions,' Heyla declared. 'Or, at least, I do.'

'Hello Merouac,' Lavilla said. 'I don't have plans to bake, but I would like to talk with you, if you have time.'

'Of course,' Merouac said. 'You're alright with her?' he asked Heyla.

She nodded. 'Of course. We have some wildflower collecting to do before we bake, anyway.'

'I'm ready,' Evra piped up, and took Heyla's hand, leading her towards the huts, behind which the wildflowers were known to grow.

'Alright then,' Merouac said. 'Lavilla, shall we head up with these two? We can sit outside the hut, it's a bit quieter.'

'Lead the way,' Lavilla said agreeably.

The Governor of the Ingrue placed herself, without fuss, on Merouac's wooden benches outside the small shack he and Evra shared. Her people, two administrative-like folk, had accompanied her and Heyla to the camp, but kept themselves at a discreet distance.

'So, you've been to Suron then?' Merouac asked, handing her a freshly brewed cup of marla tea.

'Yes,' Lavilla said. 'Heyla took me to meet Delsaine, and we spent time with Ophrin.'

'Ah,' Merouac said. 'How was that?'

'These children,' Lavilla said with a smile. 'Where did they come from, with all these talents?'

'It's a good question,' Merouac agreed, sipping his tea and leaning against the wall of his shack near the rear balcony steps. 'Ophrin is unique to say the least.'

'It was a good and timely visit,' Lavilla continued. 'Changes are underway. Sanat has started to prepare for the transition of leadership, for a start.'

Merouac whistled. 'So Gartounne is finally ready to step down?'

'He doesn't really have a choice,' Lavilla said. 'As everyone knows, it's long overdue.'

'And Tor Anale?' quizzed Merouac.

'Tor has been removed from most of his various positions, including overseeing Suron's military and railroad logistics. It turns out he had quite the string of covert operations underway, above and beyond his activities in the grid.'

'Is that right?' Merouac said. 'I have to say, I do feel for him. He's been asking the questions for as long as anyone and getting roadblocked the whole way.'

'Agreed,' Lavilla said. 'In any event, all is not lost for Tor. He will remain in his role as Head of Buntans, at least for now.'

'And any news from the mountains?'

'Some,' said Lavilla slowly. 'After we returned from High Country, and before I visited Suron, I spoke with Kultan's guardian, Qualan. We are continuing a conversation about the possibility of Kultan being officially made leader before he comes of age at twenty-five shades. That is too far away, and leadership in the mountains is needed now.'

'Afourla doesn't plan to return?'

Lavilla gave Merouac a frank look that told him she'd had a few challenging conversations since they'd last spoken. 'I've also spoken with Afourla. I suggested he think about what was best for his people. He has made many decisions of his own that have led us to where we are now. It will be less disruptive for the Faurin of the Remneur Ranges to have Kultan come into leadership than have Afourla return from the dead, so to speak.'

'I see,' Merouac said. 'Well, it's not for me to say, but it sounds like a good idea. Kultan is ready, I think. He showed us that when he challenged Afourla to be straight with everyone.'

Lavilla nodded, and suddenly stood up, digging into the pockets under her long shawl, which looked for all intents and purposes like it had been given to her by Heyla. It had the distinctly colourful flair of the Ayuherica, despite Lavilla wearing it in a more conservative fashion.

'I have something for you,' she murmured, as she placed a bundle of cloth in his hands. She held her hands over his for a moment, then released them and returned to her seat.

Merouac felt the weight of the bundle. And almost immediately, he knew what it contained.

'How …' he began.

'Aren't you going to look inside?' Lavilla asked lightly.

'It's white pala, isn't it?' Merouac said. He didn't mention this was the second time white pala had come his way in as many days.

'You can tell?' Lavilla said, a look of surprise on her face.

'Maybe let's call it an educated guess,' Merouac replied, feeling the power of the stone in his hands.

'Apparently, Tor had it on his person when we arrived at High Country,' Lavilla explained. 'It was taken from him during his recovery in the infirmary. The Faurin felt very strongly that he had not come into ownership of the stone in the right manner, and should not have it.'

'Poor Tor,' Merouac said, shaking his head. 'Foiled again.'

'Perhaps. It seems one of the mines in the Ingrue uncovered quite a rich vein of white pala a few weeks ago. Two miners got out with some and tried to sell it on the black market. So, as the Faurin understand it, since the stone was mined in the Ingrue and sold illegally on the black market, it should come to me, as Governor, to decide what to do with it.'

'And what will you do with it?' Merouac asked.

'Just what I have done. I am giving it to you. It's time we started doing more tunings here of our own, as the Raja have encouraged us to do. If the shield is fading, then it's time for us to begin researching, experimenting and understanding more about what it means for us. I want to set up a section of land, a collection of territories, if you will. This is how we will begin.'

Merouac felt at once as if he understood exactly what she meant, but also that he needed a thousandfold more detail. 'Tell me more,' he said immediately.

'Alright,' she said. 'And I should say, I've already had a number of conversations in Suron and with Kultan to test some ideas with them, should you have any concerns about that.'

Merouac nodded impatiently. 'Good. Great. Now, those details?'

Lavilla laughed. 'Well, I see you're open to my ideas, which is good. My proposal is this: you stay here at Bitroux, permanently. You divide your time between railroad duties and being my head researcher for what lies beyond the shield.'

Merouac found himself pacing back and forth along the length of the hut. He felt Lavilla's eyes on him, but he stayed silent while the thoughts raced through his head.

He stopped and looked up. 'Evra,' he said.

'I know she's your top priority, Merouac,' Lavilla said. 'Heyla has told me about the school you're building, and that you need a teacher. I've already arranged it to be funded between the railroad and the Ingrue.'

'Excellent.' Merouac paused for a moment, and thought of Heyla's words. And the sentiment he had felt reaching across the dimensions from wherever Malaena was. 'A while ago, all I wanted was for Evra to be safe,' he said.

'She will be,' assured Heyla.

He nodded. 'I know she will be. More recently, I think I've started to realise she can't be excluded. She's part of this journey too.'

'Alright,' Lavilla said. 'What does that mean?'

Merouac kept pacing. He paced until the right words came. 'I don't want her to be separated from whatever we do here. So the school will be part of the research work. The children will be able to participate in what we do, and learn with us as we go.'

'Do you think that's safe?'

Merouac threw up his arms. 'I don't know. That's what I haven't been able to figure out. But if the shield is down and our whole world is changing, I think Evra and Ophrin have a role to play as much as any of us do.'

Lavilla looked thoughtful. 'Alright, I think we should discuss that a bit more, but I'm open to ideas. Heyla, too, is committed to ensuring the children have a role to play. Delsaine has asked her to stay in Suron to help with Ophrin's development, since he will inherit the leadership of Suron one day. So, I think you are both saying similar things.'

Merouad nodded. 'Alright. Then, the territories you mentioned. Where exactly are these territories and who owns them?'

Lavilla opened up her hands, indicating the landscape around then. 'Right here. Bitroux becomes the territories, with additional tracts of land given by the Ingrue for the purpose.'

'Alright, that sounds good. I need a team.'

'Yes, you will,' agreed Lavilla.

'I have about four men who will be just right.'

'I'd like to meet them,' Lavilla stated.

'Yes, of course. When do we start?'

Another laugh from Lavilla. 'Soon. But there's something else I want to task you with, Merouac.'

'Alright, what is it?'

'The one hundred children. If what Afourla has shared with us is true, then you and your sister are two of them. Tor is a third. That makes many more of you out there somewhere. I want you to try and find them.'

Merouac was silent, surprised that Lavilla was so prepared, so ready to progress things. It was daunting but positive, but searching for others like him, when he didn't really even know what he'd be looking for?

Lavilla must have sensed his hesitation. 'Merouac, I urge you to consider this. We don't know anything about the experience of these other children. Have they simply gone on to live ordinary lives? Are they living with their talents lying dormant? Or have they discovered them by accident, not knowing what to do with them? Or are some already using their skills and experimenting with navigating between the realms?'

Merouac considered what she was saying. 'There is a lot we don't know,' he concurred.

Lavilla continued. 'It may have just been coincidence that Evra showed Heyla your sculptures, and Heyla had the imagination to ask "what if?". But chance or not, she was able to see your skills for what they really do seem to be. She was able to see beyond the parameters of the world that most people see, and imagine a new possibility. How many others of the hundred have had that kind of person in their lives?'

Heyla and Evra returned from their adventure picking flowers in the hills. Some of those flowers around were edible, so they'd picked those, choosing the most colourful varieties – very tiny pink and orange and purple flowers. And those flowers had been cleaned and sorted, later to be placed throughout the cake and sprinkled on top.

The kitchen in Merouac and Evra's shack was basic, but it had a stove. Merouac watched while they greased the bottom of the pan. They layered the pan with those flowers. They poured in the cake mix on top and put it in to bake.

Harlin and Seb arrived just as the cake was cooling off after coming out of the oven. They seated themselves at the table with Evra, Merouac and Heyla.

'What's this I hear about a celebration?' Seb said gruffly, ruffling Evra's hair and winking at Merouac.

'We're having cake because it's nearly my birthday.' The cake was flipped over deftly by Heyla so that all the flowers that had been placed at the bottom of the tin now appeared on the top as natural decoration and colour.

'I see,' Seb said. 'So, not your actual birthday, but near enough. Sounds like a good idea to me.'

The idea of a birthday celebration had been floated on the way back from Tenogru, and Merouac had been somewhat flustered at not remembering the exact date of his niece having come into the world. And so Evra and Heyla had improvised, and decided a cake was a good idea in any event.

Merouac cleared his throat as the cake was presented and admired. 'Uh, Ev, you were born in the first days of the monsoon season. That I *do* know. So this is great to have a cake and celebrate it today, but let's remember to celebrate it then, too.'

Evra grinned. 'You know?'

'I do. I came up to visit your mama when she had you. And I remember how wet it was. All Malaena's friends in the camp had laid extra tarps over her tent so she was safe from all the rain. And so you were safe as well.'

'I don't remember that.'

'Of course you don't. You were just a tiny wee thing.'

'What day of the season?' Heyla asked, approving of the fact that some details were emerging, and which would help her create a chart of Evra's stars for her.

'The fourth, perhaps.'

'Well, there you go,' said Heyla to Evra. You're a child of the monsoons. Deep blue, that will be your birth colour. That's very interesting, isn't it. I'll tell you all about that.'

Evra nodded solemnly.

Merouac felt a flush of embarrassment that it had been Heyla who had thought of making Evra a cake. He'd been so busy, so preoccupied with everything that had been happening, that it had never occurred to him Evra might have a birthday coming up that would need celebrating.

'Ev, the monsoons aren't that far away. That means you'll be six shades old very soon.'

Another grin of delight. Despite the complexities of everything that had been happening in their world, the child was easily pleased.

It was a blessing.

After cake, Evra tried to catch the hahmalites floating on the evening breeze.

'Your hair's getting long, Ev,' commented Seb.

'Uncle Mer, did mama wear her hair long when she was my age?'

'Yep, she did. Very long, in fact.'

He thought back to his twin and what they had been like as kids. Both tall and skinny. Forever entangled in scuffles, running up and down the hills of the Ingrue after school where the breezes were fresh and cooling.

'It was pretty dirty though a lot of the time. The camp we lived in got all the dust but not much wind to blow it away. We had to go up on the hills to let it all fly off. She loved running downhill with her hair streaming behind her. Sometimes she used to twist it and braid it with grasses and flowers.'

'We could do that,' said Heyla with a small smile.

'Right now?' Evra asked hopefully.

Heyla looked at Merouac, who nodded.

'Why not?' Heyla replied with a grin, leaning over to run her long fingers through the child's hair.

'After you've done my hair, you're leaving again, aren't you?' asked Evra matter of factly, plucking her slice of cake off her plate and popping it in her mouth.

'I am,' Heyla said.

'Which road is singing to you this time?' Evra asked.

'The road back to Suron,' Heyla said.

Evra considered and accepted the response. 'Everything's different now, isn't it, Uncle Mer?'

'We could say that,' Merouac said. 'But maybe we could also say that everything is the same and different at the same time.'

Seb nodded approvingly, as did Harlin.

'Same but different sounds about right,' Heyla agreed.

'Same but different sounds good to me, too,' Evra said.

'Looks like we're all in agreement,' said Merouac, said with a smile at his niece.

'You have more sculptures to make now, don't you?' Evra asked.

'It would seem that way,' Merouac concurred.

Evra nodded approvingly. 'Are we going to the Kinderrst next?' she asked.

Merouac felt himself freeze.

'That's where mama is,' Evra explained, popping another piece of cake into her mouth and munching without concern.

Heyla and Merouac exchanged looks.

'Kid, I think we're done for a bit, aren't we?' Merouac said.

'Alright,' Evra conceded. 'But not for long. It's going to disappear soon.'

'What is?'

'The Kinderrst, of course.'

Merouac swore under his breath. 'You're really testing me, kid,' he told his niece.

Heyla chortled. 'Why shouldn't she?'

Merouac rolled his eyes, but he wasn't laughing.

He knew, instantly, that what Evra had announced so unceremoniously was true. Malaena had shared with him very early the idea that her location was somehow connected with the memory planet. And legend had it that the Kinderrst did go dark from time to time. But he'd had no sense from his sister that it was imminent.

There was work to be done.

They'd start tomorrow.

MANIFESTO

Have you ever thought how amazing it would be if we could commune with all other living creatures, starting with people from other cultures and extending to animals, the ocean, trees, stars and - more ambitiously -with the universe and everything in it, including other-world and non-human intelligence?

I believe we will develop this method of communication; in fact, I think we're closer than you might think.

These new communication capabilities will allow for a far more fulfilling human experience, enabling us to perceive the world through a much more complex and generous range of filters.

I also believe they will lead us to a more balanced place where the subconscious, the instinctive and the heartfelt all play a more pronounced role in how we express and share our worlds with each other.

I believe our bodies have untapped potential to communicate in ways we have yet to fully comprehend.

It seems to me that our bodies are far more sophisticated than we realize, and that we have the capacity to transmit and receive information – and therefore, knowledge, wisdom and cosmic intelligence – through a range of signaling functions we have barely begun to explore.

The language of vibration and frequency is not a rational one. Vibration is far more connected to our 'gut' intelligence, our empathetic capacities and our subconscious, creative self.

Likewise, our ability to transmit and receive data through particle energy, likewise, is not logical. It doesn't speak to our brain, in fact it specifically diverts consciousness away from our brain, directly into our bodies.

We must understand this form of intelligence physically, not intellectually, allowing our bodies to receive and process this intelligence in our own way, through abstract ideas, instinct, creativity, and the often long and convoluted and deeply personal pathways of the subconscious.

When we use our whole bodies for communication, rather than just parts, such as our ears, vocal cords and our brains, I believe we will find our way to a place where we can commune with a broad range of sentient life energy.

Until then, or in anticipation of that time. I'm pleased to be have created a world where the inhabitants are at this tipping point themselves; where the universe is opening up to them, along with the challenges of communication, community and leadership that come with change.

CREATING THIS BOOK

Even as a writer, I often get blocked when I rely on words to express myself. Many of the artworks featured in this book came about through trying to find a more intuitive way into the story, and very often the work emerged when I wasn't paying attention, immersed instead in the happy play of splashing paint around.

So, as a way to explain the artworks; in a way, they are illustrations, or aspects, of the story that came to me as I was developing the book.

In another way they are the work of marvellous distraction, or alternatively, the process I used to descend into my own 'Maolfi state' of deep concentration, in the same way that Merouac does when he creates his metal sculptures. This is what has allowed me to trawl the energetic landscape and return with something that felt truthful for my story, even if this work is one of fiction.

The work of writing and painting the material that resonates with the intent of the *Bitroux* books is a slow journey. For that reason I'm hugely appreciative of all my close circle in Australia and Aotearoa New Zealand who've grounded me in the joys of daily living.

In particular, friends, peers and students who have made me laugh, shared stories and kept me grounded in creative practice; thank you. The workplaces, studios and learning spaces we've inhabited together are some of the richest, happiest places I know.

For those with whom I share the journey of spiritual inquiry with, thank you. Marg Rainbird, in particular, who offers such nourishing company as we explore ideas around storytelling and sacred practice. To my treasured husband and family, who are always with me on my creative adventures, thank you. In particular, I want to thank my hubby who has created spaces for many writing retreats to occur over the years, and my parents Janine and David – the last chapters of *High Country* were written in their cosy wine cellar under their house.

I also want to acknowledge the artists, writers and thinkers who so intuitively and passionately advocate for us to release the old stories that no longer serve us. This includes Mary Rodwell, Charles Eisenstein, Graham Hancock, and Dolores Cannon and Toko-pa Turner.

In the last year of writing this book, I discovered Gosia Duszak, and her direct communication with a Taygetan/Swaruunian crew in Earth's orbit. This crew shares a vast amount of knowledge, guidance and wisdom through their extraordinary contact efforts. Taygetans inhabit the four planets of the Taygeta Tau-19 sun solar system in the M45 Pleiades star cluster.

For anyone who is interested; disclosure happens softly, quietly, profoundly and deeply - when you are ready. Don't wait for anyone to tell you what's what. *Listen with every fibre of your being* and find your own way there - it's worth it.

The journey continues – thank you for reading.

ABOUT THE AUTHOR

Jordan is an abstract painter, writer and communications professional. She's passionate about all aspects of creativity, life-long learning and personal wellbeing. Over the last fifteen years she's led, coached and developed creative professionals across the Asia-Pacific region.

Jordan's books, studio workshops, courses, coaching and resources are an invitation to explore the rich landscape of creative experiences open to all.

jordanharcourthughes.com